To Dance W

To Dance With Dragons

By
Jaq D Hawkins
First published as Demoniac Dance in Great Britain in 2012
Golbin Publishing fourth edition February 2023
Copyright Jaq D Hawkins 2023
ISBN 979-821558889-5

Cover Art Credits:
Colour Drawings by Regina Curtis
Graphics Design by Jaq D Hawkins

Table of Contents

Special thanks to all of those associated with the Goblin Circle, who continue to support the book and the quest to make the film.

"And those who were seen dancing were thought to be insane by those who could not hear the music."
~ Friedrich Nietzsche

Chapter One

Namah pushed the small boat into the water, then hesitated for a moment before getting in. Most of her early childhood memories were faded, confused, but one was as clear to her as if it had happened yesterday. Men in three of the boats had been doing something wrong. She had been only a toddler at the time and did not understand exactly what was happening, but the people who were crowded around her were horrified at the actions of the men in the boats. She had been taught that they were good men until then, but whatever they were doing had upset everyone. Then the boats toppled, and the men fell into the water. Something had turned them over.

There's something in the water.

The water bubbled and blood floated to the surface. No screams were heard from the victims, but the people at the side of the river were taken aback from the horror of it all and Namah had been surrounded by exclamations of shock and surprise. Before then, the children sometimes had been allowed to swim in the river. Afterwards, they were never permitted to enter the flowing water again.

The river was tranquil now. The first light of dawn was just beginning to creep over the frosty morning, promising a warmer afternoon. It would have been a nice wedding day, only now the ceremony would be lacking a bride. She climbed into the boat, her feet slightly wet from the shallow water she had stepped into as she tried to handle the unfamiliar craft. The boats were known for being unsteady and were seldom used, but they were the only hope she had of putting distance between herself and the home that she would lose today, no matter what else happened. Too many times, Namah had heard the stories; that girls who ran away from the marriages their fathers chose for them had met the same fate as those men on the river that day. There was something in the water, and it had something to do with the goblins.

Namah remembered more about that day. Through all the confusion, Count Anton had walked right past her, and with him had been one of the creatures that they had called demons. The goblin had patted her on the head. In that touch, she felt a genuine affection that she had never felt from her own father. The goblin hadn't seemed evil at all. Yet they had seen no more of them after that day. The stories of their existence seemed to grow more legendary with each whispered telling throughout Namah's childhood.

Count Anton had been no younger then than her promised husband was now, yet he was so much more handsome. Had she been promised to him, perhaps she would have been happy to marry.

The unforgotten memories began to seem, perhaps, the over-inflated dramatisation of a child's mind as Namah looked out over the placidly flowing river. She felt much as a child now, although her first blood had declared her a woman and ready for marriage in the week past. The oars dipped into the water making little sound, and the small boat seemed less shaky now that she was calmly settled in the centre of the plank that served as a seat for the craft. As Namah reached what she judged must be near the halfway point in the river, her spirits soared with a feeling of freedom at last. The nightmare of her unwanted wedding faded behind her as a distant past event from which she was certain now that she could escape.

The first hard thump on the bottom of the boat broke the tranquil mood instantly. Suddenly alert, Namah's breathing came in sharp, hyperventilating intakes as she dropped to the damp bottom of the craft, uncaring of the rough wood and splinters as she clutched the seat for lack of any other handhold in the rocking boat.

There's something in the water.

Terror crept over her as the nightmare memories turned into a very real present crisis. For the first time, Namah understood what those men must have felt when they saw their companions' blood floating on the water, knowing they had a few seconds at most before they would meet the same fate.

'Please God,' she said aloud with her eyes shut tight, 'Don't let them eat me. Don't let it turn over. I don't want to die.'

With a horrific demise at hand, Namah was suddenly not so sure of her previous resolve. She had convinced herself that death would be a better fate than marriage to Gareth, but the thought of being eaten alive like those men in her memory was too hideous to embrace as a romantic end. She shrieked as the second thump nearly capsized the boat. She could feel the unknown creatures' attack right through the all-too-thin boat bottom. Her prayers were not going to be answered. She knew this with a surety that could not be denied. These were not creatures of the God she had been taught to pray to, and they were not going to respond to any plea she could make to Him.

She could feel the wobble of the boat increasing as the next wave came... the one that she knew would topple it and send her into the water to her doom. She squeezed her eyes shut as somewhere within her one final plea arose, but it was not a plea to God. Somehow, she *knew* that wherever they were, the magicians she sought would hear her mental scream, though she did not know what they could do to help her. No sound came from her lips as the words exploded through her mind, *don't let them eat me!*

She felt the wave of water rock the boat violently, but there was no thump. The boat didn't tip over all the way. In her mind, she thought she caught a voice that was not quite heard. There were no actual words, but she felt the meaning behind the thought, *she is one*.

Namah felt the water settle back into its gentle rhythm. Eventually she opened her eyes. She was a little surprised to find herself alive and still within the boat. After a moment, her panic had subsided enough that she felt able to move again. She released her grip on the seat of the boat and shifted herself carefully to keep the boat as steady as possible. She had dropped the oars, but someone had been wise enough to design the little boats so that the oars were caught in oarlocks and could not be lost in the water.

The one to her left was easy to reach, but the other had fallen with its full length through the oarlock so that she had to stretch across the boat to retrieve it. As she shifted her weight to do so, she realised too late that the river had not completely settled and the wave that swept under the boat as she leaned just a little too far flipped the boat mercilessly, so that she was plunging into the cold depths of the water before she had a chance to realise her error and shift her weight back.

Her first thought was that she would inevitably drown. Then she clutched her eyes tightly with her fists, trying to stem the immediate sense of panic as what felt like strong arms wrapped around her. Perhaps the creatures had decided to eat her after all. She could not bear to see her own blood float past her vision or the thought of the pain to come, but instead of pain she felt the sensation of water rushing past. Soon she felt a welcome blast of air in her face and the arms disappeared as suddenly as she had felt them wrap around her. She breathed in deeply, realising that it had been her panic that had made her forget to attempt to breathe in the brief moment that she had been under water. It had probably saved her from drowning, yet she was still floating in the water and whatever had thrust her from beneath the boat was still there as well.

The boat floated helplessly just a little distance away, but there was no way she would be able to retrieve it, or to turn it over and climb in if she could manage to catch it. She would have to swim. The distance to the north shore was daunting. She hadn't got far enough before the boat had tipped. Swimming back to the southern shore might be a little closer and would make more sense, but she wasn't going back there. The time it would take to swim back and try to launch another boat might well be enough for a search party to come along and take her back to her unwanted wedding. She was not free yet.

The morning sun reflected gently from something that moved beneath the surface of the water. Sparkles seemed to move and dance just out of visual range in the murky depths, teasing her senses. Whatever was in the water had apparently decided not to eat her, but it was still there. She began to swim towards the northern shore.

It wasn't long before she began to struggle. The river had been forbidden for most of her lifetime and what little swimming practice she had gained in the small swimming pools her people fashioned had not prepared her for currents. Her determination was strong, but her body was weak. She felt herself sinking lower and lower, losing her will to the river as it flowed strongly over her exhausted body. She slipped beneath the surface, too weary to fight the inevitable death that awaited her. Then once again, strong arms enfolded her. Namah felt water rushing past her body, then something enfolded her face and air was blown into her deprived lungs.

She was too exhausted to feel fear. She gave herself over to whatever fate awaited her, hoping dismally that she was not destined to be painfully ripped apart for some unknown water creature's meal. There was something about the creature who held her that was distinctly humanoid, and male. The feel of the arms that held her against the firm chest reminded her of her awareness of some of the younger men amongst her people, those who might have aroused her interest if they had been considered to be of marriageable age. Here at death's door, pressed against the body of another living being for the first time since infancy, Namah became aware of another new feeling of arousal as well – one that told her that she had indeed become a woman.

Namah's confusion over the panorama of new sensations was abruptly halted by a sudden whoosh as she was thrust flying through the cold, damp air, and then landed with an unmerciful impact on the unyielding solidity of earth. Her breath was knocked out of her for a moment and she started to gasp for fresh air, but there was plenty to be had. She was on the northern shore. She felt completely drained of strength and allowed herself the luxury of collapse for a moment. She dared not sleep. She was still within view of the other shore where her people would look for her all too soon.

It was unspoken among them, but the Southerners all knew that when a young girl went missing on her wedding day, the river was the first place to look. Indeed, Namah was grateful that her parents had not locked her in her room as some of her friend's parents had the night before their weddings. It was her cleverness in feigning interest and excitement about the impending marriage that had circumvented suspicion long enough to escape, but now she had to find somewhere to go. She knew little of the land beyond the river, except that there were people like her own who lived less severely. There were also the magicians. Fear as she might, she knew that it was to these that she must appeal to for help. It was only an instinct, but her feelings had always served her well. There was something which drew her to the world of the magicians, as if there were a connection between them and herself.

Namah became aware of a presence. She opened her eyes to see an ordinary pair of human feet in front of her face. She lifted her head to see flowing skirts and long, auburn hair framing the face of a woman with a kind expression. *So beautiful*, Namah thought as she looked up at the pretty red-haired woman. Namah had always admired her own mother's beautiful auburn hair as well, so unlike her own dull blonde tresses.

'It isn't every day that the river spits a girl at my feet.' The woman's voice was melodic, soft, almost mocking – yet she spoke with sympathy. 'Perhaps you had better come with me.'

Namah nodded. Whoever the woman was, she was kindly. Namah was also very aware that help to find her way in this new world was going to be essential.

'What is your name, river spawn?'

'Namah.'

There was a flicker of something in the woman's eyes. Recognition? Surely news of her escape could not have reached the Northern people so quickly. Could she trust the woman not to turn her over to her parents?

'Come, Namah, you are safe now. My name is Laura. You can rest at my cottage, then we can talk about what to do with you.'

There was no sense of deceit about the woman. Namah decided that she could trust Laura. She reached to accept the hand that was offered to help her to get up. As soon as their fingers touched, images came to Namah's inner sight. A young girl, no older than herself but with bright red hair, ran among the trees and bushes that she had come through herself just that morning. The boat wavered in the water, but this time it did not topple. It landed on the northern shore and a frightened girl stood alone, looking like a scared rabbit as she chose direction bravely, on the very spot that the woman was now standing.

The images faded and Namah looked into the eyes of the grown-up Laura. The woman nodded acknowledgement. Somehow, she knew that Namah had seen her own childhood flight across the river, so long ago. Namah knew then that she would not have to hide her visions from Laura.

'Yes, Namah. I am a magician and see visions of past and future, like you.'

There. It was said. After a lifetime of being told by her mother that she must never speak of her visions to her father or anyone else, someone had said it as naturally as if everyone had them. The short walk to Laura's cottage seemed tiring, but it didn't take nearly long enough to learn all that Namah wanted to know. She was too exhausted to ask all the questions that begged to pour out of her, but Laura told her enough during the walk for her to believe that her silent cry in the boat had somehow reached this woman... that her presence on the shore had been no accident.

It had been very early when Namah had left her parents' house to run away. Laura's offer to let her sleep a while was welcomed with as much enthusiasm as Namah could muster after the morning's events. She ate just a little porridge, then accepted the offer to rest in Laura's room. She felt complete trust for the strange, yet familiar red-haired woman. In no time at all, Namah was asleep.

When she awoke, the light from the window had faded. Namah assumed that it must be very late in the day, nearly nightfall. The time for her wedding would have long since passed. Had she stayed in her parents' home, she would now be a maiden no more. Namah shuddered at the thought. Gareth, the man that her father had chosen for her, was considered to be a good man. He worked hard producing tools for the other men to use and could probably be described as kindly.

Still, his round face and balding head were not appealing to a young girl who had only just started noticing that some of the younger men could stir her attention. She also did not like the way that he had behaved in the weeks leading up to her wedding day. He often stood too close to her, the smell of his sweat permeating her senses. He had looked at her in an odd way that had made her feel uncomfortable. His words had been polite and acceptable enough, but he had seemed somehow predatory. Namah could feel an urgency behind the pleasantries that would no doubt have been expressed physically had she become his wife.

She was no child. Namah knew what took place among the animals and the married couples, and that compliance was expected. She remembered her friend Judith who had been married just a week before. The day after her wedding, Judith had been seen at the Sunday gathering with two black eyes. Her own parents had pretended not to notice.

Namah pushed away the disturbing thoughts and looked around Laura's room. It was a simple room, decorated in artistic hangings made of wool. Namah had never seen wool used for decoration before, only for sweaters. Her people were practical. Her old room had had no decoration at all. Her mind drifted back to the sheep that her family kept. Most families had a few sheep, as well as other animals which were used for food or other practical purposes. In history lessons she had been told that the Southern families had been taught farming by the ancient Count Victor and that this had saved her people from starving during the Dark Times.

Now it was his descendant, Count Anton, who looked after the interests of the people. Namah pulled the coverlet closer under her chin as she thought of her resolve to see Count Anton, to ask for his protection. The childhood memory came back to her again. The goblin patting her kindly on the head... Count Anton stopping for a moment to smile at her. He had been a dashing figure. Again, Namah wished that she might have been promised to such a man, but now she must find the courage to speak to him, knowing that he was no longer the bachelor that had stopped to share his smile that day. The news that he had married the Countess Ariane had reached Namah when she had been still a small child, intruding upon her childish dreams of growing up to marry him herself someday. Their child, the young Prince Alaric, had turned ten recently. Not so much younger than herself.

As she lay musing, the door opened gently and Laura entered carrying a tray with food on it.

'I sensed you were awake and thought you might be hungry.'

Namah suddenly realised that she was indeed hungry, but she was more intent on Laura's choice of words.

'There is no point in pretending, among our kind we often know things. We develop it and learn to use it properly. We are discreet among the people of course, but when we gather, we can be freely what we are. When you have eaten, we can go to meet the others.'

Namah sat up, pondering Laura's blatant admission. She nodded to the woman as she accepted the tray of food, lost for words to express the onslaught of feelings that stormed through her mind. This woman knew her thoughts, which was a little scary. More significantly, she was openly acknowledging the magicians in a way that suggested that she was speaking to another of their own kind. That thought was exciting. Despite a lifetime of teachings that their ways were wrong, Namah knew that she wanted to be among the magicians. She knew nearly nothing of what their lives must be like, only that she wanted to be one of them. Surely it must be more interesting than life among the ordinary people.

Laura smiled at her, as if yet again, she had read her mind. Then wordlessly she turned and left Namah alone with her food. It was simple fare, a small plate of meat and vegetables that had been freshly cooked, but Namah was used to simple food. It was almost disappointingly similar to what she would have eaten at home, or at least she thought so until she tasted it. There was something different about the food... a flavour that was sweet and unfamiliar in the vegetables. The meat also seemed subtly different, yet she could not identify the exotic new taste. She would have to ask Laura about it later.

Namah finished the food quickly and got herself out of bed, straightened her simple black dress, and borrowed the hairbrush on the dressing table to tidy her hair. By the time she was ready, darkness had fallen over the world, yet a bright full moon lit the sky like an eerie beacon as Namah followed Laura trustingly into the cool night air. She did not need to know exactly where Laura was taking her. She knew only that she was being taken to meet her new people, *the magicians*.

Chapter Two

Rested and fed, Namah was full of questions for Laura as they walked in the cool evening air. Many of them were about Count Anton. Laura smiled indulgently, recognising the young girl's fascination for the romantic figure whom she would have seen in the dashing Count. The real man would no doubt dazzle her with his charm and quick smile when she met him. All women who encountered him were at least a little in love with Count Anton and most men wished that they could be him. He ruled by charisma as much as by birthright. No previous ruler had ever been so admired.

Namah told Laura of her encounter with the Count when she had been little more than a baby.

'I remember his smile most of all,' Namah explained at the finish of her tale. 'The goblin might have frightened me, although it was only kindly patting my head, but when the Count smiled at me I just knew that it was alright and that I was safe. My father was pulling me away...'

'You trusted the Count more than your own father?' Laura queried.

'He knew the goblin, my father did not.'

'Here,' said Laura, removing a ring. 'Take this in your hand and see if you can get any impressions from it.'

Namah obeyed, taking the simple ring into the palm of her left hand. She closed her eyes and watched the images dance. It was something that she had always been able to do. She need only close her eyes and flickers of light and shadow would begin to take shape into mental images. If she watched them undisturbed, they would form into moving pictures. Often she would not know what the images meant, but they fascinated her and sometimes she would learn later that visions of people she knew would depict something that they had been doing at the time that she was watching them behind her eyelids. It was one of those things that her mother had told her not to talk about.

The images from the ring flickered back and forth, Count Anton and a goblin cavorting in some form of rhythmic spectacle, but soon it became apparent that this was no dance. The sword of the goblin barely missed the finely sculptured cheekbone where Count Anton already bore a small scar. He turned so quickly that Namah could hardly see his intent, then dropped and rose swiftly with the blade thrusting towards the stocky goblin. Namah saw that it was the same goblin that she had seen as a child. The goblin parried, stepped and suddenly it was Count Anton who had the end of a blade touching his throat. Namah caught her breath, but she relaxed again as she saw the familiar smile spread across the Count's face. The goblin blade dropped casually and immediately Namah understood. They had only been sparring.

'What did you see?' Laura had observed the changing reactions of the young psychic, but was too well trained to interrupt her before the vision had finished.

'Sword practice. It was them... the goblin who patted me and Count Anton.' Namah looked up at Laura. The woman was smiling down at her as if she had achieved a personal triumph.

'The ring was given to me by Count Anton, just a token.' Laura slipped the ring back on. For a moment, she looked at it wistfully, as if she was remembering something from long ago. Then she continued chattering gaily as if she had just come back to the present.

'Touching it gave you a connection to him, more so because you had a memory of him in person. He will be pleased that you reach visions so easily. We need more like you.'

Namah opened her mouth to speak, but no words were forthcoming. After a lifetime of hiding her ability as if it were something shameful, she had at last come home to a place where it was valued. *Yes*, she thought to herself. *That's exactly what it's like. Coming home at last.*

After a few moments Namah began to chat freely with Laura, which continued for the rest of the walk. She asked many questions about the magicians – what they were like and how many there were, what they did, even what they ate. Laura tried to answer as many as she could. She told Namah that there were children among them that she would be introduced to right away. Namah noticed the odd look come across Laura's face again as she mentioned the children, as if there were something that she wasn't saying. Namah could sense a little trepidation from her benefactor and wondered what there could be about a group of children that would cause such a reaction. Certainly they would be different than the children she had grown up with. Even the ordinary Northern children knew different ways than the children of the Southern people and these were the children of magicians.

Namah felt excited as the bonfire became visible in the distance. She could hear sweet music drifting on the air currents and saw the flicker of people dancing in front of the flames. As they drew closer, she felt something in the air that was somehow different, as if the magic itself was a tangible substance that created a different world within the space where these people sang and danced. Namah felt as if she was about to step within a separate space from the outside world, far away from that land where she was meant to have been married this morning. She felt an indescribable joy and sense of freedom. She had never danced in her life, but now she felt as if she wanted to.

Laura led her to the circle of people sitting around the fire just as a song was coming to a close. There was applause for the musician, then Laura commanded the attention of the onlookers.

'We have a new one among us, my friends. This is Namah, whom the river practically spat out at my feet this morning.'

There were a few seconds of silence, then a man asked.

'Spat out?'

'Yes, Brion, spat out from the river itself.'

The emphasis on the words and the significant look that passed between Laura and Brion said far more than the words. Namah looked from one to the other. They knew. They knew that there was something in the water and the fact that it hadn't eaten her was what was causing the uncomfortable silence and odd looks that they were all giving her. Then it all changed. The music began again and the others returned to speaking amongst themselves.

'You are most welcome among us, Lady Namah.' Brion stood and emphasised the words with a formal bow, as if he were speaking to royalty.

'Don't tease, Brion.' Laura remonstrated gently. 'She's had a very trying day. Where are the children?'

'Lurking in the shadows, as usual', replied a young female voice from the darkness. Then a slim girl who looked about twelve or thirteen stepped into the light.

Namah had been struck by the melodic, even sonorous, quality of the voice that came from the girl. As she saw her better now in the flickering light of the bonfire flames, her attention was drawn in by her straight stature and a pair of eyes that seemed to penetrate right through her. The girl's eyes were the most interesting spectrum of colours, so that it was difficult to determine their colour at all.

First green, then brown and blue and yellow, and then all colours all at once.

The spell was soon broken by the arrival of a boy bounding into view from out of the shadows. He was dark and lively, smiling and playful as boys were inclined to be.

'A new girl! Come with us, you can meet the others. We were just having a game, but we can start over if you want to play.'

Namah smiled. The boy had a presence to him that was hard to resist. It was as if he were welcoming her into his own private realm of play.

'I see you've met Alinea already. Is it true? Were you actually thrown out of the river?' The boy stepped closer to Namah before she could answer and looked into her eyes, as his tone turned suddenly very serious. 'Did you see them?'

Once again, Namah was captivated by the multi-coloured eyes, but they were the boy's eyes. They were disturbingly similar to those of the girl called Alinea.

'Come.' Alinea interrupted the scene almost as if she were doing it deliberately before Namah could answer about whatever it was that was in the water. 'There are others for you to meet, and you mustn't think about the things that might frighten children.'

She gave a significant look to the boy. He grinned back as if he had been caught at something, but Alinea had taken Namah's hand and was pulling her towards the darkness before the conversation could continue.

Namah liked her new companions. She instantly trusted Alinea. Laura had allowed the children to take charge of her, so Namah knew that it must certainly be safe. She found that as they moved farther from the fire, her eyes adjusted so that she could still see the adults around the bonfire clearly and also could see for a distance in the darkness around herself. With no light to shine on them, the children would be hidden from the adults in the darkness. Namah smiled, remembering what Alinea had said to Laura about lurking in the shadows. It had seemed like a joke, but the girl had meant it literally.

The boy chased after them, then skipping playfully past them and ran ahead. Namah wondered if he might be related to Alinea. Such unusual eyes could not be so similar otherwise, unless there was something about magicians that made their eyes sparkle in such colours. Laura's eyes had been an ordinary green, although her gaze had been powerful.

The sounds of more children laughing and playing reached Namah's ears, followed quickly by a glimpse of moving shadows that could only be the children they sought. Alinea had known the place where they would be with uncanny accuracy.

'It's my eyes,' said Alinea, as if the question had been spoken aloud. 'I see in the dark like a goblin.'

Namah didn't answer. She did not find Alinea's figure of speech funny at all. She was sure that she would be terrified if she ever actually met a goblin, despite her childhood experience. She had been too young to react when the nice one had patted her head by the river, but even that kindness was associated with the memory of his frightening appearance. Rumour had it that the magicians actually spoke to goblins regularly... demons as some of her people still called them... and her one fear had been that seeking life among the magicians would result in encountering one.

Alinea stopped just before they reached the children. She turned and looked deep into Namah's eyes. She spoke seriously, again as if she had heard Namah's thoughts.

'You will like my friends. There is no reason to be afraid.' Then she nodded, dipping her shoulders as if it were almost a bow, and led Namah into the circle of children.

Namah looked around at their faces quickly, half expecting to see goblins among them because of Alinea's assurances. She saw only children, much like herself, and one small creature that was certainly no goblin. She had seen pictures of such creatures in her lesson books. The funny little animal was called a monkey. It jumped onto the shoulder of the boy, who was now leading the others playfully in a game of singing and slapping hands that had them all giggling hysterically. The monkey screamed along with the childish squeals of laughter. Namah decided she quite liked the boy and that she would certainly like the others. There was no restraint in their play in order to seem 'proper' as there was among the children of her own people. They played un-self-consciously and their laughter had real joy in it.

The boy danced impishly among them, charming them all. Alinea had waited with Namah so that they wouldn't interrupt the game, but the boy saw them and ran over, grabbing Namah's hands and pulling her into the centre of them. He mouthed the words of the song to her and showed her the hand movements patiently, without breaking the rhythm of the game. Alinea integrated herself in gracefully, also without disrupting the play.

The song and hand movements were actually quite easy. After a couple of verses, Namah had caught on and she was slapping hands with the others randomly, but her attention kept returning to the boy. He was younger than herself, perhaps nine or ten. Far too young for her to have any romantic ideas about him, yet something about him was compelling and drew her in. His long dark hair bounced from his shoulders as he moved and those multi-coloured eyes sparkled with warmth, even in the darkness. An unbridled joy emanated from him and seemed to magically encase the circle of playing children. He was an attractive child and would be a real stunner when he was older.

Then Namah remembered that these were the children of magicians. Part of the spell in the game was his doing. He was probably unusually powerful among his peers, charming everyone into his own rhythm and even extending the charm to the monkey on his shoulder. Namah had paid a lot of attention to the whispered tales of magicians. Her own people spoke of Count Anton as a particularly powerful and charismatic magician when they thought the children could not hear. What she felt from this boy was similar to the feeling she had all those years ago, when the Count himself had smiled at her. It was not a babyish crush she had felt for Count Anton, but a feeling of recognition. To some extent, Namah could feel it towards all of her new friends, especially Laura. Still, there was something special about how it expressed itself with the boy.

The game came to a natural end as the song finished and the children all collapsed on the grass in laughter. Alinea was the first to speak.

'As you can see, we have a new friend among us. This is Namah, a child of the river.' All eyes turned to Namah then. The sudden silence and look of awe made her nervous for a moment, until a pretty, dark haired girl who looked about her own age stood and walked over to Namah, offering her hands. Namah took them and the girl bowed slightly in an odd undulating motion and looked into Namah's eyes warmly as she spoke.

'Welcome among us, Namah, child of the river. I am Lolari, you already know Alinea. These are Damon, Saffara, Emily and Jase.'

Each of the children nodded acknowledgement as they were named. Damon and Saffara were fair and looked to be close to Namah's age as well, or perhaps a year older. They had the look of nobility about them, in contrast to little Emily who looked like a very common eight-year-old with her shaggy, black hair falling into her eyes. Jase also looked very ordinary. Namah realised that some of the impressions she was forming were based on the clothing the children wore. There appeared to be a mix of classes among the magicians.

'Where's Drazek?' Alinea asked the group.

'Lurking among his own shadows, as usual. You know how he is.' Lolari answered. 'He's probably watching us right now.

The boy she had first met had still not been named. As Lolari released her hands, he rose and came to Namah, kissed her cheek and sat casually next to her.

'Your sense of rhythm is remarkable, Namah, I shall have to fall in love with you and grow up and marry you someday.'

Namah laughed.

'Just because I have good rhythm?

'You would be amazed at how important that can be among our kind,' he answered seriously. 'Magic works in patterns and I could only love a girl who could feel the rhythm of *The Dance*.'

'But you're a little young to be thinking of marriage anyway, aren't you? I'm sure you're younger than me.'

'That won't matter when we're grown,' he answered her confidently.

'And I don't even know your name.'

The boy turned and looked at her in surprise then, as if he had expected her to know it. He stood and took her right hand in his, made a sweeping bow and spoke formally. The impish smile lit up his face as he answered.

'Alaric. At your service, My Lady.' Then he kissed her hand, his eyes looking up into hers with mischief gleaming from every pore.

Namah's mouth dropped open.

'*Prince* Alaric?' She managed to remember to close her mouth after saying the words, but her expression was aghast.

Namah had no idea how to respond properly. Prince Alaric! The son of Count Anton and the Countess Ariane was the romantic fantasy of many mothers of young girls, although he had only recently turned ten. The idea that he would be playing amongst ordinary children had not occurred to Namah during the game, but here he was ,speaking to her of marriage... albeit in jest.

Namah gathered her wits about her, then found an answer that she hoped would not make her seem too much like an ignorant commoner.

'Well, kind sir, I hope I will have the chance to know you better before you speak to me of marriage again!'

The other children laughed at the rebuff.

'Told *you*, didn't she Alaric?' Laughed Jase.

Alaric joined in the laughter, but his eyes twinkled even more at Namah. She had evidently gained his respect.

'As you wish, My Lady. Shall we have another game?' Alaric directed the question to the group as a whole.

'Can we play a goblin game please?' asked Emily in a sweet, high voice. 'Please, Lolari, will you teach us a new game?'

Namah looked with curiosity at Lolari.

'You know goblin games?' she asked incredulously.

Lolari turned to Namah, her eyes unreadable in the dark.

'Didn't you know?' she said gently. Then she pushed her long hair behind the large pointed ears that marked her as goblin. 'I forget that humans cannot see colours in the darkness. See? My skin is quite green.'

Lolari hovered the palm of her hand over her arm, somehow producing a light between the skin surfaces which clearly showed very green skin. Namah looked at this, then she looked up at Lolari, seeing for the first time how the goblin girl's golden eyes shone in the darkness.

The shock, and almost horror, were all too apparent in Namah's unguarded expression.

'I thought...' Namah gathered her words unsure what to say to her new friend. Her new *goblin* friend. 'I thought that goblins would look... different. Like the one I saw as a child. He was...'

'Goblins are of many types.' Lolari explained patiently. 'You saw one of the *Deep Dwellers*, who are very different in appearance from humans. I am a *Betweener*. We are not so removed from our human ancestors that we have changed to become like the rocks in our natural environment.'

Namah blinked.

'Goblins have human ancestors?'

Lolari nodded assent in the undulating goblin fashion.

'I am not surprised that your people do not tell you. The magicians teach their children of us, but most of the humans only pretend we are not there. We stay out of sight so they forget about us. It makes them happy and keeps us safe.'

'Are people so dangerous that they would harm you without reason?' Namah asked incredulously.

Alinea looked sad as she joined the conversation.

'Humans will harm what they do not understand. I look entirely human, yet the humans tried to drown me as a baby.'

Images returned to Namah's mind then. The baby thrown into the river... the boats being knocked over by some unseen creature in the water. *Creatures* she reminded herself. They had been in the water with her that morning, yet they did not kill her as they did those men.

'You were that baby,' Namah stated in understanding. 'You're a goblin.'

Alinea nodded assent as Lolari had done, with the undulation of the shoulders that was customary among goblins.

'I was seeded by a human, so I look like one.' A conspiratorial look passed between Alinea and Prince Alaric. Alaric's eyes glinted. Namah could see that he shared some secret with Alinea that they were not yet going to tell her.

'But in the dark I see with the eyes of a goblin, and I grew up among my mother's people so I know the ways of our kind. Still, I have always been welcomed among these humans, the magicians, and I know their ways also.'

'How did you survive being thrown in the river?' Namah asked. Again, a look passed between Alinea and Alaric that was difficult to read. Alaric was attentive, awaiting her answer to the question, but Alinea answered very simply.

'Some goblins can swim.'

The smirk she gave Alaric was enough for Namah to see that this was an old game between them. Alaric didn't know the answer, yet Alinea obviously did and wouldn't tell. Namah decided she would ask Alaric about it sometime if she could find an opportunity to talk with him away from the others.

'The goblins live in harmony with the earth, feeling its natural rhythm and reflecting it in the music we make,' continued Alinea. 'This is why we often know things that are occurring in other places. If the rhythm feels wrong, we know there is trouble and we will help our own kind in whatever way we can. Sometimes my people have even been known to help yours, although mostly we stay out of sight because the humans will kill us.'

Namah was fascinated by all that she had seen and heard amongst the children. She quickly grew used to the greenish tinge of the young goblin girl's skin and began to get to know her just as she did the humans. Alaric was a striking lad, but Alinea, with her goblin heritage and human appearance, captured Namah's interest in a very curious way. The girl was incredibly pleasant. Her mannerisms were much like the goblin girl's, yet if she had walked among the people of Namah's village, Alinea would only have been thought a little odd at most and might well have passed as one of the Northern people, with their different customs.

Namah closed her eyes, trying to feel the rhythm that Alinea had been describing. It was faint, but she thought that she could sense it a little. It seemed somehow familiar, as if she had experienced it unconsciously all of her short life. Some scrap of memory came to Namah of that morning, when she had awakened to what had been meant to have been her wedding day. In the quiet of the pre-dawn hours, she had felt... something. The unheard rhythm had enveloped her in pure sensory instinct. It had told her to run.

Something else began to entwine itself through her senses. It contrasted with the irregular rhythm of the earth, embroidering a high pitched resonant melody that seemed to lace itself between and at peace within the rhythm. It was several minutes before Namah realised that she was actually hearing the melody with her ears. It was coming from the group of adults who were gathered round the bonfire.

Nobody spoke to Namah as she quietly got up and walked towards the fire. She had to know the source of that music. She followed the sound as if she were in a trance, unable to resist, following the tune with both her mind and her body. Some part of her felt as if it were observing her movements from afar, no longer in control of this young girl in an alien world. She wondered for a moment if there would be goblins among the adults as well, but as she came upon the adults she saw that they were nearly all humans. *The magicians.* There was only one green skin among them. He was playing an instrument which she could see now was the source of the music.

It was some sort of flute-like device that looked as though it had been carved from bone. *Bone of what creature?* Namah could not help but wonder. There were holes drilled into it, just four in a row and one on the side that the goblin blew into. *How do goblins drill holes in bone?* Her inquisitive nature soon gave way to pure sensory enjoyment as the sonorous music enraptured her.

Even in the trance-like state, Namah was astounded at the beauty of the goblin. He was slim, yet his toned muscles spoke of strength and agility. It was then that she noticed how little he was wearing, nothing more than a reddish-tinged skin loincloth stood between him and complete nakedness, yet he looked so like an animated statue that she had not immediately noticed. His dark hair fell only just past his pointed ears and had a texture like some of the bigger fluffy dogs that her father kept. There was a long plait that hung down in back between his shoulder blades. His skin, although green, was a deep shade that looked as though it was what green skin would be like with a suntan. Namah knew this was a silly idea. Goblins lived underground where there was no sun, but it was the only way she could describe it to herself.

She felt confused. She had always been told that goblins were ugly. The vague memory of the goblin she had seen when she was two was not of a very ugly goblin, but it was not one with this kind of slim beauty that she had seen first in the younger men of her own people and now in this lovely musician. She could not help but admire the delicate line of his straight nose as his fingers moved gracefully over the instrument. He seemed completely at one with the music, the instrument a part of him as much as the elegant fingers that moved across the air holes so expertly. She wondered for a moment how old he really was. If he were human, she would guess him at about nineteen, but goblins were... different. After all, the man that her father had intended to marry her to had been thirty.

What am I thinking! She was aghast at her own thoughts. *He's green! And... another species!*

Just at that moment, the song came to a finish and the people around Namah applauded. The goblin bowed in response, dipping his shoulders while still sitting. When he looked up, his eyes met Namah's. She caught her breath before she could stop the reaction. His eyes were large and almond shaped. The naturally dark lashes lined them as if he were wearing the cosmetics that some women used to frame their eyes. It gave them a dreamy sort of beauty that touched a young girl's deepest appreciation. Most disarming though, was their colour. They were a deep golden hue that sparkled like fire, yet pulled her into their depths like the secrets of the deepest pools.

He bowed again, especially for her this time. Then he sat back and smiled at her before he began to play another tune. Namah knew that the smile would haunt her as much as the look of amusement she saw in the beautiful goblin's eyes before he turned his attention back to the music. His mouth was broad and yet shapely. The full lips had parted to reveal sharp teeth, the one reminder that there was more than skin colour to separate their species. Slightly embarrassed by the feeling that he had somehow read her mind or seen her girlish reaction to his beauty, she furtively backed through the crowd of adults and left the fireside to rejoin the children.

The night was brightly lit by the full moon. The shadows created by the moonlight lent an eerie feeling to the new surroundings that accented the unprecedented experiences that the day had brought. Namah walked slowly across the comforting grass of the heath, the one familiar substance in a world that had changed so completely for her in a single day. She took her time, giving herself a few minutes to assimilate all of the new experiences before rejoining her new friends. It was odd looking around the site. It was obviously a familiar meeting place for the magicians. She wondered for a moment if Count Anton himself would appear soon.

Namah's eye fell on an object standing erect against the darkened sky. She had not noticed before. It was an abnormally shaped object, tall and striking, yet not quite visible in the shadows of moonlight. She walked towards it. When she was quite close she could see that it was a carved wooden post. There were figures carved on it of various animal-like masks. On the top sat a very detailed figure of a gargoyle. It was ugly, with the sort of features that she would have expected to see on the goblins. It had broad leathery looking wings that accented its demon-like appearance.

Namah wondered for a moment why the magicians would carve such a frightening figure. The eyes were particularly alarming. They looked predatory... almost evil, yet they had a similar quality to the beautiful goblin's eyes. They were like deep golden pools to draw in the soul, much like those of the musician... *a carving with colour?* The expression in the eyes changed to one of inquisitiveness as the gargoyle cocked its head to the side, studying the girl who gazed upon it.

Namah began to hyperventilate in absolute, soul encompassing fear. She felt the vibration of the scream as it rose through her diaphragm, then escaped through her throat into the open air in a blood-curdling shriek that might possibly have awakened the dead.

Chapter Three

C ount Anton felt agitated. He did not yet know why, but he had been a magician far too long to expect anything other than a very good reason for his unease. Somewhere, something was happening that would require his ability to balance chaos. Nothing less would have him feeling nervous enough to pace the floor of the receiving room. He wasn't entirely sure why he had come to this part of the castle at all. He had spent far less time in this room since... the trouble. His eye fell on the disused chess set on the table. He was almost grateful when he heard the knock.

'Enter, Dani,' Anton called. He looked up at his faithful servant expectantly. *So. Now it comes.*

Dani strode into the room with the formal air that was reserved for visitors. He was clearly not alone.

'Sir, there is a man to see you about a matter of some importance.' The look in Dani's eye told Anton that the matter was surely of importance to the man outside the door, but that Anton would probably be less than delighted to have it brought before him. Anton braced himself. Worse, the degree of formality indicated it was one of those from across the river. The Southerners.

'Show him in, Dani, and serve wine.' Again, the eye contact between them was communication enough. Dani was to stay close and listen. Anton's closest counsellor and second in command might be needed.

The man was shown in and introduced as Rab from the Southern shore. The servant fetched wine from a nearby cabinet while Count Anton greeted his guest. The change in Anton's demeanour and expression was more genuine than a casual observer might have believed. He simply invoked a memory of more carefree times when the characteristic smile spread across his face. The wolfish grin never failed to put such visitors immediately on the defensive, yet that too was genuine. Whenever a man from across the river brought a matter to Count Anton the game was on, and the stakes were probably high.

'Good morning, sir,' said Anton jovially. 'Now what could bring a man of the South all the way across the river to my castle? Is there a matter with which I can be of service?'

The man looked uncomfortable from the time that Anton referred to him as 'sir'. He was obviously unused to such honorifics. The tactic had achieved the desired effect. Thrown off-guard by the Count's manner and apparent willingness to treat him with respect and to be of assistance, Rab stammered a little as he began to explain his plight.

'It-it's me daughter, Sir. She was to be wed this morning, b-but the silly girl got a case of nerves and fled the safety of her own bed last night. I was hoping to find her here, maybe come to you to... to plead for sanctuary.'

There. It was said. Rab had acknowledged that his daughter would run away from a planned marriage. Few of this man's people would admit so much.

'We found a boat floating loose in the river, Sir. I fear for her life. Please, Sir, if you know anything at all, I would rather know she was safe and hiding from me than to think she was lost to the river.'

Dani chose that moment to offer a glass of wine to Count Anton, then to the guest. The man stammered a 'no thank you' as expected. Anton and Dani knew very well that Rab's people did not drink wine, but it served as a delaying tactic, plus feigning ignorance of the prohibition was Anton's way of offering insult in a suitably subtle manner.

Count Anton looked at the man for a moment. He was familiar in some way. Anton wondered for a moment if Rab had been directly involved in the incidents a little over ten years before, when Ranalf had died. His thoughts towards the Southern peoples had never been kind since that day, although his words and mannerisms towards them never showed his true feelings. This time, however, he was in the mood to speak his mind.

'Perhaps if you did not marry your girls at so young an age to men far too old for them, your daughters would not run away from their weddings.' Anton looked at Rab sharply, accusingly.

'Please, Sir, do not blame me for the ways of my people. Tradition is not an easy thing to break. I've lost two daughters already, many years past. I had hoped the little one would be happy with the husband I chose for her. She seemed so enthusiastic.'

Count Anton looked at Rab a little more sympathetically then. He knew what a father feels for his daughter. Anton had been so afraid of losing his own daughter when she was a baby. The horror of watching her thrown into the river by those men, the Southern men, had never left his memory. Then there had been the fear of losing her in the goblin world, but Talla had been generous. Alinea had been brought to see him regularly in the levels where he was allowed. Later, when she was old enough, she had become a regular visitor among the magicians. She had come of her free will to see him, although she would never call him 'father'. It was not the way of goblins.

'Why is it that you have never come to me to ask about your other daughters, yet you come to me now?' Anton watched Rab's expressions closely for a reaction, but a twist of his eyebrows spoke only of pain.

'When Lana left I was shamed. All I could think of was my promise to the man I would have given her to and what it would look like in the community. You must understand, if a girl disobeys her father so, she is dead to us. Disowned. So I promised the man my second daughter, Laura, as soon as she was old enough. She was only two years younger than Lana, so he waited. Then Laura ran away as well and the man married a girl from another family.'

Anton looked at the man coolly. He knew who he was now. He also remembered where he had actually seen him. So, this was Laura's father.

'And what about your third daughter?'

'Namah was much younger. My wife learned she was pregnant just before Laura ran off. The shock nearly made her lose the baby.'

Anton sensed something not quite true in Rab's last words. No doubt Rab had chosen to over-dramatise the event to gain sympathy. Rab looked up at Anton then, imploring.

'Sir, if you have information about any of my daughters...'

'I can tell you about Lana,' Anton answered, choosing his words carefully. Some information would comfort the man, but he was not going to mention Laura. She was still unmarried, and not so old that her father would not seek to trade her in marriage still.

'Lana did indeed come to our side of the river. She found her way among the people here and eventually married when she was old enough.' Again, the sharp eyes looked accusingly at the father. Then Anton's expression softened as he said his next words.

'She had a son... he died.' Anton absently picked up a chess piece from the board on the table. It was a knight.

The memory of that day came flooding back so suddenly that he had to grip the piece hard in his hand to distract him from the tears that fought to fill his eyes. He was a ruler and a magician. He could not show so much emotion to this man. Not now, in this room. Too much would require explanation. He wondered for a moment if the

man had been among those who had stoned Ranalf to death. Rab
might well have helped to kill his own grandson. If it were so, now
was not the time to tell him.

'Of your youngest daughter, I know nothing yet,' Anton
continued truthfully. 'If she ran away only this morning, it is possible
that I may hear something. But you put me in a difficult position. I
am a father as well, I know what it is to love a child, but I could not in
good conscience turn a young girl over to be forcibly married against
her will.'

'Begging your pardon, Sir, but it's different with a girl. Your
young son will grow to be a man and make his own choices, but a girl,
well, you have to take so much responsibility for them.'

'Do you?' Anton asked the man flatly. 'And what do you suppose
would happen if we let our daughters make their own choices, as we
do our sons?'

The man looked horrified. This concept was too far outside his
cultural conditioning to even contemplate. He wrinkled his brows
for a moment, thinking. Anton thought it a credit to him that he
bothered to try to work it out rather than firing off a quick response.
Eventually Rab answered.

'I suppose, Sir, that they would marry the first man that caught
their girlish fancy.'

This silenced Anton for a moment. Memories of a time when
Laura was young and fanciful came to his mind. The girl had had
a crush on him, but he had dealt with it patiently. Had he been a
man without honour, he might easily have taken advantage of her.
She had clearly had fantasies of becoming his Countess, but he had
chosen Ariane instead, and never regretted it. The darker woman's
cool head in a crisis and her unswerving loyalty had proved her worth
many times over. Also, she had never remonstrated with him about
Talla.

'Perhaps you are right,' Anton replied at last. 'The fancies of young women are not always sensible. Yet neither are the fancies of young men.' Anton thought again of Ranalf. The young man had died for his fancy of Talla. He had believed that her child, Anton's own daughter, had been his own. Perhaps it was best that he had never learned the truth.

'I will make a bargain with you.' Anton summoned his most persuasive tone for this one. It would not be easy for the man to agree to it. 'I will make enquiries about your lost daughter, and if I learn something I will come to you and tell you that she is safe.'

Anton hesitated just a moment before coming to the difficult part.

'But you must not ask me her whereabouts or try to hunt her down to take her back to a marriage she does not wish for.'

Rab met Anton's eyes. This was hard for him. It went against everything he believed in and the ways of his people, but after losing his other daughters and not knowing for so many years if they lived, he was not able to face the uncertainty a third time. After a little internal struggle, Rab nodded his head in agreement.

'Her mother will be grateful to know whether she lives,' he said, sounding defeated.

Dani moved from his unobtrusive position to guide the man out.

'I will come to you as soon as I learn anything, I promise.' Anton regretted the words almost as soon as they left his lips. It seemed a simple promise to make, but a shadow passed across Rab's face. No ordinary shadow, but one that Anton recognised. The man was doomed. Anton's premonitions were never wrong. He could sense that in some way, he would be involved in Rab's demise.

They shook hands and Dani led the man away. Anton was left to contemplate his thoughts. He still had the knight from the chess set in his left hand, fingering it absently. Again, he remembered the bloody and broken body of Ranalf in his arms, dead from the angry stoning of his own people. Then having to leave him to run after those who had kidnapped Talla... watching his baby daughter and the woman he loved thrown into the river to drown or to be eaten by the unknown creatures that Haghuf had never explained.

Suddenly Anton realised that he had tensed and was clutching his fists tightly. He released the chess piece in his hand, fumbling it slightly so that it fell under the table. There was blood in his hand where the sharp edges of the carved piece had cut into his flesh. It had fallen just behind a side table, but when Anton bent down to retrieve it, there was no sign of it. Only slightly perturbed, Anton leant the chair next to the table back to take a good look underneath, in case it had rolled or slid out of view. Then he walked around behind the chair, searching intently in every possible corner or any place that it could have gone. It was nowhere to be seen.

Slowly, an understanding smile spread across Anton's face.

The faintest hint of laughter touched his more psychic hearing, but no sound that a non-magician could detect was to be heard. Anton knew this game. He looked all around a second time, this time knowing that he would not find the chess piece, then he searched a third time.

'How curious,' Anton said, sounding less than sincere. 'Where could it have gone?' He walked purposefully out of the room closing the door behind him. In days gone by, Anton knew that he would have found the lost item on the fifth search, or in another odd place while looking for something else. However, he knew the game too well, and the goblins knew that he knew it. He pushed the door open again, unsurprised to find a goblin sitting in his favourite chair with a big grin on his face. The chess piece was dangling from Leap's fingers.

'Well met, Leap. It has been a long time.'

Leap grinned back at his human friend. The playful goblin had always enjoyed his little tricks. Yet in his own way, he had been the source of much information about goblin abilities for Anton's insatiable curiosity. That curiosity was piqued now. Leap had never openly come to the castle before. It seemed odd to see him sitting among the human finery when Anton had always encountered him in the goblin caverns before.

'I bring news of a visitor for you, Anton.' The goblin's voice was playful, teasing in his usual manner. Yet Anton knew him well enough to recognise the subtle serious note within. 'Humans come to you, from far away. Over the water they prepare to come.'

'You're slipping, Leap,' Anton replied lightly. 'I've just had a visitor from across the river.' Then a thought occurred to him, and for a moment he was very serious. 'Or do you mean that they are coming across in force? Like before?'

Leap sat up then and handed the chess piece over to Anton.

'Not from the river. Far away, across bigger water. The distant land, where your people do not go. They came from there before, but many generations before your lifetime.'

Anton contemplated this information for a moment. He was about to speak when Dani returned to the room. Dani looked shaken, yet he held his formal demeanour as he first acknowledged Leap with a bow and then delivered his message to Anton.

'Sir, you have another visitor.'

The words were simple enough, but it was the subtle expression on Dani's face that told Anton that this was no ordinary visitor. Something was up. Leap's words came back to him as he answered his friend and servant.

'Show him in please.'

Anton turned to set the chess piece back on the table, but was not surprised to find that the goblin had disappeared. Whoever this visitor was, Leap was not going to show himself any more than he had with the Southern man. Keeping out of sight from humans was a skill taught from birth to the goblins, and they had a long history.

How long even Anton didn't know, but he did know that none of the staff would have seen Leap enter the castle.

Anton turned and adopted his most formal stately posture. He was glad that he had had some warning as the new visitor was ushered into the room. His mode of dress and bearing left no room for doubt. He was an emissary from over the sea. From the place where, as Leap had put it, his people did not go. Anton bowed formally to the visitor before he spoke.

'Welcome to my castle. Will you take wine?'

The stranger nodded acknowledgement and Dani moved to serve the wine, and to listen.

'Please sit,' Anton invited, gesturing towards a chair. 'You must be weary after your long voyage.'

'Thank you,' the man replied as he sat in the fine tapestry chair that Anton had indicated. The foreigner's strangely accented form of the human language was apparent even in those two words. 'As you probably know, our boats are very good.' The man met Anton's eyes as he said this. There was an implication behind the words. 'But the voyage still takes a full night to make the crossing, and travelling from the shores of your country even with the best horses has taken us until nearly nightfall, as you can see.'

'Where is your escort?' Anton wondered how many the man had brought with him, and whether they had a camp setting up even now.

'I have brought only half a dozen to your castle. They are looking after the horses in your own stable now.'

This did not answer the question. The man was good. Half a dozen in the stable, and how many more outside of the city? Was it an invading force, or just an emissary?

'What brings your people to my land?' The slight emphasis on the word 'my' was subtle, but not lost on the visitor.

'My apologies, Count Anton. I am afraid I have the better of you. I know who you are, yet I have not introduced myself.'

Artful Anton thought to himself. The visitor had implied an advantage through an ordinary phrase that would have a less sinister meaning if it were spoken by one of Anton's own people.

'I am the Count Michel, emissary for King Niklas. He sends greetings, and a sincere wish to renew contact with our little brothers across the sea.'

Anton flicked a glance at Dani, meeting his eyes briefly. The servant had remained out of the way, busying himself with seemingly small tasks in the far corner of the room. Unknown to the visitor, one of these tasks was to prepare a white powder to add to the second glass of wine, should it be required. The situation was delicate.

'Is this a purely social call then?' Anton kept his voice steady as he probed for answers. 'Or is King Niklas seeking trade in other lands, now that you have such good boats?'

Count Michel smiled, yet it came over as a sinister expression.

'As you probably know, Count Anton, only half a dozen generations ago, this island you inhabit was part of the larger continent that King Niklas rules.'

'Much has changed since then,' Count Anton interjected quickly.

'True', replied Count Michel. 'But not so much in many ways. We still come from common ancestry, one people, and we all benefit from sharing resources.'

There. The point of the exercise was becoming clear now. Anton spoke quickly to intercept the direction of the conversation.

'According to what my father and father's father passed down, much of the land that was once Europe is under the sea now, and what you inhabit was largely raised from the bottom of the ocean during the Turning. Old borders are meaningless now.'

The wolfish eyes studied the visitor coolly. A barely perceptible nod to Dani escaped the notice of Count Michel. Count Anton could not help but remember that if common ancestry was to be invoked, then they could all claim kinship with the goblins and have as much right to live their anarchic lifestyle as to be subject to some fool who called himself King.

Count Michel smirked, displaying his discoloured teeth in a wry smile that suddenly made Anton feel as if the room had become filthy.

'And yet the remains of old civilisations rose from the ocean beds along with those lands. The histories are preserved well enough. We were all one land once upon a time.'

'Things change with time.' Anton kept his voice confident, authoritative. 'The rulers of those ancient lands died out. Their descendants may well have been peasants among the people who inhabited our lands before the Turning.'

'Yet still the descendants of royalty continue to rule them,' Michel answered quickly. 'Except here. You have no king in this land *Count* Anton.'

Count Michel looked Anton in the eye steadily. It was a challenge. His emphasis on the word 'Count' was not an insult – he shared the rank himself – but it was a declaration of station. Count Anton's rulership of what was left of the island nation once known as Britain was not recognised by the European descendants.

Count Anton returned the steady gaze. He felt 'wolf' stir within him. A low growl on a level undetectable by ordinary humans escaped his slightly parted lips.

'I think you will find that a ruler is defined not by the name of his title, but by the recognition of his people.'

Count Anton's boots echoed on the wooden floor as he paced steadily towards the window, taking another glass of wine from Dani as he passed. He gazed coolly over the courtyard, towards the distant river. No boats were to be seen. The invaders had been clever enough to dock out of eyesight of the castle. Count Michel took the remaining glass from Dani politely and downed the full glass with a flourish as Count Anton spoke in the confident tones of a true ruler.

'Tell your king that I will be happy to discuss trade with him. He can send his lackey with messages if he likes...' The dismissive hand gesture towards Count Michel was demeaning... an insult far beyond what any words might have conveyed. 'Dani will give you a list of those provisions which we have in surplus. You may take some samples back with you if you like.'

Anton turned, meeting eyes with the foreigner again. Somehow his eyes had turned yellow, revealing a hint of the wolf. 'But now you must excuse me. I have business to attend to among my people.'

Count Michel opened his mouth to speak. He had taken a step back when he saw Count Anton's eyes, but now Dani was at his elbow guiding him to the door.

'We will speak again,' Michel stated weakly as he passed through the doorway.

Anton smiled wolfishly, enjoying the expression on Michel's face. The obvious confusion he had caused in the stranger was only a small victory, but a victory nonetheless.

'You can come out now Leap.'

Anton turned, and found that Leap was already sitting in the favoured chair as before.

'How many came with this human?'

'Two boats,' Leap answered at once. 'Not many men, small boats that sail on the river.'

'Perhaps your friends in the river will see that only one boat returns,' Anton said flatly.

Leap looked truly frightened at first as the words penetrated. A human, speaking openly of... *them*! Then the customary grin spread across his face.

'You think like goblin, Anton. When your ears grow and you turn green, perhaps we may speak of such things.'

Anton returned the amused smirk. He had never before gone as far as to mention the *Kol'ksu* directly to Leap. There was clearly no chance that the goblin would speak openly of them lightly. As much as Anton's burning curiosity wanted to know the nature of the creatures that he knew populated the watery places, pushing it would only lead him back to the wall of silence surrounding them. It was time to change the subject.

'What news of the Southern humans, Leap? Have they been behaving themselves?'

Leap looked thoughtful for a moment, so much so that Anton started to become a little apprehensive. Leap had nearly always been in good humour. To see him look so serious, even for a moment, was disconcerting.

'These humans across the river are not like you. They do not feel the rhythms of the Earth, Anton.'

Anton nodded in understanding. To the goblin, the Southerners would always seem out of sync and discordant. Leap continued.

'We stay far away from them, keeping to the deeper places on that side of the river. We feel them, they feel wrong. Like... humans.' Leap looked up at Anton at this analogy to be sure that he understood.

'Somehow they feel more wrong now. They have done nothing unusual, but they feel as if they might. They feel angry, Anton. We can feel their hatred, and we don't know why.'

Anton contemplated this for a moment. He knew the feeling of which Leap spoke. That tension when something was about to happen. The goblins would feel it even stronger, living close to the Earth's rhythms as they did.

'Anton,' Leap asked quietly. 'Why do they hate us still? They know we are not the demons of their superstitions.'

'They fear your freedom,' Anton answered sadly.

'Perhaps that is it then,' said Leap. 'When their female took her freedom, they blamed goblins. Yet all we did was let her pass. Perhaps those humans would be happier if she had been eaten when she fell in the river.'

Anton's eyes widened at this remark. He looked up at Leap slowly.

'What do you know about a girl crossing the river?'

The grin spread across Leap's face again. He had the better of the human once more.

'Your network is too slow. Goblins would have had a runner tell you right away. But no runner came, so Leap came to tell Anton. The young female dances among your people even now.'

Anton reflected on this piece of information. He did not feel surprised. Somehow, he had seen the inevitability. Even as he had spoken to the girl's father, he had felt the expectation that his own circle of magicians would somehow absorb the girl.

Anton contemplated the meaning of what Leap had told him, that she had been in the river where her people no longer allowed their children to swim. A memory of the song of the siren came to him as he let his mind slip back to his own experiences near the water, so long ago now. The river, always so safe, and yet filled with unknown creatures that could topple boats and devour men horribly. The sparkles of lights just under the surface in a dark, underground pool and the hypnotic song enticing him closer... the lure of the light reflections in the ripples on the water surface... his own steps taking him closer to the edge even as he lost all sense in the song that called to him...

'Anton!' Leap's voice startled Anton out of his reverie. He looked at the goblin in confusion for a moment. It had been the same sharp tone that Haghuf had used to rouse him from the trance before.

'There is no lake or river here in your castle, Anton. You must be careful near the water. You have been too close to... something very dangerous.' Leap looked concerned, almost as Haghuf had looked that day in the underground cavern with the sparkling lake.

Anton nodded. He did not ask for further explanation. Somehow he knew what Leap meant. Few heard the siren song and lived. It was in the legends of the humans as well. He felt it every time he gazed on the placid waters of the river that separated his people from the Southerners. Somewhere, within those waters, were unknown creatures that could kill. Yet they had chosen to let him live. For a moment, he thought he could feel throbbing in the bite marks in his ankle, though they had long since healed. He gazed out of the window towards the river now as he asked a more direct question than he would normally hazard with a goblin.

'Leap, I know that your females carry venom for mating. You know how I know this. Do the creatures in the water also carry a venom, one that might have a lasting effect?'

Anton turned towards Leap for his answer, but the goblin was gone. He hadn't simply disappeared into a shadow this time. Anton sensed that Leap was no longer anywhere in the room. He took a deep breath and let it out in a sigh. The goblins would continue to keep their secrets. Even his friends.

The night called to Anton. Somewhere in the night, his people danced in the moonlight as he sat in a room dealing with matters of state. The sun had faded and it was time to revel in the magic. He threw on a cape against the cold of fading summer and strode out of the castle into the night air. None saw the wolf who traversed the distance, then resumed man shape at the edge of the heath where the magicians met.

Count Anton walked along the wooded path, enjoying the peace and the stillness of the cool evening air. He had nearly reached the meeting site when the shriek of a young girl cut through the night stillness like a banshee's dying wail.

Chapter Four

F*ear*. *Heat*. There were no words, only emotions as Haghuf watched his own image torn limb from limb in the searing reflection of volcanic fires. The claws, rending and tearing. The other, his twin, shredded into nothing but meat for the dragon's feast. Blood everywhere. *Fear*. No words, just emotion. *Fear*. Run, run, run...

Haghuf awoke with a start. His eyes opened. His body flinched as if he would run, but he lay safely among the sleeping furs in the coolness of his familiar cavern. There were no dragons here. No fires. The world of the *Foringen* had been left behind long ago. Haghuf had never gone back to his mother's people again.

The dream had been more than a dream... it was a memory. For a moment, Haghuf lay still, shivering. For the first time in a very, very long time, he allowed himself to remember what life had been like in the *Foringen* caverns. It was accepted among them that some would be lost to the dragon's feast, just as many of the dragon's eggs would feed the goblins, but this did not prepare Haghuf to actually watch his twin being eaten.

Twin birth was very rare among goblins. Haghuf wondered if his grotto had allowed themselves to mourn that loss. Unlike other deaths, feeding the dragons was accepted as part of the cycle of life and death. For this, they were more fertile than many of the other species, yet Haghuf was still seldom chosen in the Dance. Talla had once told him that it was because the females found him too distant and unapproachable. Haghuf accepted that having been a part of the grotto at Krapneerg for many generations, his bloodlines already filled the veins of many of the younger goblins.

Haghuf had never been one for conversation beyond necessity. Among the *Foringen*, there were no names, no verbal language. Haghuf didn't remember how long it had taken him to learn to speak when he first came among the *Deep Dwellers*. The first noises he was able to form were no more than guttural grunts, which is how he gained the name that was the only sound he was able to utter for long after his acceptance within what had become his grotto amidst the *Deep Dwellers*.

He had been accepted easily among them. Haghuf had the look of the ancient earthen goblins, enough to suggest that his mother had likely been seeded by one of them. Sometimes the *Foringen* were known to travel to other levels, to bring weapons among the fighting goblins and collect gifts of food to take back with them. Dragon eggs would be a stale diet on their own. All forms of goblins did as they needed to for survival. That had no doubt been how the symbiotic relationship between dragon and goblin had started. Goblins needed underground fire to forge weapons to protect them from humans. Both dragons and goblins needed food.

Now Haghuf was not sure if he would be able to tolerate the heat. So much time had gone by. To go among a people who had no names, no language to speak aloud, was his task alone. He knew their unspoken language still, as he had remembered when the *Foringen* had brought the sword to Count Anton. Some terms he had to struggle to remember, but the knowledge was still there, as was the fear.

Much time had passed since the sword had been bestowed on the human... an unprecedented event. Those who had been younglings then were nearly grown now. Haghuf had never understood the reason for the gift. He wanted answers. His resolve to seek them among the *Foringen* had remained since that day, but still his feet did not travel the deepest passages.

It came down to this: He was afraid of the dragons.

The nightmare had not been his first, but there was only one way to make it his last. It was time to conquer the fear and to go among the people of the dragons, the *Foringen*. Weapon forgers, fire goblins... his mother's people.

Haghuf roused himself from the sleeping furs and took the first step. That one was hardest. The rest would follow more easily, but not *too* easily. As he passed the opening to his sleeping space, his instincts cried out to turn left, not right. So it was with every choice where passages converged. Haghuf knew these caverns as well as anyone – better than many. Every junction gave him visions of possible destinations and imaginary business that he must attend to that would distract him from his path. He had, in fact, tried this route twice before and had allowed himself to be distracted by other diversions.

Not this time. For this journey he allowed himself only one detour, to collect a bag of apples to take with him as a gift to the *Foringen*. The golden apples that the goblins grew specially on an island that only one human had ever seen and lived to remember. These would be a welcomed gift indeed.

By force of will, Haghuf kept himself on the path that would take him to the deepest places. Nothing was going to distract him this time. No excuse would be allowed to stop the journey that must come. He had delayed it far too long already.

He needed to know. And that drove him forward. Forward and down, down narrow passages that grew warmer and noisier as he drew closer and closer. The walls themselves seemed to change as he travelled, growing redder in hue. The sound of sizzling and bubbling things permeated his consciousness increasingly, as did the smell of sulphur. It was no wonder that the humans thought of the deepest places in the Earth as a place of punishment in their mythologies. If only they knew the truth.

Sweating, feeling the heat too strongly as his destination drew near, Haghuf began to wonder if he was on a fool's errand. What matter was it if the *Foringen* should choose to bestow gifts on a human? The sword could never be used on a goblin anyway. Let the creatures kill each other more efficiently. What was it to goblin kind?

But that was exactly the point. Haghuf knew well that 'goblin kind' did nothing without reason. It had been too long a journey to the surface just to bestow a gift on a creature that was of no importance to the forgers of metal. A human would not have thought to offer food in return. Only the goblins kept the metal forgers supplied with food besides their staple diet of giant eggs. Haghuf was grimly aware that the dragons must not be allowed to die out, or the forgers would starve.

The rhythm of the earth had changed steadily during his journey. Now suddenly the intermixing of the rhythms of hammers echoing off of volcanic rock became noticeable. He was near the world of the forgers. The heat was almost unbearable. How had he lived here as a youngling? The larger cavern openings reminded him all too well of his fears. He felt exposed, more here even than on the surface world. There was much more room in the spacious passages here than in the comforting enclosed caverns of his adopted grotto. Room for a dragon to move about.

Even as the thought occurred, Haghuf turned a corner and found himself face to face with a pair of huge, fiery golden eyes. He froze in place. Thoughts of retreat mixed with realisation of futility... there was no escape. But the dragon turned and ambled away nonchalantly. It had obviously eaten recently.

It was then that Haghuf identified the blood stench mixed with the sulphur on its breath. He clutched the wall for support. His knees wobbled shamefully. Such abject terror was unfitting to a goblin, especially one of his mother's people, but it was in the nature of all living things to fear death at the claws of such a beast. He wondered for a moment how many of his people knew such fear when the dragon actually took them. It was too easy to be philosophical about something that happened to someone else.

A few more turns and suddenly he was amongst them – the forgers. Dozens of the dark, fire toughened goblins were to be seen working among the cacophony of noisy hammering that had been the only sound Haghuf had known in his youth. One of them broke away from an assembly line to greet him. They bowed to each other casually, then Haghuf handed the bag of apples to the *Foringen*. The dark goblin bowed again in thanks.

Then the dance began. Haghuf remembered the movements he needed. He had indeed run them through his mind many times over as he had descended the paths to this realm. The *Foringen* answered in his own dance of communication. The explanation was straight-forward. No riddles this time, only answers. At last, Haghuf understood.

Chapter Five

T he scream pierced the night, sending terror into the hearts of all that heard. Not least of all, the gargoyle creature who hopped down from his perch and offered his hand to the girl who had issued the alarm.

'No fear, human girl, *friend*!' The creature exclaimed in her own language.

Alaric was the first to run out of the darkness to investigate the commotion. He took in the scene with the creature and the still hyperventilating girl. Namah looked at Alaric with terror in her eyes, pleading wordlessly for rescue as her whimpers tried to form coherence, threatening to escalate into another scream. Then confusion crossed her expression as the creature also looked to Alaric in consternation.

'Fear.' The creature spoke only the one word to Alaric. Then Alinea appeared from the darkness and reached to stroke the little gargoyle's head in a comforting gesture. Alaric turned to Namah.

'It's alright, Namah, this is Drazek. He is one of our friends.'

Namah looked confused for a moment, then pained as the other children and adults from the campfire appeared through the darkness, rushing to respond to the alarm. Most melted immediately back into the shadows as they discovered its cause. Namah heard low murmurs, even giggles, as references were made to the new girl having just met Drazek. He was apparently well known among these people. She began to feel severely embarrassed.

'It's ok.' Alinea spoke comfortingly as she laid a gentle hand on Namah's shoulder. 'They understand. Everyone here had to learn to accept him when they first joined the circle. Even among the magicians, not many are used to encountering goblins who look very different from themselves.'

Namah looked at the creature tentatively. *Drazek* they had called him. He still looked like a living gargoyle to her, yet the expression in his deep, golden eyes was not threatening. If anything, it pleaded for acceptance. Alinea was stroking him like a big dog with obvious affection emanating from her sympathetic eyes.

'Namah, please meet Drazek. He is perhaps my closest friend among my own people.'

The creature smiled, an odd expression from one with upper and lower fangs showing over his lips, and pressed his head against Alinea's hand. Once again, he held his own hand out to Namah. This time she took it, if perhaps a little nervously.

'I-I am very pleased to meet you, Drazek,' Namah stammered. Images from the teachings of her childhood flew through her mind. Demons, winged creatures that looked so much like this gentle goblin. They had said the creatures were evil and harmful, yet Drazek seemed so much like a loved pet that she almost wanted to reach out and stroke him herself. The affection that clearly poured from Alinea towards this creature was stronger than a lifetime of superstition. Namah's fear had already begun to turn to curiosity.

'Come,' invited Alaric. 'Let's join the fire and listen to the music.'

Alinea and Drazek immediately moved to follow, but Namah hesitated for a moment. She remembered the beautiful musician... and her discomfort with her own reaction to him. Confusion threatened to overwhelm her as she began to fully appreciate how many goblin friends she had made in one night and how easy she had found it to want to know them better.

'It's alright, Namah.' Alinea's voice was so soothing to Namah's ears that she could not help but feel comforted. 'You have nothing to fear... from any of us.'

Namah looked into her friend's eyes. She knew. Somehow in the tone of her voice, Namah could tell that Alinea knew about her attraction to the musician goblin. Yet it was alright. With her new friend next to her, she was sure she could enjoy the fire without doing or saying anything to disgrace herself. She would just have to avoid looking too closely at the beautiful goblin's eyes.

As they approached the fire, Namah could not help but look for him. One of the human magicians was playing a stringed instrument now and singing a song that sounded like a beautiful saga. The children sat together at first just outside of the ring of adults, forming a small ring of their own. Namah's eyes wandered through the adult circle, searching.

'Listen, they're singing about Alaric!' exclaimed Alaric. This confused Namah for a moment. She looked at him quizzically.

'The historic Alaric, from long ago, before the Turning,' the boy explained.

Namah nodded. It made sense now and she turned her attention to the words of the song. Alaric and Drazek moved closer to the musician to listen.

> *... Out on the Western reaches a Goth tribe*
> *They raised up a king of a noble line*
> *Though Alaric sought the glory of Rome*
> *He was King of the Goths who had crossed the Rhine*
>
> *He sought position, they approached the walls*
> *The great city knew fear and shut him out*
> *Fear of the Barbarian Gothic King*

Would lead to Rome's fall, on the second rout...

Eventually Namah's attention wandered from the song, despite its beauty. Again she searched for the goblin musician, this time among the shadows just beyond the circle of magicians. Her eyes had adjusted to the night now. She began to see that small groups of people sat away from the fire, in private conversation. She could not see well enough to pick out individual features, yet she hoped that the pointed ears would stand out among the shadowy shapes in the moonlight.

In the end, it was her ears rather than her eyes that detected the alien creature. His melodic voice would have given him away easily, but it was the words in another language – a broken fragment of conversation – that caused Namah to spin round and try to stare into the darkness at two shapes speaking privately. The words sounded something like; "Namu yrak nug."

'Alinea, is that the goblin musician we saw before over there?'

'Yes, Namah, but we must not listen too closely to his conversation with Count Anton. His name is Ja'imos. He's a runner. We'll be told if anything they speak of concerns us.'

'What's a runner?' Namah asked, trying even harder to penetrate the darkness with her inadequate vision. The revelation that Count Anton himself was sitting so close to her now piqued her interest as much as her fascination for the goblin. She wondered for a moment if either of them had been among those who had seen her embarrassment when she met Drazek.

'Every grotto has runners,' Alinea explained. 'They do what the others of their grotto do, but they travel to other places to spread news. Ja'imos is the only one of his grotto who will come to the surface among the humans. He has an interest in them, because rumour is that he was seeded by a *Betweener*. They are closer to human than the *Deep Dwellers*, like his mother.'

Against her conscious knowledge or will, Namah wrinkled her nose in distaste.

'You mean his mother was a goblin like a gargoyle, but a human-like goblin would couple with her?'

Nonplussed, Alinea answered in a steady voice. She turned to look at Namah as she spoke.

'I understand your meaning. You see ugliness in goblins like Drazek, but we do not see it so. Your clan keep animals as pets. You would not couple with them... I understand.' Alinea nodded, dipping her shoulders goblin style to emphasise her words. 'And you would find ugliness in another human whose face resembled that of a dog. But when you look upon your beloved pets, you see them as beautiful within their species. So do we see others of our kind who are unlike us in appearance.' Alinea looked affectionately towards her friend as he sat peacefully, listening to the human musician.

'Drazek is very beautiful for one of his species and beloved of many for qualities that do not require a similar appearance to ourselves. Perhaps you have seen me scratch his ears, as you would a dog. I look on him lovingly, seeing him as a beautiful creature of his kind and with love for the friendship we share, but he is not a pet. He is one of our kind. If we were mature, I would not hesitate to choose him in *The Dance*.'

This statement shocked Namah. Despite her lack of knowledge of goblin customs, something in Alinea's voice had made her meaning clear.

'You would couple with him?'

Alinea nodded in response.

'If we were mature enough to do so, yes. I think when the time comes, he will be my first. We share much already in our friendship.'

'Your first?' Namah said incredulously. Alinea smiled patiently, and answered patiently.

'Among the humans, mating is often done with one partner for life. I understand this. But goblins do not have such a luxury. We do not breed easily, and we have many fewer females than males. If we are to survive as a species, we must have diversity in our breeding habits.'

Alinea looked closely at Namah, searching her face for comprehension.

'We also do not have a concept of ownership of another, as seems to be the attitude within the agreement that you call marriage. Neither do we own our children. We are all individual beings, with thoughts and desires of our own. It is not necessary to feel abandoned if one we love also loves another, or even many more.'

This concept was confusing for Namah. Her strict family background simply had not prepared her for such an open society.

'You mean you couple with just anyone, wantonly?'

'There is choice,' Alinea answered with forbearance. 'The females among us choose to mate with those we feel close to, or might potentially breed with. The visitor you noticed for example, because he is from another grotto, has different blood lines and would be likely to breed more easily with one of our grotto. He will almost certainly be chosen in *The Dance* before your sun brings light over the human world again.'

Namah was not pleased with this revelation. The pretty male goblin had looked at her in a way that suggested that he had noticed her attraction to him. Would he be thinking lustful thoughts towards her? Or worse, would he have an ugly goblin woman tonight without giving it a thought? Namah felt both outraged and jealous, and most of all confused. She wanted to change the subject.

'What did you mean that you don't own your children?'

Again, Alinea explained in her patient, steady voice. She could see the consternation in Namah's expressions and tried to explain as gently as possible.

'When a child is born among us, the mother has the right of life or death over it in the first few moments. This custom is based on viability. If the child is malformed and unlikely to live, there is no sense in wasting resources and emotion on trying to force it to live for a little while. The pain of its death will only be greater when those of its community have come to know the personality.

'If it is healthy, the mother cares for it until it is weaned, but as soon as it can walk it is considered a child of the community. All help in its care and teaching. As soon as it is old enough to understand how to run through the caverns without falling into traps, it is effectively a full member of the community and can make decisions about what path to follow.

'A child younger than Alaric might choose to go to another grotto, to go to learn from *Those Who Protect* or go adventuring with *Those Who Provide*. None say that the youngling can or cannot do these things, just as none say when I am old enough to breed or who I will choose in *The Dance*. That choice is mine, when I know myself to be ready.'

Namah was astonished. She was older than Alinea, and among such people would never have been assigned a marriage of her father's choice. Soon her shock gave way to the memory that in fact, she had made the choice to reject the marriage her father had chosen for her and was now among people who were giving her free choice over her future, even the humans. Nobody had told her what to do at any time. They had brought her among themselves and demanded nothing.

'Are the magicians much like the goblins then?' Namah asked innocently.

'In some ways. They choose life partners as humans do, but those who have not yet chosen do not keep to the ways of the people south of the river. I do not know all the details, but it seems that these humans live somewhere between the world you knew and that which I live in. They feel *The Dance* and they allow themselves to respond to the rhythms of the Earth. I think perhaps they would find *The Dance* within my world too intense, although Count Anton has visited places where no other human has been.'

Namah thought about this for a moment. She looked among the magicians round the fire, some of them swaying to the music alone or in pairs. Some had got up and were dancing near the fire, taken away by the music. It had grown in tempo now. The lone musician had been joined by others, many playing drums. Namah began to feel the pulsating rhythm within herself. She began to sway with it, and to feel something else. A deeper rhythm that felt as though it was driving the audible drumming... something coming from the Earth. It seemed to grow louder in her ears and in her being. For a moment she felt more alive than ever before... and she felt desire. Then it was gone. The music continued, but she had returned from what felt like another place. For a moment, she believed that she had understood about *The Dance*.

'Alinea, would it be possible for me to visit a goblin *Dance* sometime?'

Alinea acknowledged the question with a nod.

'It could be difficult. Humans are not often allowed in the caverns.'

'But Count Anton was allowed...'

'He was given the status of *guest* by Haghuf.' Alinea thought for a moment. 'Technically there is nothing to stop me from giving the same to you, but it is not often done. There are reasons. To do so would be to take responsibility for everything you do while in our world, as well as for your safety... and ours. It is not a thing done lightly.'

Namah was more interested than ever now.

'You can trust me, Alinea, I won't do anything to disgrace you, I promise!'

Alinea hesitated for a moment before answering.

'I will consider this idea. Perhaps in a few days, when you have become more accustomed to different customs among your own people. Then it will be easier for you to come among a very different culture with an open mind.'

Namah looked sheepish as she asked her next question.

'Do you think the visitor, Ja'imos, will stay that long?'

Alinea grinned.

'You would choose him yourself, would you?'

Namah blushed. Could she be thinking such wanton thoughts? Yet she wanted to see him close up. How close, she wasn't yet sure. She turned to see if she could pick out the place in the darkness where he had been speaking with Count Anton, but they were both gone. Namah felt disappointment.

'You are right, Alinea. I need more time to become accustomed to differences among the magicians before I could trust myself among people who would ask such questions. But... tell me Alinea, do you see beauty in Ja'imos the same as you would in Drazek?'

Alinea tried to suppress a smirk. The girlish attraction was too easy to understand.

'Such a one as Ja'imos I think is beautiful to all, among both of our species. If I were to choose a male tonight, I might cast my eye on him as easily as on my close friend, but I think I would find other females in the way.'

Namah contemplated. Ordinarily, such a revelation might have made her feel jealous of her own friend, yet what she had said before put it in perspective. Ja'imos was attractive and his bloodlines would add diversity to the community. It made sense to a girl who was accustomed to breeding farm animals. Yet the thought of him coupling with a goblin female was too much to bear. Namah pushed the thought aside, refusing to think about it.

COUNT ANTON BOWED APPROPRIATELY to the runner goblin as he gestured his farewells and left to return to his people. Anton had much to think about now. The visits from the Southern man and the foreign emissary each brought their own problems. The incident when the new girl was frightened by the younger goblin seemed to have resolved itself, yet she was almost certainly the Southern man's lost daughter. Young girls didn't appear from nowhere so frequently that her origins couldn't be guessed, and her mode of dress identified her easily enough as a Southerner.

The report from Ja'imos was more alarming though. The overseas emissary was part of a flotilla of potential invaders from across the channel. It seemed that history was destined to repeat itself. Such invasions from overseas had been common in historic days, long before the Turning. Now that technology had moved so far backwards, the attractiveness of the fertile island nation was drawing the vultures once more.

Count Anton had hardly had time to think about the intertwining troubles facing him when a movement in the brush revealed the presence of another goblin visitor. Anton turned towards him and smiled before expressing his greetings with the customary bow. It wasn't often that Haghuf emerged into the surface world, even to visit the magicians.

'What news, Haghuf?'

'I think you've had news,' Haghuf replied in his usual gruff manner.

'Indeed I have,' Anton said seriously. 'You saw Ja'imos then?'

'Our kind are always aware of each other, you should know that by now.' Something in Haghuf's manner suggested he was remonstrating with Anton, like a teacher whose student had forgotten something important. 'His people don't come among yours without good reason. What did he tell you?'

'Which are his people?' Anton asked curiously, but just then Alaric and Drazek came bounding up to them.

'Father!' Alaric shouted as only boys can shout. 'Come dance with us! It's a beautiful night!'

Anton smiled broadly at his son and his goblin friend. Then he lowered his voice to answer Haghuf quickly as the young ones skipped far enough ahead not to hear.

'Invaders. Humans from across the water. Not the river, the channel.'

Haghuf nodded in understanding. He would learn the details from his own people. The goblins kept a close eye on any movement of humans. Had he not been journeying to the deepest places, he would have already known.

Haghuf had wanted to speak to Anton about the sword, but the young ones were pulling them into the circle to dance. It would have to wait a little longer. He smiled to himself at the thought that Anton's other question had gone unanswered. He would have told him openly this one time. The look on Anton's face would have been worth it. But Haghuf had a feeling that sooner or later, Anton would have his answer. Those who came to the surface even less frequently than he did himself would be taking an interest in the movements of the invading humans. Whatever happened on the surface world affected them all.

The dancing and revelry took over the night. Lost in the rhythms of all that was right in the world, the conflicts of men were easily forgotten for a time. With morning would come the need to act. Among the actions that human and goblin must achieve together, Haghuf had two matters to discuss with Anton. One was what he had learned about the goblin sword that the *Foringen* had presented to him when human and goblin had last come into conflict. The other matter was the current actions of Anton's old enemy, Latham.

Chapter Six

Ariane slowly climbed the stairs that would lead her to the bedroom she shared with Count Anton. She moved unhurriedly, carrying an armload of freshly washed and folded clothing, going about her domestic duties. The faint morning light spilling from the castle windows told her that it was still very early. The night's revelries had left little time for sleep.

Anton had risen much earlier, even before the sun had glinted with the first light of morning. Ariane felt uneasy. It was unusual for her husband to rise in the early morning hours after a bonfire night, but his explanation had worried her more. The goblins had brought news. Trouble on all sides – invaders from overseas were gathering forces. First two boats, then more joining them and a man from overseas upstairs in a drugged sleep who could give the word that would start a war for which they were not prepared.

As if that weren't enough, the Southerners were making trouble again as well. Anton had said that Haghuf himself had come above ground to bring word that Latham was crossing the river regularly again. Whatever Anton's old nemesis was up to, it couldn't be good. It was for that reason that Anton had risen so early. He had gone to cross the river to see what was afoot and to keep a promise. Anton had explained to Ariane about the visit from new girl's father and the dilemma of knowing that he was also Laura's father.

How Anton would convey to the man that his daughters were safe without turning them over to him she did not know, but Ariane felt that they must be protected. Forced marriage was not necessary in their society, or acceptable for magicians. She would hide them herself before allowing their lives to be wasted in that form of slavery. Without love, marriage in the culture of the Southerners was no more than that.

Ariane was distracted by these thoughts as she entered her bedroom. She placed the clothing on the bed, then some instinct made her turn towards the window. In the dim light, she could just see a woman sitting quietly in the chair next to it. Even in the morning darkness, the iridescent greenish hue of the woman's skin was distinctive by the glimmering shadows that it cast, yet even her breathing did not cause any movement to draw the eye. She might easily have been sitting there for a very long time without drawing notice. Ariane had never met the goblin woman face to face before, but the white hair and milky white irises of her eyes marked her identity. They could only belong to the mother of her husband's other child.

'Hello, Talla,' said Ariane calmly.

Talla nodded, dipping her shoulders in goblin fashion, to acknowledge the greeting. Ariane was not sure what to say in the moment of silence. The presence of the goblin woman alone was disconcerting. Talla had not been seen above ground since the birth of Alinea, Anton's daughter. This was the mother of her husband's firstborn and that too brought emotions that Ariane could not define, but the silence demanded some attempt at conversation.

'If you seek Anton, he has crossed the river to look into some trouble from the Southerners...'

'My mother's people know his movements, always.' Talla's answer only increased the tension. The look in the goblin woman's eyes was difficult to interpret. Ariane felt as though she were caught in the gaze of a predator. In the eerie morning light, she almost thought that she could hear singing... a high female voice just on the edge of hearing that flowed through a dissonant, yet intriguing melody that drew her closer. This was not the Talla that had been described to her. The light-hearted young woman that Anton had spoken of so fondly was not evident in the serious, disquieting creature before her. Ariane decided to try a more direct approach.

'Why are you here?'

Suddenly Talla smiled. It transformed her as if by magic. She stood up and stepped into the light where the playful sparkle in her eyes dispelled the frightening apparition of the predatory creature who had occupied the chair a moment before.

'You and I should know each other.' Talla spoke lightly, as if nothing had ever been amiss. 'You have an important part to play in the futures of both of our peoples, as do the young ones we have spawned.' Again, Talla nodded in the peculiarly goblin fashion. It seemed to signify that her words were fact, as if Ariane should have known the future of which Talla spoke.

'I bring you this.' Talla handed her a flask. 'It will be more effective than what you have to give to the rehto, the man who comes to your castle unwanted.'

Ariane looked at the flask in her hand. She thought of the mushroom potion that had been used just over ten years before, when the clash between human and goblin had threatened her world. Somehow that crisis had resulted in her marriage to Count Anton. Even now she wondered if in fact, the marriage had been contrived... nothing more than a substitute for the love he would have shared with the alien creature standing in her own bedroom – the bedroom she shared with Anton.

Ariane looked up, intending to thank Talla for the gift, but the goblin woman had vanished. She glanced at the open window. From what she had been told of the goblins, that was all that was needed for escape. High tower walls meant nothing to them. Ariane had seen few of them, and even then only at the bonfires. They continued to stay out of sight, allowing the common people to forget they existed once again.

If only they all would forget, Ariane thought to herself. Latham had taken every opportunity to remind people about the goblins living under their city over the years. Even after the old priest had died, Latham's fanaticism in the Temple, his attempts to stir the people to dig out the goblins and rid the world of 'demons', had gained him a reputation as a would-be redeemer of the community.

Fortunately, many also remembered the horrible death of Paul, the previous redeemer. Those who were to young to remember those horrible deaths found it easy to think Latham mad. *But for how long?* Ariane shivered at the thought of Anton crossing the river, alone. None of the humans knew what creatures had caused the boats to capsize, but the memory of the blood floating to the surface in the chopping waters of what could only be a feeding frenzy, the gasps of those who witnessed, left no doubt of one simple fact. There was something in the water. Something that was very dangerous.

ANTON PULLED THE LITTLE flat bottomed boat onto the shore. The crossing had been uneventful, for which he was grateful. Somewhere in his awareness, he knew that something was wrong. Floating across the river, above whatever goblin-spawned horror he did not know, had left him feeling exposed... vulnerable.

The morning hours were always quiet. Those who believed in enjoying revelries, like the magicians, would still be asleep. Those who led a more austere life would be solemn and respectful of the peace and quiet. Only the children north of the river would be up and about at such an early hour, soon to be followed by their disgruntled parents. The children here, on the southern shores, were taught to be silent and maintain the façade of spiritual thoughts as their industrious parents found work for them to do and to do themselves.

Still, Anton tried to listen. He didn't know what he expected to hear, but it was one of his most acute senses. He naturally relied on it when searching for something. Exactly what he was searching for he did not yet know, but he needed to be completely alert to any clues.

His attentiveness was quickly rewarded with an unexpected sound. Men... shouting. Too far away to make out the words, but men certainly, and they were excited about something. The sound carried from downriver. Anton started to run towards it, keeping to his man form. Changing to *wolf* would be too dangerous so near to where he might be seen. Reminding these men of his magician status would detract from his authority as their ruler. This had already been proven long ago. His position would always be precarious against the fanaticism that infested the Southern people.

The shouting grew louder as Anton neared the source of the noise. Soon he began to be able to make out the words.

'That one might o' got clear across the river if the water didn't slow it,' shouted one voice excitedly. Another answered.

'Just like shooting fish in a barrel. Whatever's been eating our people, it won't have a chance if it gets anywhere close to the surface again.'

Anton felt a lump in his stomach. Whatever the men were doing, it was certainly an attack on the creatures in the water... creatures with some connection to the goblins. The trouble was going to start over again if he didn't stop them quickly. Anton ran harder towards the voices, panicking now.

As he rounded a corner past a tree on the shore, he saw the device the men had referred to. It was a large crossbow, probably salvaged from one of the old museums. It was cocked to fire and a group of six men were intent on aiming it and watching for a target in the river... a moving target. Something in the water was about to feel the bite of the bolt.

A man pointed towards a flicker of lights in the water and shouted.

'There's one!'

At nearly the same time, Anton howled in panic.

'Noooooooo!'

But the bolt flew, and it hit its mark. The men, without taking any notice of Anton in the distance, excitedly started pulling on a rope attached to the bolt, dragging their target onto shore. Anton continued running towards the scene. His eyes watered in distress. He had been too late to stop this blood hunt that could potentially destroy the hard-won peace that had settled between his people and the goblins. These men had to be stopped before they did any more damage.

He opened his mouth to speak as he sprinted the last few yards to the riverside where the men were hauling their prey onto shore, but as the creature was pulled from the cloaking darkness of the water flowing down the river, Anton could not find the words.

It had been one of his most burning questions about the goblins. What creatures were in the water? He had overheard the name once... *Kol'ksu*. As the glittering scales of the man-like fish creature appeared above the water, Anton was dumbfounded. The long white hair, so like Talla's, was flipped angrily from an almost human face where narrowed white irised eyes turned to glare at him. The creature was alive. The bolt stuck out of one of two fishtail-like limbs where a man's leg would be. Blood stained the sand. Red blood, like any other human or goblin creature.

'Stop this now!' Anton ordered in his most authoritive voice. He was still breathing heavily from his run. One of the men grinned at him and answered for the group.

'Count Anton, Sir, we're just doing a little fishing.' The man's flippant tone told Anton that his authority wasn't going to carry much weight with this bunch.

'Don't you see?' Anton pleaded. 'Disturbing these creatures will bring disaster on all of us. We've made peace with the goblins, you'll start it all again!'

Anton turned to the injured creature again. There was something familiar about him... something disturbingly familiar. At first he thought it might just be the hair and eyes that were so like Talla, and the implications of that resemblance. Anton met the creature's eyes with his own and saw images in his mind – images he had tried to forget. Darkness, the cold, wet hour of death – then strong arms snaking around him like tentacles. The *Kol'ksu* song in his ears as the deep pool enveloped him in its cold, deathly embrace. A sharp pain on his ankle, and then air, the breath of life forced into his lungs within that sensory void.

'No Sir, Count Anton, they started it.' The man's voice cut into Anton's momentary reverie. 'They ate Rab's youngest daughter.'

'No,' Anton answered quickly. 'The girl is alive. I came to tell her father.' Anton regretted the words as he said them, but the men had to be diffused from their hunt at any cost. Another of the men looked all too self-assured and amused as he answered Anton.

'And besides, they're not so powerful out of the water.' The man drew a hunting knife and moved towards the weakened creature. The *Kol'ksu* watched them intently from the shore, lying very still.

Anton looked at the creature's eyes again and stepped between them. With his back to the creature and the river, he faced all of the men defiantly.

'You will not touch him.' The man faltered at the menace in Anton's voice. He opened his mouth to speak, but there were no words. Suddenly his eyes were looking past Anton, towards the river.

The other men, glaring at him only a moment ago, also looked towards the river with their mouths open and fear in their eyes.

Chills went up Anton's spine as he recognised the song, just on the edge of hearing, and yet louder than ever before with many voices. He turned slowly, keeping an eye on the men as he sought for the cause of the sudden change in them. He crouched slowly as he turned, resting a shielding hand on the shoulder of the creature he protected, but he understood immediately that there was no need. What the men feared was no danger to this creature.

Anton was frozen in both fear and fascination as several more *Kol'ksu* shuffled onto shore. They emerged from the water as if birthed from their watery home in response to the need of one of their kind. The double-finned protuberances of their lower bodies acted as legs, allowing them to trundle on land with little grace, yet with purpose. The ghostly white hair and eyes appeared cold, even more frightening than the long webbed and taloned fingers of the hands that waved casually at waist level, apparently compensating for balance.

The creatures before him brought to mind names he had read in old mythologies. Mermaid... but no, the tail was split into two. Melusine... but Anton had never heard of them walking and they were not known to be meat eaters or to kill. Siren... the women who sang and lured sailors to their deaths on the rocks. One of the creatures, a female, opened her mouth as if to speak and Anton saw the perfectly even row of sharp teeth. The curved row was shaped in a crescent, very much like the punctures on an old boot that Anton had saved from another time... a time when something had made a conscious decision not to eat him. *Something in the water.* Yes, the sirens were sometimes reported to have eaten the shipwrecked sailors. Perhaps, Anton thought, all of these creatures of mythology were only what he saw before him. After all, no one had ever brought back a live specimen from the sea as far as history recorded.

It was the needle sharp teeth that drew the gaze of the Southern men most... the teeth that had eaten men. The same teeth that had once pierced Anton's boot. The perfect half-crescent of identical needles, meant for ripping and shredding meat, was unmistakeable. The men began to take a step backwards, but suddenly the creatures sprang with unbelievable strength. The air was rapidly filled with flying fish-creatures and the high screeching sound of their voices mixed with the terrified screams of dying men. There was blood everywhere. Anton didn't move, but held his position over the injured creature.

It was done in a moment. The men were gone. Their bones littered the beach, licked nearly clean of all trace of blood or flesh. The *Kol'ksu* had fed well. In unison they all turned to look directly at Anton, and for the first time he realised that he may well be the next course. Several pairs of eyes looked at him coldly, perhaps even angrily. It was difficult to tell with the white irises and the slit pupils, the one feature that differentiated their eyes from Talla's.

They began to shuffle towards him and the injured creature. Thinking quickly, Anton decided that his only chance was to speak to them in the goblin dialect and hope that they realised that he had tried to protect the still silent creature.

'Tahw nac I od ot pleh mih?'

The creatures stopped, then just one female among them, the same one Anton had noted before when she had shown her teeth, shambled a little closer to him. She moved slowly, as if they had all the time in the world, or as if time itself had stopped in this moment. She came within reach of him, then looked at him, turning her head first one way then another as her eyes held his steadily. It was something Anton had seen Haghuf do when he was examining something closely. At last, she answered, speaking an accented form of the human dialect in a voice that sounded unused to verbal speech.

'You can do nothing to help him! Except to burn all such weapons. They are of no use to you.'

The female trundled to the creature's tailfin and examined the injury. The bolt was still stuck through. Her eyes met his, and a barely perceptible nod passed between them. Then she reached out and snapped the bolt off right at the skin. Anton flinched in pain. He wondered if the obvious psychic abilities of the creatures had projected the injured *Kol'ksu*'s pain into his consciousness, then he realised that actually he was feeling the talons of the young creature. He had clenched Anton's leg when the bolt broke. Anton nodded to the *Kol'ksu*, not begrudging what comfort he was able to give.

The female knelt over her charge and pressed her mouth over the wound. Her lips extended, fish-like, so that the entire area was covered. What was happening beneath the extended flesh Anton did not know, but he remembered a similar seal made around his face in the dark pool, so long ago. Air, the breath of another. He looked at the injured *Kol'ksu*'s eyes again. He looked very young, yet somehow Anton knew. This was the same creature who had given him breath. This creature had given him his life back.

The female finished her ministrations and pulled her mouth back. She stood and shuffled around to the other side of the young male. Anton knew this was going to hurt even more. She would have to pull the bolt through the injured flesh. Anton prepared himself. He held the creature like a child, holding him close and allowing him to wrap the deadly talons around his back. It would hurt less there than on an arm or a leg, and the position allowed the female to reach the back of the tailfin better. Anton was aware that this placed the deadly teeth of the creature near the delicate flesh of his own throat, but he also knew that if they had intended him harm, he would have been bones on the beach already.

The female began to reach for the bolt, then stopped suddenly. Her eyes glazed, as Anton had seen eyes glaze when one of the magicians entered the trance of prophecy. She turned partially towards him and spoke.

'In your hour of most need, the only weapon that will serve you is one that you cannot use against us.'

Then without further ceremony, she yanked the bolt from the wound with unbelievable force. The injured *Kol'ksu*'s talons dug into Anton's back. Blood trickled through the back of his white shirt, but it wasn't that pain that held him frozen in place as the wounded creature recovered itself. It was the needle sharp teeth dug into Anton's shoulder. Teeth that might easily have taken all the flesh off that shoulder in that moment of searing pain. But the teeth had only just punctured the flesh. Little droplets of blood beaded on his flesh. They were quickly covered by the stretched fish mouth of the male creature who had caused them. The female stretched her own mouth over the injury of the young creature's more extreme wound.

In the midst of this vampiric scene, Anton became aware that the other *Kol'ksu* had moved in closer. Any one of them might have reached out and touched him at any moment and he would be helpless to defend himself from sharing the fate of those other men. He hoped that the shark-like teeth did not indicate a shark-like bloodlust among the species. They had not attacked him yet.

The young, male creature pulled his mouth away. The puncture wounds were healed over. Still visible, yet closed as if they had healed over a few days. The female finished her ministrations as well, leaving the wound with fresh scales grown over where the open wound had been, and two of the others helped the young male to stand. It was hard to tell if the injured *Kol'ksu*'s shuffle held an extra limp as they moved closer to the water.

For a moment, Anton thought they were all just going to disappear again into the safety of the river, but at the last moment the female turned to him.

'Do not assume that you have any special protection. You have seen us, and that makes you a danger. You are not to speak of us to any of your kind. Not even your trusted advisor. We will know.' She nodded in a way that told Anton that it was no bluff. Her gaze could look through him as no one had ever done. His thoughts felt naked, exposed.

'You have killed men as they swim...' Anton marvelled at his own accusatory words. It was as if he could not stop his private thoughts being spoken aloud. The female answered coldly.

'And I will kill again. It is in my nature. You live now because you have something yet to do. Not because you helped Lo'udri.'

At that, she plunged into the water. There was no more sign of the creatures ever having been above the surface, apart from the bones that remained on the beach. Anton took a moment to recover himself. It had been a horrific morning, even with the sun barely touching the sky. There was no promise that it would get better.

Remembering the words of the female *Kol'ksu*, Anton gathered the pieces of the weapon and built a small fire on the beach. This one, at least, would cause no more trouble. The thought crossed his mind that it might have been useful against his more human enemies, but the creature had prophesied. There was no mistaking the ability. She had said that the only weapon that would save him was the one he could not use against them. Such had been said of the sword he had been given by the goblins. How they might be protected from cold steel he could not imagine.

With the fire burnt out and the weapon destroyed, Anton continued on into the human settlements. He still had a promise to keep, and now some families to inform. It pained him that rather than being sensitive with his report, he would have to use it to discourage any further attacks. He could only guess whether the families of the dead men would be devastated, or relieved. Either might be true of families on this side of the river.

74

Too many young girls, hardly more than children themselves, were still being forced into arranged marriages by these people. He should have done something about it long ago. His own daughter would be considered old enough to be promised among them. Anton smiled at the thought of anyone trying to force Alinea to marry against her will. There was too much of her mother's world in her to expect anything but disaster from such an attempt.

The wives of these men were likely to be not much older. Perhaps as widows, they would be allowed to return to their mothers and finish growing up before the next marriage was thrust upon them and whatever children they had produced to perpetuate this culture.

Anton frowned now. He was suddenly very aware that he had allowed this society to thrive unchallenged, as had his father and grandfather before him. Perhaps there was a time when progeny were needed so badly for the continuation of their species that such marriages could have been justified, but that time was long past. With war threatening him on all sides, Anton vowed to himself that among the inevitable changes to come, he would find a way to free the young girls of the Southern people from this barbaric custom.

Somehow, his boots felt heavier as he trudged the path that would take him to the Southern settlements to deliver his news.

Chapter Seven

Namah awoke smiling, although she could not remember what pleasant dream had brought her such feelings of contentment. In the days since her arrival into her new life among the magicians, she had adapted very quickly to their ways and was feeling very much a part of this new world now.

Meanwhile, rumour had got round that Count Anton had found the bones of men on the southern shore on the morning after the bonfire celebration. Namah's smile left her for a moment as she wondered if they had included anyone she knew.

Her father, at least, was safe. Laura had brought news from Count Anton that he had spoken privately with her parents and assured them that she was safe, but had refused to return Namah to them. The other people among her parents' people would probably be left to assume her dead – killed by the creatures in the water like those men.

Namah remembered the voices, not quite heard, as she had crossed the river. The creatures might easily have killed her, yet they had chosen to assist her. What were they? She felt guilty that they should take the blame for her death when they were completely innocent. That they had killed others didn't change the fact that they were guiltless of her death. Whatever they were, they had seen in Namah the abilities that the magicians were helping her now to discover.

Laura had taken a special interest in her, although she had not explained why. Perhaps it was only that Laura had found Namah that first day and felt responsible for her, but she had treated her gently and guided her patiently as if she were a second mother to the younger girl. It was Laura who had taught Namah how to sense the gentle balance of the breeze and to call up a stronger gust, or redirect the wind without upsetting the balance of nature's forces. It had been so easy for Namah to unfocus her eyes and look into the still air until she saw the little lights swimming before her eyes, then to mentally draw them to her, release the trance and feel the breeze cool her face. Laura had promised that next full moon, she would teach Namah to direct the fire as well.

Namah spared a thought for her real mother. She was glad that her mother had been told that her daughter still lived, although their closeness had always been limited by the strictures on women in their society. Namah might have wished that her mother would have tried to protect her from the unwanted marriage, yet she understood that there had been no choice. Speaking up against the tradition would only have brought public shame on a woman for displeasing her husband.

That her father had agreed to keep the secret of her safety surprised her. Namah began to think that perhaps he cared for her more than she had realised. In their own way, the men were also under the control of public expectation.

There had been no sign of the goblins since the bonfire. Namah wondered to herself if there was a way to contact Alinea or the others, perhaps with the touching of minds that she had felt with the creatures in the river. She found that very easy with Laura, but more difficult when she tried to send or receive thoughts with any of the other humans. There had been no opportunity to try it with her goblin friends.

Namah smiled again. *Goblin friends*. A few days ago, such a concept would have been disturbing. Now it seemed perfectly natural. She understood now why Alinea wanted to wait a few days before taking her into the caverns. It didn't take long to acclimatise to new conditions really, but those few days had allowed Namah to assimilate rather a lot of changes. She felt ready now to experience more differences... and more adventures. She wanted to see what life was like in the goblin world.

Throwing the covers off, Namah leaped out of bed. She had chores to do after her morning meditation, but they wouldn't take all day. If she got cracking on them now, she could be ready to explore soon after lunch. She had made up her mind... she was going to the heath. That would be the place to try to contact her goblin friends.

Laura was already outside chopping wood. She smiled at Namah as the girl passed, waving and returning the smile. Laura could see that Namah was up to something – there was no mistaking the purposeful step – but the girl was a good helper and didn't shirk duties. Laura thought to herself that their parents had taught her well. Laura finished her own task and prepared to travel to the castle. It wasn't all that far, but walking would take too long. She prepared her little pony for the journey.

Anton would be pleased to hear that Laura's little sister was fitting in so well, but there were more important matters to discuss at the castle. There was the captive from over the sea and the ships that waited, growing impatient. There was also the gossip from across the river and the peoples' reaction to the loss of those who had foolishly hunted the river. The council needed to know whether there would be a next move from the bereaved Southerners.

Laura had told Namah that she was going to the castle to seek news. She hadn't yet explained about the Inner Circle. The girl was too keen to be a part of everything new that she discovered. Telling her that there was a council of magicians that actually made decisions as a collective was perhaps a little premature. Let her continue to think that Count Anton made executive decisions on his own for a bit longer, as the people were generally led to believe. There would be time to teach her how things really worked as she grew older.

As Laura waved goodbye, Namah finished the simple lunch of bread and cheese that she had prepared after finishing her chores. She hadn't mentioned her intentions to her surrogate mother. As much as she trusted her benefactor's guidance in everything, she didn't want to take any chance that Laura would advise her not to seek the goblins on her own. Besides, there couldn't be any real danger. They were clearly friendly and it had come out in the conversations by the bonfire that Count Anton regularly visited them and had even danced among them. Alinea would be her best guide among them. She had grown up among the goblins after all.

Laura had taken the pony, so there was no choice but to walk. It was just as well, as Namah would have to remember the way to the heath on her own. It had been dark when they had come home that night. She had noted landmarks, but they would look different in the daylight. Namah took paper and pencil with her. Though the items were precious and rare, she could use them to mark the way she travelled in case she became lost and had to return the way she had come. She had never been taught to read, but could make symbols that would have some meaning to her. Enough old buildings still stood from before the Turning to identify significant landmarks.

Those that she remembered appeared periodically, confirming that she was on the right track. She walked for what seemed like a very long time. Eventually things began to look familiar. Namah noted streets that she clearly remembered marking in her memory just after they had left the heath. She was close. Her feet guided her up one last street. It had been a major road once, with a pond built in the middle of it. Ironically, the night's rain had filled the pond enough to make it appear as it once might have, in another time. So quickly the ducks came back. Then, almost before she expected it, there was greenery to her right. She had reached the turning into the heath.

The next challenge was to find the right path to the place where the goblins had gathered with them. That too had a pond, a natural one. The path from the street would come to a turning. The trick was to take the right one. She could not remember clearly if they had passed more than one crossing of paths, but she could remember the strange, twisted tree that they had passed halfway from the turning to the pond. It would have to do for a landmark.

The first crossing she came to looked right. She couldn't be absolutely sure, but she would have to try the path to know if it was the correct one. She took the turning, searching every tree and bush for any sign of familiarity. Her scrutiny was rewarded quickly when she saw a log off to the right side of the path. She hadn't consciously remembered it, but now that she saw it she remembered seeing people sitting on it and talking on that night. She was on the right path. Very soon after, Namah came to the odd tree. She stopped to look at it, remembering the sound of the drumming and music of that night. Without thinking about what she did, she walked up to the tree and touched it, examining the gnarled contours.

It felt peculiar. Not so much to the touch, but to her deeper senses. Her sense of direction had taken her to the right place, now her sense of... something else... had been awakened. There was more to this tree than its irregular contours... she was sure of it, but it would be something to think about later, now that she definitely knew the way. The day drew on. Namah had come to this place on the heath for a purpose.

It wasn't much further down the path to the place that Namah sought. It was easy enough to recognise. Not just because of the pond, now populated with ducks playing in the daylight. The place itself had an unmistakeable shape to it. It was like an opening among the paths of the heath. The trees that lined up like a backdrop to those facing the pond, the slight incline of the terrain, were all completely familiar. Now all Namah needed was a means to contact her friends.

Laura had begun teaching her to use the telepathic ability that had allowed Namah to mentally shout out to the magicians when she had crossed the river. This would be a good time to practise the basic meditation in a situation where she sought an actual result. Namah found a comfortable spot and sat down, crossing her legs. Her hands reached to physically feel the grass growing on the soft ground. Once men had used machines to cut grass so that they could have nice places to sit. Now it was used as feed for the sheep, with a similar result. Namah wondered how her species had ever become so dependent on machines and artificial ways of living.

She tried to concentrate, then realised that she was trying too hard. She needed to relax into the meditation, not to strain the muscles in her head and give herself a headache. Laura had said to listen... and to feel. Namah felt the grass again and tried to reach out her non-visual senses. At first the earth felt still... peaceful. Namah listened to her surroundings, becoming aware of the birds in the trees and hearing the quacking of the ducks she had seen in the pond. Soon she began to perceive less obvious sounds in the brush; scurrying creatures, gathering things. Squirrels no doubt.

As she strained her ears to hear more, she became aware of a light vibration in her fingers. The Earth thrummed in an irregular rhythm, one that felt not unlike her own heartbeat. She found herself rocking gently to the rhythm, taking up the cadence. She felt her surroundings in a way that was very like visual perception, yet in her mind she could see the things in hidden places that eyes would not penetrate. The squirrels and other small creatures going about their business among the trees. The insects that crawled on leaves. The fox in the distant brush that watched the ducks, yet would not make its move with a human in the vicinity. The gargoyle perched in the tree just over her head.

Namah's eyes flew open in shock just as Drazek dropped from his perch right in front of her.

'Human girl sees well, almost like goblin.'

Despite her surprise, Namah smiled at the compliment. Drazek's fearsome appearance didn't have the same effect on her now that she knew him. She actually felt happy to see him.

'Well met, friend Drazek.' Namah smiled as she spoke. 'Are the others lurking in the trees as well?'

Drazek's shoulders shook as he made a gulping sound that Namah interpreted as laughter.

'Others at the storytelling, others away to *The Dance.*'

'Why aren't you at *The Dance*, Drazek?' Namah leaned forward, genuinely interested. Suddenly Drazek's dragon-like wings spread to their full capacity, stretching to maximum wingspan.

'Drazek comes out to stretch his wings.' Namah was certain she saw him wink as he spoke. She wondered for a moment if he could actually fly, but she had to stay focused on her purpose.

'Will Alinea be at *The Dance*? You see, that's what I came to speak with her about.'

Drazek's expression became serious very suddenly. The look he gave her could almost be interpreted as suspicion. Then he closed his eyes a moment and seemed to sink into another part of himself – a part that connected closely to the Earth. Namah's new sensory awareness allowed her to follow much of the internal grounding that came so naturally to the goblin. Then his eyes flew open as he answered her question.

'Alinea hears you. Alinea will come.'

Namah turned to look around the area, but when she turned back, Drazek had vanished. She sent her awareness into the trees to see if she could sense him there again. She felt something, but it was far distant. Either he had cloaked himself psychically, or he had travelled a great distance in a short time. Namah wondered again about the wings. *Could* he actually fly with them? She vowed she would try to find out, but not yet. It was still too soon in her association with the goblins to pry very far into their business. She was stretching things as it was, coming here to ask if she could be allowed into the caverns.

Namah returned to her meditation, becoming aware of her surroundings again and trying to sense Alinea. Surely she would feel her as soon as she came near. Drazek's assurance that Alinea would come heartened Namah. She did not doubt the goblin's words for a moment. It might be a long way to travel. She would have to be patient, yet sitting and waiting grew tiresome. She had just begun to wonder if Drazek had been mistaken when the voice of her friend right beside her startled her almost enough to jump.

'Well met, Namah.'

Namah opened her eyes and smiled, accepting Alinea's offered hand to help her up.

'Well met, Alinea. Why didn't I sense you coming?'

A glint of mischief sparkled in Alinea's eyes as she replied.

'My people must learn to move unseen, unsensed, for our survival. I practise it at every opportunity.'

'Oh.' Namah laughed. 'So you thought you would sneak up on the head-blind human did you?'

'Not so head-blind.' Alinea spoke seriously. 'Drazek tells me you touched minds with him as he watched you from the trees. Only one other human has shown such ability to do so among us, although Alaric shows signs of becoming like his father as he grows older. He is far too distractible to listen as a young one.

'Do you know why I'm here?' Namah asked, half wondering if Alinea could read her thoughts. Alinea nodded, goblin fashion, as she answered.

'You wish to see my world.' Alinea looked thoughtful for a moment before she continued.

'We spoke before of this. It is a serious matter to bring a human into the caverns. Are you sure you wish to do this?'

'Yes, please Alinea. I will follow your lead and stay close to you, I promise!' Namah's words tumbled out in her excitement. Alinea looked at her with that unblinking stare that had disconcerted Namah on the night they had met, but this time it did not unsettle her. Namah knew she was being examined, down to her deepest motivations. She felt her friend's consciousness penetrate her physical self and touch minds with hers. It was a wordless exchange, the emotion behind the intent was clear to them both. It was a necessary test.

'Very well then. Come.' Alinea motioned gently with her hand. It was a graceful motion that might have been inviting the breeze to follow her, yet pulled at Namah's spirit through their recent mental link. Namah followed obediently.

She felt no surprise when Alinea led her to the strange, gnarled tree. Namah had recognised that there was something different about it all along. Alinea led silently, climbing into the hollow tree with the familiarity of one entering a path well known. Namah followed, amazed that she had not seen that the inside of the tree could lead anywhere. It had appeared as just a twisted, hollowed tree. Namah followed Alinea through a downward climb within the trunk that seemed impossible, passing far below the tree's roots and through the ground towards a different world.

It wasn't as far as Namah had expected such a portal to drop. Goblins were too clever to create passages to the outside that would require extended confinement within a narrow opening. Namah speculated that the distance beneath the ground was no more than twice a man's height. The subtle hand-holds that Alinea showed her within the tree made it easy. Then there was a short drop, and the girls were standing in a tunnel that led severely downwards in two different directions. Namah could see that it would be an excellent escape route for a goblin running from surface enemies. One of the passages immediately split into several directions. The other was where Alinea led her. It soon forked as well. There was no enemy to run from now, so Alinea led her slowly, allowing her eyes to adjust to the dim light that reflected from the iridescent stone walls.

Namah shrank closely to her friend, nearly blind in the increasing darkness. The unfamiliar closeness of the caverns frightened her. She tried to remember that this was home to Alinea, a place where the goblin girl travelled confidently and knew the way. A place where Alinea and her other new goblin friends belonged. Still, Namah felt like a trapped animal. She was completely dependent on the guidance of her companion not only for direction, but also for protection. Despite meeting the child goblins on the surface, Namah was not prepared to deal with coming across an adult alone in the isolated atmosphere of their own realm.

She ran her fingers along the rough texture of the walls as they descended deeper into the unknown world. They vibrated. Within these walls was a rhythm unlike anything Namah had encountered before. She had learned enough of goblin ways to know that somewhere, someone was drumming, yet the drumming was accenting the rhythm that already existed within the stone itself. It called to something deep within her... something primal. This is what they had meant. This was the rhythm of *The Dance*.

'Alinea, what would happen if you took me with you to *The Dance*?'

Alinea turned and looked at Namah in surprise. She could smell the fear in the human, yet she had asked this of her. Looking within herself, she did not know the answer. What effect might the power of *The Dance* have on a child human? Namah was one that had been nurtured in an atmosphere of extreme restriction against all that was of nature.

'I do not know,' Alinea answered honestly. 'I think that it may not be a good idea.'

'Would the goblins... hurt me?'

'No!' Alinea exclaimed quickly. The human girl had misunderstood her concern. 'My people would not lay hands on you. You are *guest*. Only... I am not sure what effect *The Dance* may have on you. You are not accustomed to it.'

'Count Anton is human. He dances among your people.' Namah had set her chin stubbornly. Alinea recognised the determination. She had behaved so at times herself, as did all of the young ones. The goblin attitude was to let them learn through experience, so long as they did nothing to seriously endanger themselves. She had said it herself; her people would not harm the girl. It was only herself that Namah had to fear.

'Anton is a magician. He came to *The Dance* naturally, and in his own world.' Alinea turned to Namah, meeting her eyes to emphasise her words. It was almost a challenge. 'I will take you to *The Dance* if you will promise to stay close to me, so that I can look after you if things get... frightening.'

'Is *The Dance* dangerous?' Namah's voice came out in a high note of surprise. She had not expected a warning of this nature.

'No, not dangerous,' answered Alinea calmly. She looked away for a moment as her thoughts drifted to a distant memory. A memory only of a story as she had been too young to remember it herself. Then she met her friend's eyes again, this time just to emphasise the communication. 'Your people do not need real danger to react to fear.'

Namah nodded. She felt some embarrassment for the actions of the humans, especially of the Southerners... her own people.

Neither of them needed to say the words aloud. They both had heard versions of the events of the day that some of the Southern men had thrown the baby Alinea into the river to drown. Indeed, Namah's people still believed that the baby had died. It was all because she was different... alien. She had looked completely human, but the knowledge that she was half goblin was all that was needed for them to label her an abomination and send her to her death. Their fear had driven them to murder.

But the men who actually committed the act are dead now thought Namah. They had been eaten by whatever horror it was that lived in the river. A horror that somehow was responsible for the goblin girl's survival... and for her own.

Alinea saw the train of Namah's thought and knew that she must change the subject before the human asked what she could not tell her. Every adult goblin she knew emphasised that they do not speak to the humans of the *Kol'ksu*, not even those humans who were most trusted. To do so would bring disaster, for everyone.

'I will take you to *The Dance*, Namah, but you must promise to stay close to me.' The girl's eyes brightened as she nodded assent. Alinea wondered what the others would think. No other human besides Count Anton himself had ever danced within the caverns. Her eye fell on the severe black dress that Namah wore... a style that was peculiar to the Southerners. What would they think indeed...

'We must dress you as one of us, so you won't draw attention to yourself as so obviously human.'

'Oh yes!' Namah shouted excitedly. 'Maybe they will think I am like you. That I just look more human. I can't wait!'

Alinea smiled at the girl and took her hand to lead her through a different passage. She automatically led her through a few false twists and turns so that she would not remember the way to where she was led. Humans were easily confused by the caverns. Alinea had no false hopes that Namah would be mistaken for a goblin, not for a moment. The smell of human would draw attention to her long before they entered *The Dance*. At least dressing her properly might seem less offensive.

'*This?*' Namah's voice rose in consternation. 'I can't wear *this*! It's... immodest!'

'It is what all goblins wear, apart from when we go to the surface.' Alinea's calm tone seemed to pacify the girl a little, but she realised too late how goblin clothing would seem to a young girl of Namah's background. The humans wore clothing that covered more of their bodies, especially the Southerners.

Namah's own black dress covered her from neck to toe. The goblin children she had met had dressed for the surface, except for Drazek. The human girl's fear of his physical form had probably prevented her from noticing the exposed flesh of his body. Apart from his posture and the wings, he was actually formed much like any young goblin, or a particularly muscular human child for that matter. The girl had even turned away as Alinea had changed into the loincloth and the strip of fur that kept her small breasts from bouncing painfully during *The Dance*. The constant temperature within the caverns did not require dressing for warmth.

Namah looked up from the skins she had been given. Her eyes looked like those of a rabbit that had been caught for the feed pot. Alinea nodded to her.

'I will leave you for a moment, to change.' Alinea didn't really understand the human's shyness, but she recognised that it caused her genuine distress and so left her alone. She did not want to leave her for very long in the strange world. For a moment she thought, and perhaps hoped, that the distress over the clothing would cause Namah to change her mind, but when she returned to the cavern

Namah was dressed in the skins and examining the effect they had on her young body.

'You're sure all the goblin women will be dressed this way?' Namah asked. But the need for reassurance wasn't as pronounced as Alinea might have expected from the human girl. There was a glint in her eye. The goblin dress did suit her, and it was easy to see that she recognised that this was so.

'Many will be wearing less. The mature females only wear skins across the breasts to stop them bouncing too much in *The Dance*, and a short kilt like the one I wear. They will be openly seeking to mate. Are you sure you are ready for this?' Alinea looked intently at her human friend, looking for a reaction. The girl must understand the ways of the goblins as much as possible. *The Dance* would be very different from the world she knew.

'Yes', Namah answered confidently. 'I understand. No one will approach me?'

Alinea shook her head.

'Among my people, the female chooses. Those who are too young only dance. They will take no notice of you, although they will be aware of a human in the caverns.'

Namah grinned.

'I am ready then. Let's go.'

Chapter Eight

N amah's excitement gave way to nervousness as she walked along the dark caverns with her friend. The rhythm seemed to vibrate from the very walls and called to her to dance, yet her fear of encountering a demon-like goblin was exacerbated by the knowledge that she was walking straight towards a cavern filled with goblins of all kinds. There would be no way to avoid seeing some with fearsome appearance.

However, she knew that appearance isn't everything. Drazek, the gargoyle-like goblin boy, was a sweet creature. Haghuf, the ugly goblin whom Namah had seen as a child, had been kind to her. Her mind told her that she was perfectly safe, especially with Alinea to look out for her, but her instincts and a childhood of training in prejudices told her to run.

Namah forced herself to breathe deeply, as Laura had taught her. Then she pulled her shoulders down, noting that they had unconsciously tightened to make her neck sore. The teachings of the magicians were already making a difference in her life. Simple exercises in relaxation allowed her mind to think clearly, overcoming the barrier that separated real instinct from learned responses.

The rhythm that echoed from the walls soon became soothing, calling to Namah's more primal nature to join in with the celebration of life. Just at that moment, they turned a corner and the music blasted at full strength as a sea of goblins of every description danced in front of her eyes. The rock wall had efficiently insulated the brunt of the sound.

Alinea took Namah's hand to guide her among the dancing green creatures, most of whom were much taller than the girls. Namah was used to adults being taller, although the green skin caused a slight tremor in the steadiness of her nerves. Try as she might, she could not immediately lose the sense of alieness that the goblins' physical appearance aroused. She tried to keep her eyes on her friend, joining her in the free expression that was *The Dance*.

It didn't take long to become caught up in the unconscious movements. The music pulled Namah into its tribal cadence, weaving a spell through flute-like notes from some instrument or other, perhaps the same type as the attractive goblin had played by the fire. The notes permeated her body... her being. It was as if the music itself was a life form, penetrating years of civilised learning to reach the innermost instinctual centres of her most fundamental nature.

As the music took her through the freeform unhindered movements of *The Dance*, Namah became more aware of her surroundings. She did not fear the green creatures who danced all around her any longer. They were part of *The Dance*, all sharing this moment in time together as one entity, celebrating the pure joy of being alive and part of the symbiotic rhythm of nature.

She turned to see Alinea dancing just a little away from her, wrapped up in her own spiritual reverie within *The Dance*. Namah could sense that her friend remained aware of the short distance between them, staying in sight despite the wild nature of *The Dance* and the sometimes huge dancers who were pressed so close to them.

Most of the goblins were male. It was far too obvious in their minimal clothing, and even more so from their musky odour. Namah became very aware of the scent of manliness that surrounded her. An adult female goblin danced nearby, drawing the attention of potential mates. Namah was glad that Alinea had explained the ritual to her. She was intrigued by the subtle body movements that emphasised the state of arousal that the female shared in much less restrained ways than the males dancing closest to her. Thoughts of Ja'imos, possibly dancing here in this very cavern with females wantonly expressing their desire for him in this primitive mating custom, brought Namah's own blossoming sexuality to conscious awareness.

Then the female chose. She touched a male goblin with a familiarity that would have made Namah turn her head in embarrassment in any other situation. Yet now she was fascinated, watching the custom play out in the way that came naturally to this strange society. The blatant sexuality of the chosen couple – touching, dancing closely, the female licking the male goblin's skin and nibbling gently – felt both voyeuristic and exciting. Namah had seen animals couple, but she only knew what happened between adults from what her mother and married friends had told her. Despite knowing that her thoughts would have been enough to embarrass her in her old world, here in *The Dance* Namah felt excited, sensual, and ready to see what it was like to touch a man herself.

Her eyes scanned the crowded dancers. Was Ja'imos here? Would he already be chosen? Would she be able to get near him with other females wanting to get there first?

The rhythm drove her movements as she spun into the crowd, away from her forgotten friend and protector. Her body brushed against other dancers without concern. Desire for the young goblin was her only thought... her sole motivation as she pressed her way deeper within the throng of dancing, primitive sexuality.

Then suddenly she became aware of the effect her sensual thoughts were having on the goblins around her. She was surrounded by male goblins, dancing closely. Their attention was on her as they moved their hips towards her in the same way that they had tried to entice the female goblin. They were waiting for her to choose among them. They wanted her, as Gareth had wanted her. All of them thrusting, undulating, reaching out just short of actually touching her, trying to draw her attention. All of them at once, wanting her, reeking of animal sexuality. Visions of being taken by a gang of lustful goblins out of control flitted across Namah's mind and without warning, she panicked.

She felt herself scream, although the music was far too loud for anyone to hear. Then she ran, hoping that it was in the direction she had come. There was no time to think. She had to get out of there, away from the aroused goblins. A path opened, allowing her easy escape. She did not have the presence of mind to wonder why, although later she would realise that the change in her would have been obvious to the psychically sensitive goblins. She ran blindly into the nearest opening, hoping it was the one that would lead to Alinea's cavern where she had left her demure human clothing.

The cavern seemed too straight, yet she didn't care. She had to get as far as she could from that press of unbridled sexuality. She hadn't been ready for such intense erotic expression. Somewhere in her more rational mind, Namah realised that Alinea had been right to dissuade her.

The sensible thoughts didn't stop her feet. She ran on, although she was beginning to feel winded. Then suddenly Ja'imos dropped in front of her, seemingly from nowhere, and halted her progress. With her momentum she ran straight into him, wrapping her arms around him before she realised she had been immobilised. He was speaking to her urgently, but she couldn't follow the words in the goblin language. All she understood was that she was in a dark cavern, alone with this beautiful goblin man, wrapped around him like a lover and breathing heavily into his chest.

Her earlier excitement at thoughts of him returned and she reached her face up and kissed him roughly. The goblin's words stopped suddenly as she pressed herself into him, bringing a physical reaction not unlike that which she had aroused in the other goblins, yet infinitely more desirable in this one whom she would find so pleasing.

At first he reacted instinctively, allowing the female to express her willingness... all too willing himself. Then he pushed her away gently, holding her arms as he tried to speak to her again. His serious expression and insistence eventually impressed on Namah's consciousness so that she tried to understand what the urgency was about. Eventually he gestured just behind him. Namah looked and saw the pit. He had stopped her to save her life.

She held his arm tightly as she imagined what might have happened. She didn't know how deep the pit was or where it led, but the danger was clear. She found it difficult to take her eyes away from the gaping chasm then. Full realisation of how close she had come to falling in began to dawn on her. She began to shake. She felt Ja'imos tugging at her, encouraging her to follow him away from the pit. A moment later his strong arm encircled her and turned her in the opposite direction, forcing her to come. His strength was undeniable. She had no choice but to move where he guided her.

He held her gently and spoke soothingly to her as he guided her through the passage. The darkness of the caverns was confusing. Namah could not be sure if they were going back the way she had run or through another passage entirely, but she felt safe with Ja'imos. She felt a thrill at being alone with him, feeling his touch. She wondered for a moment if he was leading her to some private cavern somewhere, then realised that it was more that she was hoping he was. She stopped a moment. She was calm now, so he did not force her on but turned to meet her eyes and try to understand why she was stopping here.

Several thoughts went through her mind at once as she looked up into his beautiful golden eyes. Had she done her father's will, she would not be a maiden now, yet she felt young still. She was not sure if she was ready to be a woman as yet, but she felt drawn to this creature. Without thinking, she reached her hand towards him, gently stroking his bare chest as she had seen the goblin woman do with her chosen mate. For a moment she abandoned her thoughts, moving closer to him so that they might embrace, no longer caring if she were ready or not.

Ja'imos took her hands and gently but firmly held them together, stepping back just a little so that she could not stroke him further. He was speaking to her in his own language again. Namah could not understand the words, but the meaning was too clear. He would not accept her advances, despite the look of wanting that was so clear in his eyes.

'He is saying that you are too young,' said Alinea's soft voice from the darkness. She stepped closer, so that Namah could see her. 'Among my people, a female may befriend a future mate when she is not yet ready, and Ja'imos offers you this. But there are subtle differences that change a young one to a mating adult, and he will not touch you before your time.'

Namah felt a little embarrassed, but she was not sure if it was because she had offered herself to a man who turned her down, or because she had a witness to her indiscretion. She was not even sure if she need feel embarrassed among goblins, whose customs were so different from what she knew.

'Alinea, what is the custom for accepting his friendship in this way?'

Alinea spoke in the goblin language then, although she seemed to address herself to both Namah and Ja'imos. A smile flashed across his face as he listened, then he embraced Namah, much as a brother might. Namah began to wonder if she had promised herself to him in some way, but she did not get a chance to ask Alinea.

'Oh!' Alinea exclaimed suddenly. She walked a few steps away and picked up something from the floor of the cavern. Her eyes widened as she turned to hold it up for Ja'imos to see. It was a length of chain. Alinea looked almost frightened.

'What is it Alinea?' Namah felt Ja'imos move away from her gently, suddenly alert to Alinea's obvious concern. She spoke to him again in their language. Namah caught the word 'Drazek', but could not understand the significance of the discovery. Ja'imos sprang away, running down the cavern corridor at a seemingly impossible speed.

'Jezza has slipped his chains again,' Alinea explained. 'Drazek is too far away for us to wait. We are halfway to Legna now. Namadla must be told he came this way.'

'Who is Jezza? What does Drazek have to do with it?'

Alinea looked at Namah with a calculating expression. Namah caught a feeling of caution from her friend's mind. Apparently she had already said too much. Alinea answered the question carefully.

'Drazek is the only one Jezza will follow. He is *of the blood*.'

'I don't understand.' Namah was becoming frustrated.

'It must remain so.' Alinea sighed. 'Yet there is no choice but to take you with me to see Namadla. No human has gone so far, but it would take too long to take you back and I cannot leave you alone in the caverns. You must come with me.'

Namah nodded. Her fear of all that was strange in the goblin caverns was assuaged by her trust for Alinea. For a moment, she wished that Ja'imos had not run to seek Drazek. She would have been happy to have been left in his charge. Despite her weariness from all she had experienced so far in this alien world, Namah made up her mind that she would take the adventure a little further and help her friend in whatever way she could. Besides, knowing that she was to see things in the goblin world that even Count Anton had never breached appealed to her sense of discovery.

Alinea had gathered the heavy looking chains and wrapped them expertly so that they were contained in a tied ball of iron. Namah was astonished at how easily her friend had accomplished this, and at the ease with which she carried the heavy ball. Goblins were certainly stronger than humans, but Alinea's human appearance made such strength seem out of place. *Perhaps*, Namah thought, *there is more goblin in her than anyone might have guessed.*

They walked quietly but quickly, not stopping to talk. Namah did not know why there was such urgency, but she could see that this was something important that couldn't wait. The paths where Alinea now led her looked as though they sloped downwards. Not radically, but consistently. Namah imagined that the caverns were becoming darker as they travelled, moving deeper within the Earth. Every step made her feel both more scared and more excited.

After a while, she began to wonder how far they had yet to go. Alinea had said they were halfway to their destination when they started, yet it seemed to be taking much longer than her run from the cavern where she had bolted from *The Dance*. Namah had speculated that the distance she had travelled afterwards with Ja'imos must have been back in the other direction, returning her to Alinea.

Somewhere in the darkness, she heard singing. It wasn't the same odd sort of song that she had heard from the river. She remembered now that there had been some sort of hypnotic song when she experienced being close to the river creatures, although she had forgotten it at the time. This singing was similar, but somehow more real, perhaps because it was a male voice singing in falsetto. The echoes of the cavern walls made it difficult to determine what direction it came from, but it still sounded tangible in a way that the river song did not. It became louder as they moved closer. Namah guessed that whoever Namadla was, she must be in the company of whoever it was that they heard singing. Alinea was leading her straight towards the source of the voice.

The singing stopped abruptly. Alinea quickened her pace. Namah kept up, aware that her friend might have moved faster if she did not have to wait for a slow human. She wondered if Alinea possessed the skill which had allowed Ja'imos to pass her and drop in front of her so suddenly. It had been as if he could crawl along the ceiling itself.

They turned a corner and suddenly there was light. Dim and flickering, but light nonetheless. Namah could smell candle wax... and something else. There was a pungent scent, one which she could not identify. It became stronger as they moved towards the flickering light, which Namah could now see was emanating from another cavern. She had no doubt that Alinea was going to lead her into that cavern and to whatever awaited them within it. This would be the home of the one they called Namadla.

Namah was imagining some kind of witch living alone away from the others, but nothing prepared her for what she saw as they turned the corner into the lit cavern. A young man was kneeling, holding a large candle in each hand. His arms were outstretched and his smooth face turned upwards, eyes closed, looking very much like a young acolyte in prayer. But what was most shocking to Namah was that he was undeniably human. He wore chains and a goblin loincloth. There could be no doubt that he was here as a slave. For the first time, Namah was genuinely afraid. It had not occurred to her before that goblins might keep a human as a slave.

'What have you brought me, fair Alinea?' The voice, deep but decidedly feminine, seeped out of a shadow cast by the candle light.

'Namah is *guest*, a friend from the world of the magicians above.' Alinea's answer was calm, emphasising the word '*guest*'. She showed no fear of whatever creature dwelt here. Alinea dropped the bundle of chains with a clamour. 'Jezza is loose... again. A runner has gone to find Drazek.'

Namah noted that Alinea sounded remonstrative. Whatever was going on, there was some history, perhaps even a dispute in the air.

'My pet causes too much concern. Perhaps he feels the need to hunt.' Namadla's voice sounded unconcerned, almost defiant.

'That is exactly what we fear, Namadla. He grows bigger. Some of the young ones may not be too big for him to look on as prey even now.' Alinea spoke patiently, but Namah sensed that there was more behind the words. This 'pet' was obviously of a different nature than the one she had chained to hold her candles. If it were a creature that could hunt 'young ones', it might be a predator that Namah did not want to meet in the dark caverns herself. She began to look forward to returning to her own world, where at least she knew the dangers.

Namadla emerged from her shadow then, showing herself in the flickering light of the candles.

'A day will come, young Alinea, when you will be glad of Jezza's friendship to our kind.' Namah looked up at the tall goblin woman. She looked much like a female version of that first goblin she had met – green skin, long dark hair, golden eyes peering out of a face with ridges that a human would find ugly – yet she projected a certain magnificence in her slow, graceful movements that inspired awe. The effect seemed to be lost on Alinea.

'I must take my *guest* back to her world. We have had to come too far just to bring these chains back to you.' Namah was amazed to hear her friend speak with such authority. She might have been Alaric, issuing orders as the future ruler of the humans. 'You must find a solution, Namadla. Perhaps it is too late to return him to the deep places from whence he came, but he cannot wander freely in the caverns forever.'

'Perhaps you would have me keep Drazek as well, to watch over poor little Jezza.' The honeyed tones held a subtle threat – one that made Alinea's eyes flash in the dim light. Namah sensed anger, an emotion she had never seen in her friend. 'He too likes to fly freely, does he not?' Namadla finished in her silky voice. She clearly did not fear Alinea's anger.

There was a moment between Namadla and Alinea where nothing was spoken, but their eyes met in challenge. Namah could feel the tension. Then at last Alinea spoke in her more familiar, calm voice.

'Come, Namah, we must take you home.' Namah followed obediently as Alinea stormed out of the cavern. She heard Namadla order the young man to sing as they passed through the doorway. His clear voice rang out in a song that sounded very old and sad. Namah wanted to ask about his presence in the caverns, but decided that now was not the time. Alinea had referred to the creature 'Jezza' as something from the deep places, and that was a frightening thought. Plus she had been angered. Namah decided that she would be patient and concentrate on following her friend out of the caverns. Questions would come more easily in the light of day.

Alinea seemed to walk at an easy pace, but Namah was pushed a little to keep up with her. She had the feeling that if the half-goblin wished to move much more quickly, she could do so easily. Namah was grateful for the consideration that slowed Alinea's pace for a human's limitations. Their silence allowed Namah to concentrate on breathing, so that she could keep up as quick a stride as she was able.

Yet after a few minutes that seemed much longer, breathing was becoming hard. Namah found herself struggling. Alinea stopped and turned then, noticing her human friend's distress.

'My apologies, Namah. The caverns are deceptive. I had forgotten that we were moving uphill.'

Namah nodded, still taking deep breaths to catch up to her body's demand for oxygen. After a moment, she felt able to speak.

'Why doesn't it affect you?'

'I have lived in the caverns all my life.' Alinea smiled a little as she answered. 'The air is thinner here than on the surface and we do much running between places. As you can see, the distances from one place to another are often long stretches of empty cavern. These, near the surface, slope upwards and downwards so my lungs have had to develop capacity to feed my body in the same way that someone living very high on a mountain on the surface might. Such places also have thinner air and even more dramatic slopes to the land.'

Namah understood. The history and geography she had learned from her own people concerned only the city she knew and a few generations, then a skip in time to ancient civilisations in a foreign place where their religion had first come into being. But among the magicians, she had quickly been learning about many places and of people before the Turning. She had been told of people who lived high in mountains and had seen pictures drawn of such places. She had never seen a mountain herself.

But now she was deep within the Earth. How deep she did not know. Alinea had said they were close to the surface, which was reassuring. Namah had heard that if you travel deeply enough, the Earth became a furnace of molten rock flowing in deadly rivers of fiery lava. It sounded frightening.

'Alinea, how deep do the goblins travel?'

Alinea looked away from her friend before answering.

'This is something I cannot speak of to you. It isn't that I do not trust you, it is that we just don't speak of our world to humans. You have seen more than any other already. It is a rule for our survival. A human, a trusted one, may inadvertently say something to one less trustful, or be overheard. Or many small pieces of information may be put together like a puzzle, and the wrong humans learn too much of our ways.

'What of the human in Namadla's cavern?' Namah asked boldly.

Alinea met her eyes quickly in surprise, then looked away again.

'Mikel is one who has not known the company of humans since he was an infant, and will never know them again.'

'You mean, he's a captive?' Namah's voice rose in incredulity.

'Not exactly.' Alinea answered calmly, but she would not meet her friend's eyes.

'The chains are for show... a game he and Namadla play together. He would no more leave her side than I would leave you here alone to fend for yourself. Your people had a war – one with machines and explosions. They hid in the between places, the tunnels originally dug by men. A small child wandered, hardly old enough to walk. The goblins did not go far into the between places then, but Namadla found him. She had lost a newly born of her own and she took the young one to suckle.'

'But the last time humans had a war with machines was long before the Turning!' Namah exclaimed. 'He could be no older than twenty.'

'He is far older than he looks.' Alinea turned to her friend, meeting her eyes at last. 'Many you see have lived much longer than the lifetime of a human, yet look young to your eyes. Ja'imos, for example. How old does he look to you?'

Namah thought a minute.

'I knew that goblins lived longer, but in my mind I have compared Ja'imos to a young man of nineteen.'

'Yet your own great-grandmother may have been charmed by him, had they met,' Alinea answered calmly.

'Then, the other goblin, the one I met as a child...'

'Haghuf.' Alinea took up the thought. 'Haghuf knew the old goblin wars with humans... in a time before humans consigned the stories to legend. Many generations passed before they believed them to be no more than that. Yet in times when humans knew the smaller goblins and called them fairies and other names, Haghuf walked the deep places, staying away from the world of sunlight.'

Namah took a few minutes to assimilate the new information. Then her thoughts drifted back to the young man in chains.

'It seems an odd game to play, to chain someone adopted as her son.'

Once again, Alinea looked away.

'Among my people, a youngling ceases to belong to parents when they are younger than you and I. A female would not mate with one she knew she had given life, but there is no blood relation between Namadla and Mikel.'

Namah was shocked.

'She raised him, then mated with him?'

Alinea nodded.

'In the old tradition of the changeling, it is recognised that fresh bloodlines strengthen both peoples. Namadla's act in claiming a lost human child was unusual, but in keeping him deep within her own cavern, a place that humans knew nothing of, she fulfilled the one basic law that we must hold; that we do nothing to endanger our own. To take a child without replacing him would bring trouble under normal circumstances, but the war among the humans caused confusion. Many disappeared without explanation.'

Namah tried to read her friend's face. She was sure she could hear a note of disapproval in Alinea's voice as she explained. She could not be sure if it was because Namadla had cruelly left a mother bereft, or because she kept a mating male to herself. Namah had learned enough of the goblin ways to see that this was unusual. She opened her mouth to speak, but Alinea cut her off.

'No more questions, please. If you are recovered, we must take you the rest of the way.'

Namah nodded in assent, but just as they began to walk again a noise stopped them both in their tracks. Alinea's arm shot out in front of Namah, as if she were literally barring her way forward.

Namah tried to work out what the noise could be. It had sounded animalistic, as if a large creature had expelled something between a bark and a roar... and it sounded close. They hardly breathed as they stood silently, awaiting another sound. Soon the stillness was interrupted with a low growl that sounded almost like amplified purring. It was a rolling sound that echoed from the cavern walls and sent terror to Namah's deepest instincts, yet Alinea did not flinch.

Namah wanted to run. The intermittent trilling of the unknown creature drew closer. She was sure it was just around a corner right in front of them. There were other passages they could escape through. She tugged on Alinea's arm gently, urging her to come away from the direction of the sound. But very softly, almost on the edge of hearing, Alinea whispered to her authoritatively.

'Don't move.'

Chapter Nine

C ount Anton approached the castle slowly, setting his pace to accommodate the small group of teenage girls at his heels. Two of them carried infants. At least the other four had been spared that extra responsibility as they had been more recently married, or for other reasons had failed to conceive. They made for a drab display in their dark clothing and dark hair tied severely back for the sake of practicality.

Now they were Anton's responsibility. It had been an eventuality that he had not expected. The Southern people had never experienced several widows at once before. They had been taken aback when Anton had suggested that the girls return to their parent's homes. Widows among the Southerners were normally quickly married to whatever man wanted a wife enough to also adopt her children, or to at least receive used goods. The indignity as the group of elders had begun to speculate on which single men among them would be prepared to take the homeless girls off their hands had been too much for Anton. He felt he had no choice but to volunteer to take them back to the Northern shore and find them homes, like stray kittens.

They had nowhere else to go. Their poor houses would be claimed by their husbands' parents and prepared for the marriages of further offspring. The girls owned nothing but the clothes on their backs. Their own parents no doubt expected that Count Anton planned to arrange marriages for them and were all too glad to have the task out of their hands. Anton allowed the presumption to go unchallenged. He hoped to find people who would adopt them, or perhaps to add some of them to his own castle staff.

Namah's father had not been among the group of miscreants that had attempted to hunt the creatures in the river. At least in this, the elders had been surprised at the stupidity of the brash men. The dead men had all been relatively young, just over thirty, and full of fire and temper. No one in the Southern settlement had even known they had gone. Their disappearance might have remained a mystery forever if Count Anton had not brought the news to their community. He did not hesitate to use the episode to forbid any such further attempts to disturb the river creatures. Anton actually enjoyed relating that the creatures could move on land and frightening those who might have considered a better thought-out attack.

He did not describe the creatures in detail though. This much he knew would be a violation of what trust he had been given. Instead, he emphasised hideous sharp teeth and the ability to strip bones in minutes. The Southern people would not go near the river anytime again soon. Had they known the ethereal beauty of the creatures, curiosity might have overridden their fear.

It had taken some manoeuvring to gain a private moment with Rab. It seemed like these people never left each other alone unless it was to go out into the trees to relieve their bladders. He had met Rab's eyes and gestured, then excused himself. Luckily, the man was clever enough to recognise the ruse. Anton did not want to give much information about Namah. His promise had been only to tell Rab if his daughter lived.

'She is alive and happy where she is. That is all I can say.' The man had nodded in response and walked away towards the houses. The look in his eyes had spoken of both sadness and relief. Anton could believe that this man actually loved his daughter. Rab still had that aura of doom over him. He had not been foolish enough to join those who hunted the river creatures, but Anton was sure another unpleasant fate awaited the poor man.

Anton contemplated all of this as he led the young Southern girls into the great ballroom. Ariane would surely be able to take over this task now. He sent for her as the girls settled among the plush cushions, looking around the room in wide-eyed wonder. They had never seen opulence, only the drab existence of their world. They would always remember the day they saw the inside of Count Anton's castle.

Anton smiled at the thought. He was so used to his surroundings that he gave it little notice until a visitor brought his attention to the splendour in which he lived. Ironically, it held little pleasure for him.

He had never actually said the words before, not even with his internal voice. Now he had to acknowledge it to himself at least. He wished he had been born a goblin. He wanted nothing more than to be one of them... to live within their world. If he were to join them now, he would be accepted by some of them, treated as an equal, though there were some places that he could never go in his human body.

Anton sighed. He knew that even Haghuf would not encourage such an idea. Anton could never really be one of them. He was 'other'. Always a foreign visitor in their realms. Some of their secrets would always be kept from him. Stone walls could never really be his home. Responsibilities kept him here in the castle, and one of them would require his attention all too soon. Too much time had passed. Anton could not keep the invader, Count Michel, in drugged sleep for much longer. Soon he would awake and look for his missing guards, also sleeping, and demand to have another audience with Count Anton. There was no telling then what devilry he might get up to.

Dani appeared at Anton's elbow, as if he had been called by some silent signal.

'The Countess will be here momentarily. She stopped to order refreshment for the young ladies. Can we have a private word, sir?'

'Of course, Dani.' Anton answered, hardly remembering the servant role that his close companion played for the benefit of the common people. Then it occurred to him that he now had an excuse to escape.

'My ladies,' Anton addressed the girls formally. 'My good wife will come momentarily with refreshment. Do relax, and enjoy a well-earned rest. You have travelled far from your old homes. The Countess Ariane will see that you are safe and cared for. Please, have no worries. I must leave you now, as matters of great importance demand my attention.'

The girls' eyes gleamed as they watched Count Anton bow to them gracefully. It was at times like these that he was glad to be married, and not available for more than the most wistful fancies of young girls. Anton had been the subject of far more marriage fantasies from the daughters of common men than he would choose to remember, although there was never any question in his heart that he could only marry a female magician. Even there, he had had his choice among them.

Dani hurried Anton down the corridor to get out of earshot of the ballroom.

'Anton, another visitor came to ask about Count Michel. He was received by Ariane in your absence. She had been brought a gift by... an old acquaintance of yours... and now he sleeps more deeply than the others upstairs. How will we explain him?'

'I see.' Anton pressed the fingers of both hands together in front of his lips. He understood Dani's meaning and spared a wistful thought for the visit he had missed. Talla had avoided direct contact with him since Alinea had begun to come to the surface on her own.

Anton was at a loss for ideas. 'What did he have to say before he... succumbed to our local liqueur.' Anton smirked, amused despite the gravity of the situation. 'Have you any suggestions?'

Dani thought for a moment, then shook his head before he answered.

'It buys us a little time. He said that Count Michel had come to put the castle in order. I think he meant to take it over all along. He came with another small escort. They seem to have succumbed to drink as well.' Dani fought the smile that threatened the corner of his mouth. There were serious matters at hand.

'Even if you started training the people to fight now, they would never stand against the seasoned army at our shores. They could hardly defend from the soldiers already within the castle.' Then the mischievous smirk won the battle for his face. 'You could put the Southerners on the front lines.'

Anton chuckled.

'That might not be such a bad idea.' Anton became more serious again. 'Our choices are too few. Surrender to an unknown ruler and lose our way of life. Fight them and risk the people I am sworn to protect. Send them foodstuffs and have tribute expected of us until the demands become too great and we end up fighting them anyway.'

They had been walking unconsciously, but Anton stopped now to run his fingers through his long hair as he strained his thought processes for more options.

'What would Haghuf do?' he asked rhetorically.

'He would ask for help,' Dani answered flatly. Anton met his friend's eyes. The nod between them was barely perceptible. It was worth a shot.

The day had turned to night as they had discussed the matter. The shadows of moonlight saw the wolf leap through the gateway, running towards the one place where wisdom could be found, and perhaps even warriors.

LAURA'S PONY CLOMPED along slowly towards the castle. Suddenly she saw Namah approaching and slipped off the pony to run to meet her sister, hugging her closely.

'Namah! I've been worried about you. Where have you been?'

'Dancing... with the goblins!' Namah answered excitedly.

Laura leaned back on the pony, a look of utmost surprise engraved on her face. She examined Namah's expression, looking for any sign of a joke. She saw only a serious reply to her question.

'How...' Laura began.

'I asked Alinea to take me,' Namah answered. 'I saw so many strange things! But I promised not to talk about some of them. But *The Dance*! I was surrounded by goblins, hoards of them, dancing. It was so, so...'

Namah couldn't find the words. She had disgraced herself by running from the intense sexuality of *The Dance*, yet it had been thrilling and she had been held, if only for a few moments, by Ja'imos. No man had so much as touched her fingers before. Then she realised that she must not say too much about her adventures. She had promised.

'Come, Namah,' Laura said practically. 'You may sit on my pony. I was hoping to find you at the castle, but there is no need to go there now. We should get home before dark. There is something I must discuss with you.'

Namah nodded and did as she was bid. The change in the conversation had saved her from having to veer away from the further experiences she had promised not to speak of to any human. Not even those closest to her, or even to other goblins. Alinea had been adamant about that. The goblins must not know that she had seen Jezza, or knew of the special influence that Drazek held over the little dragon.

Namah stifled a giggle at the thought of how frightened she had been. Alinea had told her not to move and she had stood frozen, despite an instinct that told her to run. Then Drazek had appeared from around the corner, doing some sort of dance that led what looked like a giant monster in some sort of hypnotic trance. As they rounded the corner, the folded wings of the reptilian creature brought many old stories to mind. *Dragon*! Namah's inner voice had shouted. It had taken every ounce of will she had to obey Alinea instead of running away from the fearsome creature.

Walking on four legs, it had been as tall as the pony on which she now sat, but much longer. Alinea had explained in whispers as Drazek and Jezza passed in front of them that the dragon was only a baby. Drazek had stopped then and Namah had been introduced to Jezza. Alinea had been forced to explain that the young dragon was Namadla's escaped pet.

Namah had asked more questions, but Alinea had said only that they don't speak of the dragons. Not just to humans, but even amongst themselves. It seemed incongruous to be standing next to the dragon stroking it as Alinea elicited the promise that Namah must never mention it, even between themselves. Alinea's urgency convinced Namah that it was very important. The secret was one that she must keep at all costs.

The trilling noises the creature made sounded friendly. Drazek played with him as if he were a big dog. Then a moment later, Drazek had begun the hypnotic dance again and the little dragon had followed him obediently. Namah had actually felt regretful that she would probably never see such a creature again. Despite her promise, she had asked Alinea why she had been told to be so still. The serious look her friend gave her as she answered had been enough to silence any further questions.

'If you run, his instinct is to see you as prey. You are not too big to be so for one that size.'

When they had reached the surface world again, it had all seemed like a dream. Everything was ordinary again. The strange experiences of the subterranean world of the goblins were relegated to a distant memory. Namah had taken leave of her friend and headed for home, not knowing if she would ever ask to visit that world again, or be invited. The memory of strong arms holding her in the darkness, protecting her from danger, warmed her in the cool air of coming evening. Namah ran part of the way home before slowing to a walk and had then come across Laura, looking for her.

'WE HAVE HAD TOO MANY humans in the caverns. Why do you bring your wars to goblins?' Haghuf scowled, but Anton was used to his friend's surly moods.

'We have no trained fighters, you know that. We have developed farmers and craftsmen, not soldiers.' Anton waited patiently for his old companion to reply. He knew the custom all too well. Haghuf pretended to ignore Anton, continuing with the task he had been busy with when the human had first been ushered to the goblin's habitual sleeping cavern.

No goblin owned space in the caverns, but they became accustomed to sleeping in the same places and kept furs there for warmth. No matter what the weather on the surface, the caverns beneath the *Between* levels were always a little cold unless you were moving around, or went much deeper. Anton observed the goblin fingers working deftly at their task, sewing a leather pouch in an odd shape. He wondered what it was for, but did not want to distract Haghuf from the question at hand.

Anton could not resist filling the silence.

'I can hold my own with a sword, as you know from our sparring sessions. We seem evenly matched, but I am only one man.'

An old and painful memory occurred to him. He heard himself speak it out loud.

'I wouldn't want to use such a toothpick against that bloody great troll that threw me in the pit though.'

Anton thought he saw a flicker of a smile twitch at Haghuf's mouth.

'If you have occasion to meet Kahjak face to face again, do not let him hear you calling him a troll.'

Anton responded reflexively with a question without thinking of whether he really wanted to know.

'What would he do?'

'Probably prove it.' Haghuf answered with an evil grin.

At last the goblin turned and answered the question still hanging between them.

'They won't come.' Another brief silence. 'Goblins do not take orders. We have no soldiers either.'

'But you have trained fighters!' Anton implored.

'*Those Who Protect*, protect us from humans.' The answer was quick and adamant. 'They kill humans. They do not help them.'

Anton thought quickly. Haghuf had turned his back to him dismissively. The interview would be terminated if he didn't find a wedge soon.

'What makes them come to the surface?'

'When humans attack, they come.' The answer had been quicker that time. Anton knew much of the relay system that would take the message to the fighting goblins, but he would not speak of it to Haghuf now. Haghuf had objected to every piece of information that Anton had learned about the goblins. It was no time to remind him that he knew too much.

'But the humans from overseas are invaders by nature. If they conquer my people, they will surely learn of yours. There are records of the old transportation system in the *Between* places. They may try to reclaim them.'

'They will find no tracks.' A hint of a smile played on the corner of Haghuf's mouth. Anton knew very well that the old metal tracks had long since been stripped by the goblins. What they had done with the metal he could only speculate, but there had been no lack of swords among the warrior goblins. Many of them had been of designs that he was sure did not come from human sources. His own goblin sword, awarded to him by one of a species that he knew little about, was certainly not made by the hands of humans.

He was getting nowhere. Anton recognised that much of Haghuf's resistance was habitual, yet it was also because he had no authority. Nobody commanded the goblins. They would only respond if they felt their own world threatened, or if there was some important connection with future events. Anton suddenly knew how to shake Haghuf out of his stubborn silence.

'I saw some of them, the *Kol'ksu*.'

Haghuf froze. His back was still to Anton, but there was no mistaking the impact of the words.

'A female among them told me that I have something left to do.'

Haghuf turned slowly, meeting Anton's eyes. His expression was unreadable, but Anton could see that this news surprised his old friend. It was unusual that Haghuf did not know every movement that happened in the goblin world. The water creatures were very different, yet they were still goblins. Anton had seen Haghuf's fear near the water. Perhaps these creatures were separated from the other goblins by their environment, or perhaps by their predatory and carnivorous nature. He had clearly succeeded in shocking his friend.

'Then perhaps the goblins will have reason to come to you,' Haghuf stated. 'Be careful it is not you who becomes a threat.'

Anton grinned. Haghuf's warnings were serious, but his concern for Anton was real. He knew he had broken the hard shell now and Haghuf at least would help him in whatever way he could. *And where Haghuf goes, other goblins will follow of their free will,* Anton thought to himself.

ARIANE HAD THE HOUSEHOLD in hand now. It had been chaos at first, finding rooms for half a dozen girls and two of them with babies. She would get word out tomorrow to the people to see if there were homes that would make room for them.

She felt for them. Although they knew each other, they knew no one among the strangers north of the river. They had been too suddenly ejected from their homes, thrown away by their own families. It was different than the occasional refugees who came seeking sanctuary. These girls had given no indication that they had objected to their prior existence. *Perhaps,* thought Ariane, *they just don't have the imagination to reach for alternatives.*

Anton had not yet returned. The darkness had fallen while she had been busy feeding and settling the girls for the night. They were all tucked up in their rooms now, or so Ariane believed. Without being asked, Dani brought her a glass of red wine in the great ballroom.

'I thought you might need this,' he explained. Ariane smiled her thanks as she accepted the welcome glass.

'Will you sit with me a while, Dani? I think that after so much commotion, I do not wish to hear the echoes of resounding silence too quickly.'

Dani poured himself a glass and relaxed on a cushion.

'I should relax while I can anyway. We've had far too many visitors these past few days.'

'Poor Dani.' Ariane sounded genuinely sympathetic. 'At least the intruders have slept, so you haven't had to stay in role all the time.'

Dani chuckled.

'Well, we will have to let them wake naturally now and deal with Count Michel, but keeping up the façade for a bunch of empty headed Southern girls could wear thin quickly.'

Soundlessly, a young girl put her hand to her mouth as she sat quietly in the corridor, listening.

'I will find them homes... somehow,' Ariane assured Dani. 'Anton suggested that we keep one of them here, to help in the kitchen. You know that strumpet that helps Peg is useless.'

'Oh yes,' Dani agreed. 'I can't remember how we got saddled with that one. Can you?'

'She came to us, wishing to escape her dull existence among her common family. Living in the castle sounded glamorous to her at the time.' Ariane smiled at the memory. 'What concerns me about these new girls though, is that they might know Namah, or even Laura.'

The girl's ears perked up. She feared someone might come along and catch her listening, but she wanted to know more. She had known Namah when they were children, before her marriage had separated them. She had grieved for Namah when she heard the silly girl had bolted from her own wedding and had been killed in the river. Now she was astounded to learn that Namah was alive after all.

'Anton will protect Namah,' Dani said confidently. 'But if these girls are friends of hers, they may learn too much of her new friends.'

Dani looked at Ariane seriously.

'The Southern people must never learn of Anton's daughter.'

Ariane nodded.

'You are right, of course,' Ariane agreed. 'How she survived being thrown in the river by those ghastly people we may never know, but the Southerners still think she was Ranalf's child and that she is long since dead. That is enough.'

The eavesdropping girl held both hands tightly over her mouth now. She knew the story, as all of her people knew. The abomination – the half-goblin child of a man – had been thrown in the river by their religious leader. The girl had been a little older than Namah at the time and could vaguely remember the rocking boats and the horror of the river when they had been toppled... the stain of blood in the foaming water. It had been fresh in her mind as Count Anton had brought her and her companions to the Northern shore. She had wanted to scream then, in fear for her life in the unstable flat-bottomed boats, even more than she wanted to scream now.

'Alinea can take care of herself, I'm sure,' Dani said as he poured another glass of wine for himself. He offered the bottle to Ariane, but she shook her head. Dani continued.

'And of course the goblins look after their own kind.' Dani did not hear the silent creeping of the girl in the corridor as she tip-toed back towards her room. 'I would pity anyone who tried to harm her. But still, if they don't know she exists, there is nothing to fear.'

Ariane smiled.

'But who do you fear for, Dani? Alinea is no longer a helpless infant. Whatever helped her then is still out there. I wonder what Anton saw in the river this morning.'

'He said only that he was forbidden to speak of it, but men are dead. I don't think I'll go swimming any time soon.' Dani put his glass on the table as he finished speaking. 'Goodnight, Ariane. I will check on the Count Michel on my way to bed.'

He made a face as he mocked the accent as he spoke the visiting count's name. The loathing was unmistakeable.

Ariane thought of the potion she still carried in her pocket, the gift from Talla. Talla had been adamant that she must take it. It had to have been the right decision to use it, if only to keep Anton in her bed for one night instead of gallivanting around the worlds of goblins and men trying to put the whole world to rights. Just once in a while, Ariane wished he could be less of a hero and more her husband.

Yet she knew that it had been the excitement of the dashing Count Anton that had attracted her to him in the first place. Over ten years of running his household and raising their son had shown her how girlish she had been, in love with an image, when she still hardly knew the man. She envied Dani, his closest friend. At least he knew the real Anton, the man beneath the image. Ariane realised now why she had never been jealous of Talla, even when she had found the goblin woman sitting in her own bedroom. Although Ariane was married to Anton, he had never really been hers.

ANTON ARRIVED HOME to his castle well after nightfall. He had declined Haghuf's invitation to join *The Dance*, but had spent a little more time conversing with his old friend. It was late enough that he expected that the household would all be in bed. He was therefore surprised to find Dani sitting alone in the darkened sitting room, illuminated by a single candle. He sensed that Dani had been waiting up for him.

'Dani?' Anton spoke softly, not wanting to disturb the peaceful stillness of the night. 'What's happened?'

Dani lifted a glass of wine to his lips and took a sip before answering.

'He's gone, Anton. The Count Michel has awakened and escaped, without anyone seeing him or knowing when it happened.'

Anton thought for a moment. He had checked him personally that morning.

'And his escort?'

'Also gone.'

'When did you last see him?'

'After lunch,' Dani answered at once. 'He was sleeping like a baby. I didn't administer any more of the sleeping drug because we had agreed that he must be allowed to waken. I should have checked him sooner, but I didn't look again until I was on my way to bed. His bed was empty, and his escort and all their horses are gone.'

Anton took in the information slowly. There was nothing to be done immediately. He walked over and sat in the chair next to Dani, pouring himself a glass from the half empty bottle of red wine on the table. The second clean glass had been provided for him. Dani knew Anton well.

'What of the more recent contingent?'

'Also gone.'

At this Anton shuddered. The second messenger and his escort could not have wakened after Ariane gave them the mushroom potion. They would have had to have been carried. Count Michel would know beyond a doubt that he and his men had been drugged.

'What are we going to do, Dani?' Anton asked after a moment. 'We have no real fighters. The goblins are hard to predict. The invaders probably have enough soldiers to take us with what they brought along. Do we pretend to go along with their demands to save lives? Or do we stand against them and possibly face annihilation?'

Dani didn't look at Anton as he spoke, but gazed vacantly into the darkness.

'If we give in to them, we lose everything we've ever known. They will leave that slimy little git in charge of the lands your ancestors rebuilt. All of your people would probably be treated like slaves. Conquerors traditionally claim all the spoils, and the women. If we were lucky, they might leave us alive to starve after they strip the food supplies.'

Anton speculated on Dani's words. He was right, as usual.

'We have no choice then, but how will we defend ourselves? There won't be time to train fighters.'

Dani's answer was delivered in a steady voice, as if he had put a lot of thought into the matter.

'Then we will have to be more clever and pull out a few tricks.' He paused to take another sip of wine. Anton saw the hint of a smirk develop on his friend's face as he finished speaking. 'Perhaps we should start by suggesting that much of our food comes from the excellent fishing in the river.'

Chapter Ten

'I wish to see my daughter.' The woman held her shawl closely around her, clearly uncomfortable in the plush surroundings of the castle receiving room. She looked over her shoulder occasionally, as if to see if she had been followed or observed on some clandestine affair.

Jerak, long used to the discomfort of common people when the entered Count Anton's domain, smiled at her kindly. Her dour, dark dress, reaching from the buttoned up collar to her ankles, marked her as a Southerner. Jerak did not have to ask questions to deduce that the woman's daughter would be among the recent refugees.

'Of course you may see her, the girls are not prisoners here. What is her name?'

'Serina,' the woman answered without expression.

'Wait here,' Jerak told her. 'I will find her for you.'

Jerak left the woman alone. It was something he did not like to do with strangers in the castle, but Dani had slept late and there was no one else to answer the summons when the woman had pounded on the castle door at daybreak. Ariane had gone out among the common people on their own side of the river, asking who would be prepared to open their homes to the displaced girls. Jerak thought to himself that he would not be sorry to see them leave.

Serina was found and roused as she had slept a little later than the others as well. She quickly dressed and joined the servant in the corridor, then was led to see her mother. She rubbed her eyes, fighting through the fog of insufficient sleep to remember all that she had heard during her wanderings in the night. At fifteen, she was old enough to appreciate the danger that her mother had braved to cross the river to see her. Serina wasn't sure if her mother should have been more afraid of the unknown danger in the river, or of her father's anger.

Serina had been grateful that her parents had married her to a man who had been kind to her, even though she had not borne him a son. She hoped that she could be married again quickly and would be able to bear children, as was her duty. Human children... not abominations. What she had heard about the half goblin girl last night was not to be tolerated.

As Jerak led her into the receiving room, Serina could see that her mother had been crying. Jerak left them, closing the door discretely.

'Mother, you'll never believe what I heard last night!' Serina blurted as her mother rushed to embrace her. Her people had to know. The fact that her mother would have to explain where she had learned it would mean that father would punish her for crossing the river without his permission, but that was as it should be.

NAMAH AWOKE SMILING again. Dreams of Ja'imos – of being close to him – had disturbed her night, yet it was a nice disturbance. One that she was happy to let flow into her morning daydreams. It was a pity that she could not languish in bed and think of him all day, but she had chores to do. Laura would be depending on her.

Laura, her sister. Laura had explained everything last night when they had arrived home. Her parents had tried not to speak of their lost daughters in her presence, or even to mention them to each other. However, word gets around. Namah had been born after first Lana, then Laura, had crossed the river. People talk, if only in whispers. She had known that her childhood dresses were not new and had once caught her mother crying over one of them. She wondered now which of her daughters her mother had cried for, and if she was missing her youngest now.

Poor mother. She was a dutiful wife, but three daughters had run away from her to escape the system of marriage their people practiced. It must have been very hard for her. *And now*, Namah thought to herself, *her youngest daughter lay abed past daybreak musing about a goblin! Mother would be shocked.* Yet it didn't seem to matter that he was green. Namah smiled at the thought of him all the same.

Some of the elders would have her whipped and exorcised if they knew... and could catch her. They would say that she was possessed by a demon spirit, entranced not only by a demon, but entertaining thoughts of immodest behaviour outside of the sanctity of marriage. It was shocking!

Yet muse she did, remembering how it felt to be held by strong arms that refused to allow her to hurt herself. Looking up into those golden eyes, rimmed with long lashes that any woman would envy. Had he accepted her advances, Namah was sure that she would have felt no remorse for her lost maidenhood this morning. Goblins do not marry, but among the magicians the convention seemed less important than it did among the Southern people. Namah no longer felt like a piece of property to be given to some man her father chose. She would make her own choices now.

Namah threw off the covers and sat up. The time for musing was over. She had things to do. She was no stranger to work, so the few chores Laura asked of her were no burden. Still, she would have to start if she were ever to finish.

Then perhaps, she thought, *if there is time...*

But she did not finish the thought. She dressed quickly and pulled her thoughts away from the caverns and the world of goblins. Her childhood training to get on with tasks impelled her to perform her duties almost automatically.

As she worked, Namah mused over how easily word got round of everything that happened, even when events crossed between human and goblin worlds. How Laura had known exactly what had happened at *The Dance* was still a mystery. She had not remonstrated with Namah about it, but it was clear from some of what Laura did say that the details of her panic at *The Dance* had somehow reached her sister's ears. Namah wondered who else among the magicians might know.

A vision crossed her mind... a goblin speaking to Count Anton, Count Anton speaking to Laura, Laura taking her aside privately to talk woman to woman. Namah shuddered in embarrassment. The goblins would all know, including all of her new friends. Yet Alinea had assured her that there was no shame in her behaviour, only a lesson to be learned. Namah had not been ready. The raw sexuality of *The Dance* was too alien to a young human girl raised in a repressive society.

It was different for the young females among the goblins. They could glory in *The Dance* long before they were ready to choose a lover. For them, it was a natural part of the rhythm of the Earth. That was how Alinea had referred to the wild energy that Namah had felt among the all too masculine throng of pulsating goblin flesh.

Namah flushed at the memory and knew within herself that she would not attempt to join *The Dance* again. Then she smiled to herself. Laura had told her that only one other human had ever experienced this aspect of the goblin society. Count Anton himself had danced among them. Whether he had been chosen by a goblin woman Laura had not known, but she had said that it was likely. A visiting human would provide the diversity in the gene pool that the goblins needed to breed and surely the goblin females would find him beautiful, as the human women did.

For a moment, the idea that there could be more half-goblins like Alinea disquieted Namah's mood. How many? Could the goblin world be littered with half-breed progeny of the human ruler? And what of the young man who had been held captive in Namadla's cavern? Alinea had sworn Namah to secrecy about that. No human must know that such a thing occurred beneath the surface. But Namah was human, and Namah knew. More importantly, she knew now that there were many goblin secrets that Alinea would never tell her own father or brother.

Namah understood the game between Alinea and Alaric now. He was her brother, yet to the goblins he was just another human. As little information as possible was to leak to those of the human world who were trusted enough to reveal themselves to at all. It was an old custom based on survival. Namah struggled with her mixed loyalties and toyed with the idea of telling all to Laura, that she might pass it to Count Anton. He should know of such things, but Namah had sworn and Alinea had taken a big risk for her, and then rescued her from her own folly. The dragon, the slave... all of it must be forgotten, or at least never mentioned. Not even to Alinea herself.

Namah got on with mucking out the stable. It was the last task on her list for the day. Her diligence as she mused on her internal thoughts paid off, it was only mid-day when she finished.

She finished the last job with practiced efficiency and prepared to go look for her friends again. Hard work had helped the embarrassment fade, although she was in no hurry to see Count Anton himself. Her friends among the children were different. They were so completely open and accepting and even forgiving of her ways as someone who had suffered a restrictive upbringing, that she was sure that all would be well with them.

What of Ja'imos? Namah thought to herself. She pushed the thought away, blushing. He was a goblin. Her girlish fancy would have to pass. Not because his skin was green and his ears were pointed, but because his way of life was too different from human customs. Perhaps taking a lover among the magicians was not considered shocking as it was among her parents' people, but a casual encounter, a moment of wantonness, was not what she wanted.

Namah wondered as she walked the path towards the heath what love meant to goblins. Perhaps she could speak of this to Alinea, or even Lolari. Alinea had spoken of love for Drazek – the love of best friends. Yet, she had also said that a time might come when she would choose him in *The Dance*. Namah could not imagine such a thing.

She remembered her attraction to some of the young men whom she had known as boys. They had been her friends in childhood, but when she was old enough to see them differently it had become unacceptable to socialise freely with them. Young lads and girls nearing marriageable age were kept apart, only stealing glances at each other across crowded rooms.

It was only now that Namah could see how unnatural that life had been. Young men had to wait until they reached full maturity to marry, yet their interest in girls was apparent years before. Suddenly Namah pushed these thoughts from her mind as well. Some things were better not thought about.

When she reached the heath, it wasn't Alinea or Lolari she found waiting. Alaric and the other human children were playing with kites, enjoying the summer breeze that cooled the seasonal heat. Alaric was helping little Emily with her kite, showing her how to catch the breeze with it like a sail. Her light, threadbare dress blew in the wind so violently that Namah was afraid that Emily herself would blow away, although the winds were hardly strong enough to lift a child. Damon and Jase had their kites high in the air. They appeared to be playing a game of some sort where the kites attacked each other as if in warfare, but not so vehemently as to cause any damage.

Saffara sat on the grass, laughing and watching the others. Her brightly coloured kite sat next to her, unregarded. Namah approached and sat next to her.

'Why aren't you flying yours?'

'I flew mine earlier,' she answered. 'But I grew tired, and I wanted to watch the ducks.'

Namah looked at the ducks frolicking among themselves in the pond. There was a peaceful feeling about just sitting and watching them. Namah understood.

Just then Alaric let Emily take control of the kite, watching it soar lightly into the air as he walked towards Namah.

'My lady!' he exclaimed as he approached. Namah automatically offered her hand, that he might kiss it in mock formality. Alaric took the game a step further and knelt on one knee to accept the proffered hand, kissing it lightly as if he were well practiced in this form of gentility.

'Is it true? Did you dance among the goblins?' Alaric's eyes lit up with an eagerness that was becoming recognisable. 'Tell us what you saw in the caverns, please?'

'Yes,' Saffara chimed in. 'We won't tell anyone. You know you can trust us.'

'Alas,' Namah said apologetically, 'I know I can trust both of you beyond question, but I did swear an oath. I am not to speak of it. It would be betrayal to Alinea to do so, even to close friends.'

'But you did go?' The anxious question in Alaric's voice betrayed an almost desperate need for confirmation. 'You had the courage to enter right into their world...' Namah could hear the unfinished sentence in his mind ...*like my father.*

'Yes, that much I can say. I badgered Alinea against her better judgement, and proved her right. But I bolted like a scared rabbit. Hardly a picture of courage.'

'Still, you went without paying heed to natural fear. That is real courage,' he said with finality. Alaric seemed determined to worship her, no matter what she did.

'I don't know if I would overcome fear so easily,' Saffara chimed in. 'Even with friends among the goblin children. Some of the bigger ones... don't like humans.'

'So I have heard,' Namah said sadly. The truth was, she had forgotten about the warrior goblins when she had asked to go with Alinea. She had seen only Ja'imos. *I am not brave,* She thought to herself. *Only a silly girl.*

'Was it the big ones that frightened you, Namah?' Alaric asked. 'What made you run?'

Namah looked at him sharply. He was leading her as he did with Alinea. He was trying to get her to let a little information slip. He suddenly looked sheepish. The look had told him that he had been caught in the act again, but Namah wasn't going to let him off easily. She took on an over exaggerated scary story tone and began to describe a nightmarish experience without actually telling him anything.

'There are dangers beyond reckoning in the deep places where the monsters dwell! Giant creatures and slithering things, and things too shocking to speak of aloud! Few who go there return, and those who do return are changed forever for meeting the beasts and monsters of their worst nightmares!'

Alaric and Saffara had dissolved into giggles by the time she finished, Namah joined in the laughter. Her tone had made it clear that she wasn't being serious. *And yet...* she thought to herself, *giant goblins and slithering dragons... a slave kept as pet to a goblin female... have I not just described exactly what I have seen?* She wondered then about her last addition, that one came back changed from such experiences.

Just then, Damon, Jase and Emily ran to join the group.

'What's all the laughter about?' Jase asked innocently.

'Just Namah telling funny stories,' Alaric explained, still laughing. 'You're fun, Namah, not like those dour faced Southern girls my mother is trying to find homes for.'

'What girls?' Damon asked.

Alaric suddenly realised that it was his turn to be secretive. The events at the river were not to be common knowledge, even among the magicians. It was only his talent for extracting information, like his father, that had gleaned the limited details that he had learned from the Countess. Above all, he was not to mention the water goblins, especially to Alinea. She would know, but his feigned ignorance was essential, perhaps even to his father's life. Ariane had emphasised that.

'There was a fishing accident and several men were killed.' He spoke the truth, leaving out the nature of the 'accident'.

'My father brought their widows to the castle. My mother encouraged me to come out and play today, away from the castle in case any of them set their eye on a prince for their next husband.'

Alaric winked at Namah.

'Perhaps if they saw how young you are, it would discourage them,' Namah said playfully. Alaric replied in a more serious tone.

'In truth, many are not so much older. You of all people know the ways of the Southerners. I don't think there was a girl among them over sixteen.'

'Still,' Namah was serious now. 'Men among them are not considered marriageable until they are nearly thirty. A ten-year-old boy would be recognised as just a child. Even a girl at ten is considered so.'

'Never underestimate a scheming mother.' Alaric returned to his teasing. 'For a prince, they are often prepared to wait a few years.'

He winked again at Namah. At that moment, the monkey came swinging down from a tree and landed on Alaric's shoulder. Namah had forgotten about the funny little creature. Alaric handed it a piece of fruit from his pocket. The monkey looked directly at Namah as it turned the fruit over in its hands. It seemed to take more interest in her than in the food in its grasp.

Does even the monkey know? Namah mused to herself.

'Where are the others?' she asked to change the subject.

'They don't come out in the sunlight,' Alaric answered knowledgeably. 'The light hurts their eyes.'

Yet it had been daylight when Namah had come and found Drazek. Alinea had to her come as well. *Was it only because somehow she knew I had come to look for her?* Namah kept the thought to herself. This game of goblin secrets was becoming far too easy. It had seemed as if Drazek had already been out on his own before she had come to the heath and had accidentally spied her from his hiding place in the trees. Namah wondered to herself if his different form also meant his eyes were more adjustable to light.

'How much do you know about the goblins, Alaric?' Namah asked, trying to sound casually curious.

'Not nearly enough,' he answered quickly. 'My father shared the family diary with me long ago. It has notes from his father and his father before him, all the way back to Count Victor, who seems to be the first of my ancestors to encounter them directly in this age.'

He wrinkled his brow a moment, evidently thinking.

'Asking questions of Alinea is sort of a game, and I am genuinely curious. But father says that the more we know about them the easier it is to keep peaceful relations. Of course their view is that the more we know, the more danger we are to them. There was a time when humans and goblins were mortal enemies and they fear the return of such times.'

'The goblins are wise,' Saffara chimed in. 'Who can know who will rule among the humans in a few generations? People not yet born.'

'But I will teach my children and they will teach theirs!' Alaric replied defensively.

'Saffara is right.' Namah sounded sad as she spoke. 'I was hardly old enough to remember, but just before you were born the men on my side of the river turned on Count Anton. If he had been killed and someone from the Elders found this diary you speak of, they would not have hesitated to use any information about the goblins to try to kill them all.'

Alaric looked thoughtful for a moment before he spoke.

'And that would be an end to all men. At least here. My father says they have many trained fighters, more than we could muster. An all-out war would be suicide for humans.'

Emily and Jase sat quietly, listening to the conversation among the older children. Alaric met Emily's eyes. The melancholy mood had made her look sad. He suddenly leapt up.

'But my father is wise! He befriends the goblins, so we can all live in peace together.' The irresistible grin spread among the children quickly. Little Jase and Emily clapped their hands in approval.

'Come, let's have a game!' Alaric commanded. 'The sun grows dim in the sky, and soon our other friends will join us!'

'YOU'RE MAD, LATHAM!'

Latham continued sharpening his knife with the whetstone without looking up.

'I know a thing or two about these goblins. That's why you and your good lady here came to me.'

Serina's mother sat quietly in the corner, remaining silent. She looked from Latham to her husband and back again, wincing slightly at the pain from her black eye. She felt a little ashamed of the fear her husband showed as he spoke.

'We fought the goblins ten years ago, you and I. They have training.'

'We been training too, Derek,' Latham answered coolly.

'We been training *ourselves*.' Derek sounded derisive. 'If everything my woman says is true, it ain't just the goblins. Count Anton would come after us too. You think you can train yourself enough from pictures in books to take him? He knocked you for seven last time, and you're twice his size.'

'He sucker punched me,' Latham scowled. 'I'll be looking for that next time.'

'Looking for it is one thing,' Derek continued. 'Looking for who knows how many of those big warrior goblins at your back at the same time is another.'

'You saying that you and the others won't back me up?'

Derek looked at the glare in Latham's eyes. This was personal for him. Derek had never understood the reasons for Latham's fanatical dislike of Count Anton, but what he saw in that glare convinced him that Latham would see many men dead without a thought before he stopped fighting whatever private war raged within him. Derek chose his next words carefully.

'You know we all believe as you do. Letting a demon whelp live that looks human can't be allowed. A generation or two and we wouldn't know demon from human. But we lost those men that went to trawl the river for demon spawn. We have to know what we're up against and make proper plans if we're going to go after this demonspawn. She'll have protection, and we don't know what kind or how much.'

'She's just a girl.' Latham sounded confident. 'I had her mother in my grasp easy enough when we first went digging in the tunnels.'

Latham remembered beautiful Talla who had lost her glamour for only a second, revealing the putrid green flesh of the goblin seductress. That somehow Count Anton had created a child with the demon woman touched the deepest competitive instincts of Latham's being. He had come close to coupling with her himself – a secret that he had shared with no one in all the years between. But Talla knew, and he was sure that she had told Count Anton.

'How do you propose we accomplish it?' Derek was still clearly frightened of the whole idea. 'Just waltz in among the magicians and take a child from amidst their group? Not to mention the demons. If she lives among them, she ain't gonna be easy to get to! We don't even know when the magicians meet, or where. And what do we do with her when we've got her?'

'That girl of yours might be useful.' Latham said it flatly as he continued sharpening. Serina's mother gasped, but a sharp look from her husband silenced her.

'You would send a young woman to do a man's work?' Her father sounded contemptuous.

'Not to do it,' Latham replied evenly. 'Just to find out where and when. She already showed you she can listen at doors.'

Latham looked up at the man. He sounded all too reasonable.

Derek visibly struggled with the logic of it. Serina would have been punished for creeping around at night had he been in charge of her, yet the information was valuable. Intentionally spying sounded dangerous. He ought to be trying to find another husband for her rather than putting her in potential peril, but what would be the worst that could happen if she were to be caught?

If she were careful about what she said, there would be no way anyone would know why she wanted to know where the magicians met. At worst, they would grow suspicious and no more information would be available to her, in which case he could collect her and bring her back to her own people without question. They would be glad to see her go instead of interfering and trying to find her a home among the heathen Northerners.

'Alright,' Derek said at last. 'I'll go over and see my daughter. I'll tell Count Anton that I want her to come home and find another husband. If he let's me take her, I'm bringing her.' He met eyes with his wife and then with Latham, showing his determination. 'But he'll talk me out of it, and I'll let him. Then if there's any trouble, I'm taking her. I'll be looking for a husband for her in the meantime. If I find one, I'm pulling her out of there.'

Latham nodded. One of Count Anton's weaknesses was that he was predictable. He would talk the girl's father out of taking her and harbour a spy in his own castle to protect her. Latham smiled a little as he nodded again. He approved of the plan.

Chapter Eleven

Anton lined up the recruits in the closest thing he had managed to form into a military assembly. His people made for a poor imitation of a fighting force. Magicians, farmers, common townspeople had all gathered together, but to what purpose? Apart from the members of Anton's own household, none of the amassed recruits had had any real battle preparation. All the weapons in the world were next to useless in untrained hands.

Anton thought for a moment about the illusion that had saved his castle when the Southern men had stormed in, looking for trouble so long ago. It had been a simple spell. A reflection of their own expectations had made the invaders perceive ten men for every one paltry guard. The Southerners had come looking for support, not a fight. They had been taken by surprise on all fronts.

The overseas invaders would not so easily be dissuaded. Worse, they would find illusions all too easy to hack through and would find only a small population of farmers and craftsmen who had never had real need of a defensive force standing vulnerably behind that illusion. Anton cringed at the memory of the legacy left to him. Since the time of Count Victor, the emphasis of rulership had been to create. To produce food, master old crafts that would have practical application and create a thriving society out of what had been left of civilisation after the Turning. Only the royal household had been taught sword training, and that more for sport than warfare. There had been no enemy... no need for an army.

The fact that a day would come when such a need would arise had been predicted. Anton had spent many hours talking with Haghuf about the history of men. Haghuf and the other goblins knew of men in other places and had warned Anton that the other humans spent more time practising military tactics and less on food production. Like the fighting goblins known as *Those Who Protect*, Haghuf had said. It was inevitable that a day would come when they reached out to take what was produced in this peaceful and fruitful land. It had happened many times in the last age, but preparing for such an event had always been something to do 'soon'.

Anton called out names of formations. His 'army' responded. It was a little better this time. They moved in some attempt at what might be perceived as unison. Only one or two turned the wrong way and had to be turned back round by their friends to join the line. Anton sighed. *Perhaps*, he thought, *I'm going about this in the wrong way.*

Dani approached silently. There was no need to comment on progress. Any fool could have seen that it wasn't working.

'I'm no military general, Dani.' Anton said it quietly, so that only Dani would hear. 'I've always been good at organising people to do things that would produce a visible result, but military drill just doesn't inspire me... or them.'

Dani looked over the ragtag troops as he thought for a moment.

'None of our people this side of the river took much part in fighting the goblins ten years ago.' Dani stated it as a simple fact.

'But the Southern men were outmatched,' Anton answered. 'If the goblins hadn't been blinded by the sunlight, they would all be long since dead.'

'Yet their conviction could have made them a significant threat to us,' Dani replied. 'They took over the grounds outside the castle for a while, you may remember.'

Anton shuddered. He remembered. Thugs, organised into groups to watch for his return. They had chased him into Lirrewot, where no human must ever go. The dying screams of the two men who followed him in still echoed in Anton's memory, as did his own scream as he fell through the blackened pit, expecting painful death to meet him when he eventually hit bottom. Agonizing death had been the intent. The cold splash as Anton hit the underground lake was to be followed by the unthinkable pain of being shredded alive by sharp teeth. The needle-like teeth of those called *Kol'ksu*, the water goblins that he had at last seen in daylight.

Anton wrinkled his brow. Yes, it had been early morning, but daylight just the same. A shaft in the ceiling of the cavern had allowed a little sunlight to travel to those deep places, illuminating the underground cavern just enough to see the contours of the rocks and the sparkles of light in the water. Unlike the other goblins, the horror in the water showed no sign of suffering blindness from sunlight. Anton made a mental note to write the remembered detail in the family diary later, but in code. This piece of information could be dangerous.

'You've read the history books, Dani. What wins wars when a people are outnumbered and untrained?' Anton knew there must be an answer somewhere.

'It's true that a disciplined army is very effective,' Dani answered. 'But historically, many such armies have been thwarted by people who were only protecting their homes. People who became organised, but in a non-linear way.' Dani's sidelong glance at Anton was followed by the hint of a smirk.

The smirk was reflected on Anton's face as the names of peoples from the past went through his memory – The Highland Celts, the Britons, the French Resistance, the Viet Cong, the Dionysian Underground. All had held up against disciplined armies that had conquered many others, but found the chaos of organised resistance and refusal to be ruled completely unmanageable.

'I wonder,' Dani continued. 'Do the fighting goblins learn military drill, or are they trained in fighting technique and simply... organised.'

'You've cracked it Dani!' Anton was becoming excited now. 'Break out the swords and anything else we've got, let's teach these people something they can use.'

'There's one more thing to consider, Anton.' Dani looked pensive. 'You know that Latham has been busy over the river...'

'Yes,' Anton answered. 'The Southerners have been teaching themselves sword play, using pictures from the books they can't read.'

'The question is, do we teach them to be better fighters, knowing they are already practicing to use their skills against us, or do we leave them to their own devices when more properly trained fighting men may be needed to fight the invaders?' Dani clearly wasn't leading this time. There was no clear answer hanging in the silent moment as Anton considered the problem.

'We train our own people first,' Anton stated at last. 'Then we consider what to do about Latham and the others.' Anton nodded approvingly of his own decision. 'And maybe we'll call the Southerners to battle and put them on the front lines, as you suggested,' he added with a wink.

Dani nodded in approval, then went to get the weapons. There were plenty to be had. The castle had once been a museum and held weapons from many ages of mankind as decorations for the walls.

Once the men were properly armed, they trained with more enthusiasm. Some showed particular affinity for one weapon or another. Swords, pikes, spears and a number of other ancient weapons were made available and basic instruction given, more to avoid injuries than to become experts in a day.

But do we have more than a day? Anton speculated to himself. The escape of Count Michel left the question unanswered. The sleeping draft had not been as effective as a good dose of mushroom potion would have been. Had the latter been administered by the Countess' hand, the captives would be sleeping still, but perhaps permanently. Ariane's inexperience with the drug had made her afraid that adding it to the already administered drug might be fatal, and that would have been more disastrous than whatever might happen otherwise. Anton had appreciated Ariane's caution. Killing an emissary could only lead to one conclusion. Whatever force he had hidden from sight would certainly attack with full force as soon as they determined his loss. Count Michel had been too cocky for Anton to assume any less than a substantial invading force was held at the ready. *A force that might be approaching even now.*

Anton looked as far as he could see down the river. All was peaceful. His deepest instincts beheld only the calm, flowing river on a serene frosty morning. He speculated on the memory suppressing effects of the potion. Perhaps the second emissary had awakened disoriented. In fact this would certainly be the case, but how much did he remember? Only very recent memories would be affected. Perhaps his mind had been muddled enough to forget his intent when he made the ill-fated visit, but surely the fact that all of his men had also succumbed would make it obvious that they had been drugged?

Anton reflected on all of this to no avail. There was simply no way to know what to expect. He envied the goblins their information network.

Somehow the ragtag army managed to get through several hours of training with no injuries worse than the occasional finger crush between a sword hilt and a shield. It wasn't through over-caution.

With real weapons in their hands the men sparred with gusto, their natural competitive instincts leading them on to best their companions at every opportunity. No one gave quarter, until someone unexpected arrived to join their ranks. Suddenly all heads turned to regard Laura, dressed for battle in loose breeches and a man's tunic.

She had arrived on the field without warning, carrying a sword that looked too heavy for her. Yet with a two-handed swing she appeared to be able to handle it as well as any of the untrained men about her, only there was no opponent to fight. The men backed away from her, refusing to raise arms to a woman. Count Anton approached her carefully. He was well aware of Laura's headstrong nature. This was going to require diplomacy.

'Laura ...' he began. Even to his own ears his voice sounded too cajoling.

'I know what you're going to say. A woman doesn't belong on the field of battle.' She looked him directly in the eye. 'But Anton, we need every sword. A woman can die on a sword as well as a man. Would you have us cut down like cattle, helpless to protect the children? Or shelter us like property like the Southerners? Anton, the goblins have females among their fighters.'

Anton visibly winced. Laura knew how to cut to his deepest sense of convictions. But he too knew the motivations of men, and to some extent of women.

'Laura, these men are not goblins. They will not accept a woman put into such direct danger. Many would die watching for your safety instead of their own. Women can not fight beside men in our world.'

Laura began to set her jaw, an argument almost at her lips, when Anton interrupted her thought.

'However, you are right. We need every man, woman and child to be a part of our defence. In some of the battles in the history of mankind, even small children have played a part in defending their homes against invaders. Setting traps, throwing explosives, leading enemies into ambush. I think you would be the right person to train the women and train the mothers to teach their children according to their age and disposition. It would be folly to waste such a resource... and the enemy won't expect it.'

Anton smiled at Laura then, all too aware that he was using unfair influence to win her over. She was a strong woman, but still a woman who had loved him.

'You are wise, as always Anton,' Laura replied. 'Will you ask Dani to release weapons to us? There are many long daggers in the storehouses. They are perfect for a woman when she is close enough to the enemy to become the spoils of war.'

Anton nodded, struggling to maintain his pleasant expression as he looked at the cold determination in her eyes. He pitied the man who might try to ravish such a simmering volcano. There were cruel weapons with jagged blades in the storehouse. Painful castrations would await any invader who fought their way through his proletarian fighting force. It would be a kindness to train the common men well, that the enemy might die before facing the women defending their homes and children.

Anton sent Dani with Laura to find weapons, then dismissed the men with instructions to practice among themselves at every opportunity. He made no effort to shield them from the truth. The invaders could attack at any moment. The chances of another round of diplomacy could not be relied upon. The foreigners wanted their supplies and sooner or later they would make the move to take them. The ancient battle horn that hung in the castle would be used to signal when the time did come.

Anton walked back to the castle deep in deep thought. He was well aware of his limited resources for a war with humans. The weapons he had in plenty, but farmers and craftsmen were not warriors. Without knowing the numbers of the enemy he could not even conjecture their chances, but they would have to try. No matter what they faced, he would have to inspire his people to give it everything they could muster, and then hope that the luck that followed his family held out against what might well be impossible odds. There were a few instances in history of success in battle against dire probabilities of victory. They were always achieved by determined groups of men who refused to give up.

Anton climbed the stairs to the library, the one place he felt he could be truly alone. Almost before he opened the door, he became aware that he was not.

'Come out then, Haghuf, I can smell you,' Anton said as he closed the door behind him. He couldn't resist a smirk at his own joke. He couldn't actually smell goblins as goblins could so easily smell humans, but his magician's sense had recognised the calm vibrations of a goblin mind and logic suggested the one goblin who might come to visit him here.

'Are you sure you are full-blood human, Anton?' Haghuf asked as he emerged from a shadow.

'I wonder sometimes,' Anton replied as he poured himself a brandy from a bottle. 'Would you like a brandy, Haghuf? Do goblins drink alcohol?'

Haghuf looked at Anton steadily. The old game was afoot. Then both broke into playful grins, unable to keep up the pretence of seriousness. Of course Haghuf would not answer the question. The goblins must keep their secrets, and even the constituent ingredients of the sacred *Rabenis* that Anton had enjoyed during an almost unprecedented exception to the prohibition of humans at *The Dance* had never been revealed to him, although Anton had his suspicions.

'You have been too long away, Haghuf, and it is not quite sundown. You must be here for an important reason.'

Haghuf suddenly looked serious, perhaps even worried. It was unlike him.

'It is true, few things can draw me to the surface and your world of stinking humans,' the goblin began. He walked over to the brandy bottle and sniffed it, almost like a dog might sniff an object of curiosity. He poured a little in a glass, dipped his finger into it, and tasted it from his fingertip. Haghuf's expression was unreadable, but he turned and walked away from the instantly forgotten beverage.

'More stinking humans come. Many more.' Haghuf moved about the room, not looking at Anton as he spoke.

'How many?' Anton asked anxiously. On this, at least, he could expect a straight answer.

'Many more than you have to fight them, even with the others.'

Anton knew what Haghuf meant when he referred to 'others'. The Southerners, the humans who despised the goblins still, although they had made no further moves against them as far as Anton knew. As if he had heard Anton's thoughts, Haghuf continued.

'The others plan against us... and against you.' Haghuf walked up to Anton and met his eyes with the disconcerting steady stare that goblins used when issuing a challenge. 'Especially the one called Latham.'

'It's time I crossed the river as their leader then.' Anton held Haghuf's eyes, attempting to return that disquieting stare that Haghuf had used on him so many times. 'And recruit their fighters to lead my army. Perhaps I should make Latham an officer.'

This time it was Haghuf who broke into a smile first.

'You think like a goblin, Anton. I think you should study your ancestry closely,' Haghuf said teasingly.

'Perhaps it is just the good company I keep. The influence of your kind has made me more clever,' Anton returned. The affection between them was palpable. Even in times of great stress, they could still tease each other about their differences, as well as Anton's clear desire to be more like the goblins.

'What about the goblins, Haghuf? Is there any chance that your warriors...'

Haghuf looked at the floor. 'I am a librarian. I have no authority to call warriors to battle.'

'But would they respond to a request for help, to keep more humans away?'

Haghuf shook his head.

'Goblins respond when goblins are attacked. They care nothing for the affairs of humans.'

'But an invading force could be dangerous to goblins. Surely they would learn of your people, at least from the Southerners, and they would attack in much the same way as those ignorant fools did before.'

Again, Haghuf met Anton's eyes.

'Do you wish to explain your logic to Kahjak, and ask him to help you?'

Anton visibly shook as he broke the eye contact and walked a step away from Haghuf. It was a memory that disturbed his dreams still. Kahjak, the massive goblin who had thrown Anton indifferently into the bottomless pit. The splash in the underground lake... the bite on his ankle as he struggled for air... before the mysterious *Kol'ksu*, those fishlike, white haired, sharp-toothed goblins who had devoured those Southern men, had chosen not to eat him... at least that one time. The very thought of looking into Kahjak's cold yellow eyes again made Anton shudder a second time.

Yet if there was a chance... but no. There was no chance the goblins would care about saving Anton's people... the people who had tried to dig out and murder goblins. If there were any possibility, Haghuf would have spoken for him already.

'Tell me all you know about the invaders,' Anton entreated.

Haghuf held out his fingers, counting on them. When he got to the forth finger, he held them out.

'Large ships, very heavy with men. They move slowly in the river. They have travelled since the bright star lit your world today, but now they are stopped. They wait for light again. They could be here tomorrow, but not until the light begins to fade. If they are clever they will stop just out of sight of your people, then come at new light.'

Anton nodded, acknowledging the intelligence. Perhaps, he ruminated, the goblin network was at his disposal after all, if not the fighters. This was some advantage at least.

'What do you advise?' he asked sincerely. Haghuf's eyes widened a little in surprise. Anton had never directly asked his advice in such a matter before. Haghuf thought for a moment, then looked up at Anton as he answered.

'Don't let them leave the ships.'

LATHAM WAS SHARPENING a sword on a pedal-operated grinder when Anton appeared in his doorway. He looked up in surprise. The last thing he would have expected was a social call from his old nemesis.

'We need to talk,' Anton began. 'Our people are in danger. All of our people.' Anton looked at Latham sharply, emphasising the inclusion. Latham moved his mouth as if to speak, but no sound was forthcoming. Thoughts flitted through his mind. He could not bring himself to believe that Count Anton had at last realised the danger of allowing goblins to live under their very noses. He sat back and allowed Anton to continue.

'Invaders have come from over the sea. I expect you've heard something about that.' Anton looked at Latham carefully, noting his reaction. Yes, he had heard something. Anton made a mental note that he would have to work out where the information was coming from. There had been far too many people visiting the castle from the Southern side of the river of late.

'What you won't know, is that it is not a matter of a foreign emissary. There is a substantial invading force coming up the river by ship and they plan to raid us for supplies, probably killing as many of our men as they can.' Anton observed Latham again. The struggle was plainly written on his face, but he was taking it in. He just needed one more push.

'And then of course they will take the women. Our wives and daughters would be nothing but slaves to these foreigners.'

That did it. Anton had to control a smirk as Latham leapt to his feet.

'Over my dead and rotting carcass they will!' Latham huffed and puffed like a bull preparing to charge. Anton had seen him this worked up only once before, when they had fought sword to sword in the Temple after the altercation with the goblins that might have ended in the extinction of all of the humans. A large and evil looking sword lay on the grinding stone table now. It had been risky to come to Latham's home alone, meeting his enemy on his own ground while Anton was unarmed himself. But it was the only way to gain what Anton had come for.

'We must stand together, Latham.' Anton grasped the opportunity. 'Anything less would be doom to all of our people, North and South.'

Latham looked around wildly, silently cursing Anton for being here and making far too much sense instead of being across the river convincing that fool to leave his daughter in the castle as a spy. He tried to think clearly. War with humans was something he hadn't bargained on, but war was messy and led to confusion. People could disappear in the heat of battle. Half-breed girls, or even obnoxious rulers. Perhaps an opportunity would arise...

'I'd like to make you an officer, Latham.' Anton worked his pace carefully, watching every facial muscle twitch as Latham fell headlong into the trap. This would surely be the icing on the cake. A position of importance would appeal to a man of Latham's character.

'I've heard rumours that you've trained men in swordplay. We need trained men, as many as we can get.' Anton reeled him in artfully. Latham had no doubt thought his training had been done in absolute secrecy. He had no concept of goblin stealth. To reach out a hand and acknowledge the surreptitiously obtained skills as a benefit to their people, all of their people, left him with only one option.

'What rank are you thinkin' of making me?' The hint of hesitation in Latham's voice told Anton what he needed to know. A sufficiently grand title would win him over. It was an old trick; give a useful person a title and they rise to fill the place. If Latham wasn't good enough at his job, it would become apparent when the enemy slew him. Anton's playful smile slipped over his features as he made his proposal.

'I think we should start you as Captain, but if we win this war, you'll deserve a couple of field promotions. Maybe even to General.'

Latham smiled. It was not a friendly expression, but one clearly of self-interest. Both pairs of eyes flicked briefly to the sword still lying near the grinder. Anton could see that he would have to watch his back, literally, but Captain Latham would lead his men against their common enemy.

'When do we attack?' It wouldn't occur to Latham to fight a defensive battle, but in this case, a pre-emptive strike was called for.

'Before dawn.' Anton slipped into strategic mode. For the moment at least, this man had become his ally. 'Two ships will be moored just down the river from the castle, and four more further down and out of sight. We have the element of surprise... they don't know that we know their numbers.'

Latham's eyes flicked up to Anton's face. He could guess where the information had come from. Despite the unfriendly glare in his eyes, he nodded slowly. At least the demons were good for something if they brought information.

'We are greatly outnumbered,' Anton continued. 'But if we stop as many as possible from ever leaving the ships, that could change. Do you have any archers?'

Latham saw where Anton's strategy was going.

'Not many. They ain't that good either, but I got something that might be useful, something we scrounged from one of the old factories. If you got just one really good archer that could send a flaming arrow to light the fuse, I have an idea how to make it count.'

Anton blinked and looked up at Latham quizzically. Latham produced a small plastic package out of his pocket and handed it to Anton.

'I took this off one of my boys this mornin'. They was filling them up from the river and throwing them at some girls. They're old, so they break easy.'

Anton knew that Latham could not read. Few common people could. He said the word written on the package aloud, for Latham's benefit.

'Balloons.'

Latham nodded, pretending he knew the word all along.

'If they can hold water, I figure they can hold oil or anything else we can find that would burn.'

Anton smiled. There wasn't much of old technology left. Things like petrol and oil were all but gone. Even his electric car had been abandoned because the battery source could no longer be renewed, but there was one thing available that would do the trick.

'Do you still distil potatoes into liquor?' he asked Latham. This time Latham smiled genuinely.

'We got jugs and jugs of the stuff in my cellar.'

Anton grinned widely and clapped Latham on the back in genuine camaraderie. Not only did they now have a potentially very effective weapon against the invaders, but that slip of information was instantly filed in the back of Anton's devious mind. If Latham became too much of a liability, his own house was set up as a veritable bomb. It only needed detonation.

Chapter Twelve

Glynnis touched the still-swollen flesh around her blackened eye gingerly. It would heal soon enough. She should have asked permission before crossing the river, she knew this, but fear that she would have been forbidden stopped her. She had needed to see her daughter one more time.

She smiled as she remembered how her husband had pampered her when she had revealed the information that she had learned from Serina. The bruises didn't matter when they were followed by such kindness. Derek had praised her for her discovery, although he showed no remorse for hitting her for her disobedience. It was the way of things. Glynnis had known the risk.

Then Derek had gone to call a meeting with the men, but Latham had dissuaded an open meeting. He had convinced Derek that they should take a more subtle approach and that the abomination should have died years before. Perhaps if she had stayed among her goblin kin she would have been no trouble to men, but even then her human appearance would make her a danger. So it was lucky, Latham said, that she had shown herself and that her existence was known, at least among a few of the Southern people. How to find her would pose a problem, but Latham, Derek and a few chosen men would figure it out among themselves. They had a name at least, *Alinea.*

Glynnis reached for the bottle of wine. It was forbidden to drink it between Sabbaths, but she felt she needed just a little now. The danger of the situation made her hands shake. Over ten long years ago the people had learned that Count Anton knew about the goblins and was even friends with them! Yet somehow he had regained his position as their ruler and things had gone back to how they had always been. People had thought that the abomination had been spawned by a common lad, but this new revelation that she was Count Anton's daughter changed matters. The Count would protect her. Whatever the men decided, eliminating the unnatural creature would be no easy task.

Serina might come home. This thought gave Glynnis some feeling of hope, but her husband had gone to set their daughter up as a spy. There was, perhaps, no real physical danger. Count Anton was not the kind of man who would hurt a young girl. Glynnis remonstrated with herself as the wine began to have an effect on her thoughts. She was a selfish woman. What it actually came down to was that she wanted her daughter home, safe and sound, even if it was only for a little while until they could find her another husband.

NAMAH SENSED, RATHER than saw, her goblin friends. She had been playing gleefully with the other human children in the early dusk as it gave way to a bright moonlit night, then suddenly the feeling came over her that the goblins were among them.

'Lolari! Drazek! Alinea! Come out, come out wherever you are!' she shouted to the trees. At first nothing moved. Namah turned and nearly jumped out of her skin to find herself eye to eye with the little gargoyle-like goblin, Drazek.

'Your sister seeks you. Time to play has come to an end.'

He sounded so serious that Namah wondered what calamity had befallen. Little did she expect to hear the full gravity of events as they invaded her safe little world.

The soft, lilting voice of Alinea preceded her apparition as it appeared to manifest from the shadows of the foliage.

'Men come, on ships. Your people are at war with other humans.' She too looked very serious, and very sad. Suddenly a branch just behind Alinea's head shattered into splinters. Alinea didn't even flinch. It was Lolari's voice that offered explanation as the goblin girl appeared from behind the children with a device in her hand.

'We have a new game to teach you tonight, my friends. But each of you must swear that if we teach you to use this weapon, that you will never use it against goblin-kind, or teach its use to any who would refuse an oath, or be capable of breaking one.'

'I will swear, without hesitation,' Alaric announced. 'How does it work?' He took the sling from Lolari's hand and examined it.

'You fit a rock, just so.' Lolari demonstrated with a rock picked up from the ground. 'Then you sling it with a flick of the wrist, like this.'

Another branch exploded just behind Alinea's head.

'Of course such accuracy requires some practice and training in how it is done. That is what I have come to teach you.'

'But it's dark!' Jase piped up. 'How will we see what to hit?'

'That, too, I have come to teach you.' Lolari bent her knees and brought her eyes down to meet Jase's. 'That is why you must swear.'

The children each swore in turn, willingly. The children of magicians had never seen threat in the goblins, but they were all too willing to help their parents defend their land from foreign invaders. Alinea explained the full situation as each child was given instruction, not only in how to operate the slingshot to best effect, but in the art of determining a target when light was minimal. It was true that goblins had better vision in the dark in general, but they also had the ability to use such devices in the deep places where even their sensitive eyes found no light.

Drazek volunteered to get word to the parents that their children were safe and were being taught skills by their goblin friends that would serve them well in what was to come. He also assured them that they would be returned in time to sleep well before the dawn that awaited them all.

The promise was kept. When dawn came, the children awoke well rested after an exhausting evening of training that left them sleeping like the dead.

Alaric and Namah had both developed a good feel for the methods taught to them for sensing a target in the dark. The younger children, Emily and Jase, had not developed enough motor ability to master the advanced techniques, but Lolari had said that they should be trained along with the older kids as they could practice over time, assuming their parents would protect them through this current incursion. One thing that goblins always remembered was that there would always be another war.

Damon and Saffara fared well for a single night of training, if not as impressively as Namah and Alaric with their particular psychic sensitivities. They, too, could hone their skills over time, and all of the older children could teach the physical use of the slingshot to other children and even adults on this day of apprehensive watchfulness.

As the adults awoke and began scurrying about with whatever preparations had been assigned to them, Namah overheard that Jase and Emily would be among the younger children taken away from the city by a group of mothers who were ill-suited to fighting, either through temperament or inability to learn a skill that would be of use in a fight. Laura had scoured among the common people to find women who had some courage or skill to join her group, which had been dubbed the Amazons jokingly by Count Anton. He had explained that it had been the name of a historic group of fighting women. Laura had looked up the reference and found that they were indeed a fearsome warrior tribe composed of women. She didn't hesitate to share this information with the women who had shown the mettle to join her.

Meanwhile, Count Anton spent another day taking the men through fighting exercises and marvelling that Haghuf had stayed to help, even in the daylight.

'Goblins adapt,' was all that he had said when questioned. The cloud cover of early Autumn had probably helped. Still, he kept the sunglasses on at all times. Haghuf had even spent the night in the castle. Anton did not know when or if the goblin had slept. It was possible that Haghuf could have spent all night poking around and investigating the human fortress, but Anton's trust for his friend was such that he knew in his heart that had it been so, it would have been from idle curiosity rather than malice, or perhaps a goblin's sense of looking ahead. Generations from now, who knew what sort of person would rule in this castle? If the invaders had their way, at least the goblins would know every nook and cranny of the captured stronghold. Anton speculated that they probably already knew of secret passages in the castle lost to the memories of men.

Namah had elected to stay with Laura and join the Amazons. She was old enough and the goblins had shown her a few fighting moves that could be of use to the others. In particular, Alinea had taken Namah aside and explained to her how to avoid any possibility of being raped. It was something her mother had taught her, she explained. As much as Talla had an eye for a human lover, it was anathema to goblins that any female should be taken against her will and consent. Most goblin females had natural defences that could protect them in a fight with humans. Not least of all, teeth that could rip a man's throat out in an instant if he were close enough to pose such a threat. But Alinea, with her half human heritage, lacked this natural protection and had been taught alternative measures.

Namah had felt a little queasy when Alinea had explained how easy it was to incapacitate a man through the most vulnerable part of his physiology. The very thought of committing such damage on another human made her feel weak and disgusted, yet she knew that, given adequate cause, she would protect herself.

As darkness began to fall, Namah felt the exhaustion of a very active day creep over her. She had trained children in the use of the sling shot and tricks for hiding and escaping. She had trained grown women to use weapons and to use the enemy's own strength against him, though she had learned these things herself less than twenty-four hours ago and was still assimilating much of the information that she shared. She felt as if a month had passed in only a day and was grateful that the attack had not yet come, but more than anything else she wished for sleep, and perhaps to wake and find that the threat had been only a dream. The fatigue began to give way to doubts. Fighting techniques were all very well in theory, but would they hold up in an actual battle? Would she forget everything and collapse in panic when the time came?

Worst of all, she saw the same doubts on the faces of many of the people surrounding her. Even the magicians who had seen battle before shared a glint of trepidation in their eyes beneath the confident exterior each of them showed to the common people who followed them.

If only the goblins would come, Namah thought to herself, but she understood why they would not... unless there was some way to bring the battle to them so that they would feel impelled to defend their world. Namah knew within herself that this was the key, but no plan of how to go about it came to her mind as she dressed and prepared to join the adult women in the inevitable battle to come. Dawn was coming. There was no more time. Namah wondered if the child goblins she knew would come, or if they had any influence on some of the others of their kind.

THE SHADOWS OF MEN moved with as much stealth as they could muster against the first glow of red light from the coming dawn. Latham led the small party towards the moored ships, hurrying now as the sounds of preparations echoed over the river. The invaders would move soon... of that there was no doubt. Rab moved up to view the enemy from beside Latham. He had a crossbow ready in his hand, but it wouldn't be the crossbow with its accurate aiming capacity that would begin the attack.

Four more men followed, carrying ordinary long bows and arrows fitted with balloons carrying either potato liquor or gun powder. Count Anton had gone over the plan in detail with Latham, even supplying the recipe for the flammable powder. Each arrow could only carry a little extra weight. Once they started shooting, the arrows were to fly in a constant rain of combustible material with the occasional flaming arrow to set it all alight. The only flaw in the plan was that only one ship at a time could be attacked in such a way and two stood moored before them. Rab and Latham were armed to fight at closer quarters and aid the escape of the archers.

'Now!' Latham ordered. The first ship was just starting to move as sailors released it from its moorings. Arrows flew towards the open deck, raining in a sudden burst of released powder and liquid that caused instant confusion among the startled sailors. They had not expected a pre-emptive strike.

The first flaming arrow struck the deck. At first it had little effect beyond alarming the crew that there was fire on deck, then a trickle of released liquor reached the open flame and ignited, causing a flare that was sufficient to further ignite the cloud of gunpowder that had so quickly manifested on deck. The entire upper ship exploded into flames. Men jumped overboard if they were close enough to the rails and hadn't already been blown off by the explosion. More men from below deck ran to throw buckets of water or sand on the flames so that they might escape.

As the raiders had hoped, men from the other ship rushed to help their comrades, taking lifeboats to retrieve those who were in the river or carrying buckets of water by both boat and on land to help to fight the flames, although those on land found the flaming ship just a little too far from the moorings to board with their buckets. However, the ships carried well-trained soldiers. More disembarked onto land. These were heavily armed and moved towards the source of the attack. The flaming arrows had been far too easy to observe. A single horse was led down off the second ship, then a rider leapt on and rode away from the scene of conflagration.

The archers spread out and started using ordinary arrows now, becoming snipers in the darkness against their approaching enemy. Latham fired a few more flaming arrows towards the second ship to draw their attention to his own position and allow the stealth of the other archers to work its magic. This, too, had been part of Count Anton's plan. Latham had to admit that it was working well.

However, what the Count had not foreseen was the anger of the enemy when they saw their own ship attacked. Many of the lifeboats moving towards the flaming ship turned and started moving towards the hiding place that Latham shared only with Rab now. Well armed as they were, they were only two men against many. How many, they could not count. In minutes the lifeboats would land on shore and they would be overrun with trained fighters. Latham looked at Rab. It was time to run.

He took what weapons he could carry easily and sprinted into the darkness, leaving the snipers to find their own paths out of immediate danger. They, at least, had the advantage that their position was only known to those they fired at from close quarters within the darkness. Latham expected to find Rab running close beside him, but after a few steps Latham turned and saw the other man running towards the boats on the shore. There were a few of the empty flat bottomed boats sitting at the ready for anyone who wished to cross the river. Rab was running straight for them.

'He must be mad,' Latham said softly to himself. Armed only with a small crossbow, Rab didn't stand a chance in boat-to-boat combat with the swarm of angry soldiers moving towards them. Latham stood fascinated as he watched Rab push a boat into the flowing current and row straight towards the enemy. It was suicide. He couldn't possibly survive against so many.

Then Rab fired his crossbow, not at the approaching men, but into the water. Latham was even more confused as he watched Rab's madness, firing one bolt after another into the water while the armed men drew close to a range where they could fire at him with their own bows. Arrows were already just missing him, falling impotently into the water near Rab's boat. One actually struck the side of it, but still Rab alternately rowed towards the enemy and fired bolts into the water.

Just before he started to run again, Latham understood Rab's plan... and his sacrifice. Latham heard the distinctive thump on the bottom of one of the lifeboats which sent it rocking dangerously in the water. The sound took him back many years to a horror he had wished never to witness again. Another thump was quickly followed by more. Rab stood up in his little boat, facing his enemy. An arrow struck him through the heart, killing him instantly. Latham turned and ran, sprinting at a seemingly impossible speed provoked by absolute terror. Against the laboured sound of the beating of his own heart, he could hear the sounds of boats splashing over in the water and the screams of many men dying.

Whatever goblin-spawned monsters inhabited the river, Rab had intentionally invoked their fury. Latham vowed to himself that he would see that the man received a hero's memoriam.

Chapter Thirteen

'The ships are moving,' Haghuf informed Anton calmly.

Anton's brow wrinkled.

'Just the first two, or all of them?'

'One ship is in flames, the other... most of the crew met misfortune in the river.' Haghuf fought a smile of malice as he delivered his news. The haunted look on Anton's face as the river incident was mentioned was gratifying. 'Your forward guard was successful. They run this way now. Only one was slain as he attacked the other humans from shadows. The other ships move, but they will come slowly.'

Anton thought hard. It crossed his mind for a moment that he might well be rid of Latham... but no. The plan was that Latham would be drawing fire and running. The shadows would have cloaked other men that had been hand picked. Anton didn't know which of the Southerners were to go with Latham. As an officer, the newly advanced Captain was allowed to choose his own best men. Anton didn't have to ask Haghuf how the goblin knew about events before his own men could run back and report themselves. He had only seen a glimpse of the goblin called Ja'imos as he had appeared from out of the brush. The young goblin had sprinter's legs and could no doubt travel much faster than any human, and more directly. Still, Ja'imos must have been at hand to witness the events and had come straight to Haghuf with a report. The goblins were taking more of an interest in this battle than Haghuf was prepared to admit.

The men were gathered on the riverbank as the dawn approached. The goblins had estimated that the hidden four ships would take a day to reach them, but there had been no guarantee that Latham's raid would have been able to incapacitate the first two vessels. From what Haghuf told Anton, they should be celebrating a victory. The fact that his old nemesis had accomplished it with a handful of men and a little help with planning was both hopeful and disconcerting. The man could learn. As long as it was for their own side, it was an advantage. Anton noted that he would have to watch Latham ever more closely in future. The big man would become more dangerous as a result of this war... if he survived. For the first time, Anton began to entertain thoughts that it would be in the interests of their people if Latham somehow met a glorious end in the inevitable battle to come.

As the morning drew on, Anton began to wonder how much time they had left to prepare before the remaining ships would arrive. Keeping the men at the ready could wear on them if the waiting was going to fill the day. It would be better if they planned out a rota and allowed some of the people to eat and sleep to save their strength while others trained, keeping them all to hand in case of a surprise attack. He gave instructions to Dani to set up a marquee tent with Jerak and whomever else they needed to recruit for the task. They had all been up before dawn. The men would welcome the chance for a morning nap, even if they were not as comfortable as they would be in their own beds.

They could not take the chance of allowing what fighters they had to return to their homes. Many might have too much time to think and to become afraid. Besides, the extra time it would take to return to the riverside when the attack came could make all the difference in a sudden strike. The river curved. Despite the reports from the goblins, the ships could appear unexpectedly at any time.

Anton shuddered as he thought about the men lost in the river. Haghuf didn't have to go into detail to tell him what had happened to them, he had seen the work of the *Kol'ksu* at close range. He suddenly became very aware of the proximity of the river... just a few steps away. Would the *Kol'ksu* take part in the battle to come?

Not far behind the castle was the hidden entrance to Lirrewot, which held its own horrors that still gave Anton occasional nightmares. Anton wondered how much interest *Those Who Protect* were really taking in the affairs of the humans, despite Haghuf's assertions that they had no concern for human conflicts. Anton brushed the thought out of his mind. There was no time for speculation or daymares, he had men to organise and a war with humans coming to his doorstep at this very minute.

LAURA LOOKED OVER HER assemblage of Amazons with some consternation. The enthusiasm of many of the housewives had waned when they watched their younger children going away with those who had felt unable to join in battle. One of the magician women had led the children to a secret place where they would be safe, but it was not easy for the mothers, watching them all leave without knowing where their children could be found. Laura had her suspicions, but it had been agreed that none of the women who could be put into a position where they might be questioned by torture would know for sure where the others had gone. It was for everybody's safety.

Namah was beginning to wish she had been young enough to go with the children. Indeed she did have the choice – all of the Southern girls whom Count Anton had recently brought to the castle had gone to safety. Still, Namah was glad that those who knew her would not be on hand to identify her, particularly Serina as she had never liked Derek's daughter and she was sure the girl would tell everyone that she had seen Namah alive. Namah had gone to great pains to stay out of sight of the Southern girls as the group had prepared to leave. Even Laura had made herself scarce in case one of them might recognise her, despite the years that had passed since her crossing.

Not many of the housewives across the river had come to join the Amazons. Most had insisted on waiting in their homes for their men to return. Namah was both glad and disappointed. Women like her own mother were not suited to protecting themselves. Chances were that they would have been more of a liability than a benefit for the fighting group. Namah could only hope that those who did come would have too much to do to concern themselves with her presence.

Once the other women and children had gone, Namah helped Laura to organise the Amazons into a fighting force that would remember that it was their own children they were protecting. Those who did not yet have children were reminded of those yet unborn. Namah was painfully aware that the future of their people depended on the events of the day. Having a surprise rear guard of fighting women might supply a crucial advantage.

Namah was in the process of taking a group of women older than herself through a drill in spear fighting when she suddenly became aware of Alinea standing beside her, wearing a dark coloured human dress.

'Alinea! I didn't expect to see you in daylight... in front of all of these humans. They'll know they haven't seen you before.' Namah spoke in low tones that would not travel beyond Alinea's hearing. 'What if...'

'It's ok, Namah,' Alinea responded calmly. 'You have a mixed group of Northern and Southern females. Each will think I come from the other. The news I bring is worth a little risk. It is unfortunate that the others like Lolari cannot show themselves in the light with their goblin skin and ears. They would come to help if they were not such a distraction to your training.'

Namah nodded sadly. The prejudices of the humans would prevent them from accepting the help freely given by goblins when they needed it most. It could mean their doom.

'What news did you bring, Alinea?'

The training stopped as Alinea took Namah aside.

'The distant ships come slowly, but there are riders on land. Horses come with well-armed soldiers on their backs... much faster than the river would carry them. It is a new development. The runner who took news of the ships' movement to Haghuf will not know of it as yet.'

Namah felt the weight of adult responsibility as she deliberated what to do.

'We must tell Laura,' she said after a moment. 'She is in charge of us after all.'

Alinea nodded in agreement, then helped set the newly trained spear maidens to sparring among themselves before following Namah to report to her sister. As Namah related what Alinea had told her, Laura looked over her inadequate fighting force with despair.

'Anton must be told this right away.' Laura's features revealed the internal struggle as she tried to rationalise the need to deliver the information against the knowledge that women appearing when a battle was in progress would distract the fighting men from their task. There was no way to know how far the rear ships had travelled, or if the forward guard might already be engaging in battle with her friends and fellow magicians. Laura wanted desperately to help them with the abilities she had to offer, yet she also knew that the simple matter of a woman on the field could instead result in unnecessary deaths.

'Alinea, do you know how soon they will arrive, or if they may have entered the battle field already?'

Alinea thought for a moment.

'Humans move slowly, even those on horseback. Still it is possible that their fury will have made them cross the distance, or that they will do so before we could get there.' Alinea looked directly into Laura's eyes. 'You are needed here, Laura. I can move faster on my own and remain unseen.'

Laura shook her head.

'A young girl alone and one unknown to any of the men around Anton? How quickly do you think the Southern men would suspect your goblin heritage?'

'I can go with her, Laura,' Namah offered hopefully. 'I am small and know some of Alinea's ways, and at least some of the men will recognise me. If they see us together, they will assume she is just one of my friends... from one side or the other.'

Laura looked at Namah sadly.

'You know the price of showing yourself among the Southern men.'

'Things are going to change after this,' Namah insisted. 'I will not allow them to force me back, and I don't think it will be asked of me. If nothing else, the men of my father's village will see me as unruly and undesirable as a wife. I am prepared to prove it.'

Namah's eyes flashed with a fierce determination that Laura could see would brook no argument.

'Go then, Namah. Deliver the message and get yourself back here as quickly as you can.'

Namah nodded goblin style without realising that she was going to do so until the act was already accomplished. Then they were gone. Laura looked at the place her brave sister had been with pride, not least of all because she had disappeared as efficiently as Alinea herself in the blink of an eye. Namah's brief time among the goblin children had apparently been well spent.

NO HUMAN BEFORE NAMAH, not even Count Anton, had ever been shown the secret ways of the goblins. The only exception was the time that Anton had been led to the big Temple by one of *Those Who Provide* who made sure that the human would not be able to find the way again on his own. Even the old stations to the underground rail system of another time had been either blocked up or were guarded in the case of those few that the goblins chose to use as passages to the *Between* levels.

Namah knew that she had been bold in assuming that Alinea would take her through the goblin ways to reach Count Anton as quickly as possible. She also knew that Alinea would agree, as the half-goblin girl had an ability to somehow see into the hearts of humans and know them to be true or false. Alinea would not have come at all if she did not intend to do all she could to help their cause.

Still, Namah would not be able to find the passage again easily. They had walked round a tree and taken a step down, then suddenly they were in a narrow passage of the caverns. Such passages were free of traps, Namah understood now. They were for quick escapes or travel near the surface. Had she known more of goblin society, she might have identified the digger claw marks on the rock face and also recognised their other purpose, for *Those Who Provide*. Many human gardens and fields had been raided by goblins travelling near the surface and the scratched symbols of digger claws identified what sort of bounty might be found in a particular location. Whole herds of livestock had received a healthy cull and left no trace on occasion.

Namah struggled to keep up as Alinea ran lightly through the apparently straight passage. She didn't have much time to analyse the contours of the tunnel as she focused on breathing as efficiently as possible so she wouldn't slow the stronger half-goblin girl. Speed was important now. Studying the goblins would have to wait. Namah noted only that there was just enough room that another goblin coming the other way could pass them, if a bit closely. A stray thought that they could come across Ja'imos flitted through her mind, but they saw no one until suddenly they emerged into the light and trees. By the time Namah had taken two steps and realised she was on the surface again, she could not see the entrance back to the passage just behind her. She had made a point of turning to look.

More important things required her immediate attention though. Alinea was urging her on. The sudden stop as she realised she was in the light had broken their pace, something that she now recognised would not have occurred if Alinea ran alone. The goblin girl's eyes had spotted Count Anton among the throng of men and she was leading Namah straight to him. Namah broke back into a run to keep up.

Battle was not yet in progress. Namah was grateful for that. She had pushed her mortal fears aside in the urgency to get the message delivered, yet now she could imagine her terror if they had come out to see swords flying and blood being spilt. There was a sense of immediacy among the training humans. Namah had honed her sensitivities enough in her short time among magicians that she could feel her own fear mirrored in the nervous dispositions of strong men. They, too, had lives that could be lost in battle and the desire to live. The sudden reality of the danger to all of them made Namah's stomach feel as though someone had tied it in a knot.

She didn't have much time to think about it before she found herself standing breathlessly in front of Count Anton. It was an odd moment to remember that she had never actually spoken directly to him before. The goblin standing next to him, the same one that had patted her on the head as a toddler, turned his eyes to her first. Part of her was transported back to her childhood perception of them together as she stammered out her news between intakes of breath.

'Count Anton, there are men riding horseback from the rear guard ships. They could be upon us at any moment.'

Anton turned at the sound of his name. He had been speaking so intently to Haghuf that he hadn't noticed the girls approaching. The message had been clear and direct. There was no need to ask how the girl knew this as Anton saw Alinea standing next to her. He looked his daughter in the eyes, wanting more than anything to hold her and keep her safe. It was something he had never felt able to do with his alien child, but now was not the time. He must deal with her as a goblin and a response was required.

'Dani! Get all the men ready, we've got riders coming!' Anton laid his hand on the goblin sword sheathed at his side. 'You girls disappear. You know you can't be on a battlefield.'

Just at that moment Latham came running from round an old building that blocked their view from the path along the river. Anton had a fleeting thought that the enemy could appear just as suddenly.

'Anton!' Latham shouted. 'We burned it, we burned it good!' Latham crossed the distance to stand in front of Anton and gave his report. His eyes flicked to the goblin standing at Anton's side and to the two girls who had no business standing before Count Anton when battle was immanent. The small group looked at him expectantly. Among them were two pair of identical eyes... characterised by the multi-coloured iris and the wolfish shape of the brow that Anton shared with his mixed-blood daughter. The resemblance was striking. Understanding stole over the face of the beleaguered man.

'Come, Namah,' the girl said. 'We must get back to Laura.' Alinea reached for Namah's arm gently.

'It's ok, Alinea, I can run again now,' Namah said softly. Latham tried to keep his expression rigid. His suspicion had been confirmed.

Namah and Alinea nodded simultaneously to Anton and Haghuf and ran back the way they had come. They vanished as quickly as they had appeared. Anton and Haghuf blinked as they noted the implications, but there was no time to think about it now. Latham waited until the girls were out of hearing range to continue.

'We lost two men. Derek took an arrow and Rab...' Latham's eyes flicked to Haghuf again. 'Rab sacrificed himself. The men from the second ship took to lifeboats...'

Anton laid a hand on Latham's shoulder. He had not known until now that it had been Namah's father who had stirred up the *Kol'ksu*. She would have to be told, but he was glad that Latham hadn't blurted it out just then while she was in hearing.

'I know what happened,' Anton said gently. He saw Latham's eyes on Haghuf. The less that was said all round, the better.

'One rider got away,' Latham continued. 'Rode like the blazes down river. My men were picking off survivors as I ran, just like we planned.'

Latham cringed at the thought of running while his men did the work, but it had been part of the plan. The enemy was to chase him and fall into the sniper traps. Unfortunately Derek had shown himself as he had prepared to take a shot and had fallen into Latham's arms with an arrow through his chest. Latham had had no choice but to drop him where they stood and run for all he was worth, hoping the others would cut down his pursuers. He wouldn't know how they had fared until they also arrived back to report, if they arrived at all.

'I've had news that riders from the rear guard ships are coming.' Anton explained. 'Get some food and rest as best you can, we may be fighting any minute.'

Latham nodded and jogged towards the food tent. He had earned a good breakfast with the morning's work. He only hoped that he would have time to enjoy it before more was required of him. His eyes darted momentarily to the place where the half-breed and Rab's daughter had disappeared. He would need to keep his strength up for more than battle with humans. The abomination must be hunted down. At least now he would recognise her.

Anton turned to Haghuf.

'Do we assume that the rider was Count Michel?'

'Never assume anything,' Haghuf answered in his characteristic gruff tone. 'But you can be sure that news of the attack was carried to the other ships. Whether it was Michel or a messenger, your enemy will know they underestimated your resourcefulness.'

Anton looked thoughtful for a moment before he continued.

'My guess is that it probably was him. He's the sort of leader that would go for the reinforcements himself and re-establish order.'

'What would you do in his place?' Haghuf probed.

Anton thought a moment before he replied.

'With two units scattered and mostly destroyed, I would ride down river until I could flag down the rest of the fleet, then join them and report what happened.'

Anton's eyes suddenly widened as a new thought occurred to him.

'You know it never occurred to me, we don't know if Count Michel is the commanding officer. He was sent as a messenger. There could be someone else in charge of the battle ships.'

Haghuf's expression was unreadable as he replied.

'If that is the case, it makes no difference who the rider was. The message was carried. Your human concerns with hierarchy are distractions, Anton. Be careful you do not project your own thoughts of strategy onto others who may act very differently.'

Anton nodded, acknowledging the deserved rebuke. He looked over Haghuf's shoulder towards the food tent.

'Latham is coming back. I don't like the way he looks at you.'

Haghuf didn't bother to look at the man approaching from behind him.

'You know to watch your back with that one, Anton. You also know why I find him distasteful. I wonder if he would be worthy of becoming food in the river. Perhaps we should test the idea.'

Only Anton saw the subtle wink as Haghuf walked away towards Dani. He had to stifle an urge to chuckle as his friend found business elsewhere. Latham closed the distance quickly, carrying a bowl of food that reminded Anton of the meals at Storytelling in the caverns.

'I'm wondering if something happened to my archers.' Latham wrenched his eyes from the back of the retreating goblin to address Anton. 'They shouldn't have been far behind me.'

Anton frowned. 'Who did you take besides Derek and Rab?'

'Rolf, Dawid, Matthew and Zak,' Latham answered. Anton noted Latham's straightforward response. It was becoming more difficult to remember that the man was not his ally.

'We can only wait and watch for them, as we watch for the enemy.'

Latham looked at Anton appraisingly. Anton noted the assessment and wondered whether it was his leadership qualities or his vulnerabilities that Latham mulled over.

'I know your instinct is to go after them.' Anton nodded to acknowledge that he shared the impulse. 'But we must wait. We can't afford to scatter our inadequate forces.'

'What about the survivors from the other ships?' Latham insisted. 'Some might have got away. Somebody had to have killed Derek.'

Anton thought for a moment before responding.

'There was likely a plan in case men got out of communication with each other. The river is the key, it's easy to see men from the shore.

'If I saw my comrades goin' under like those boats did, I'd put a lot of distance between me and that river.'

Anton looked at Latham, suddenly remembering the stripped bones of men who had been too close to the river not so long ago. *It's a pity we have to be at odds with each other*, Anton thought. *Latham remembers the instincts of men, while I think like a strategist. He could be almost as valuable as Dani as an advisor.*

'They'll feel safe on land,' Anton said aloud. 'Any military strategist would regroup and attack as a solid force. If the snipers escaped, they may have run further inland rather than coming straight here.'

Latham appeared to take that in. Whether he caught the implication that they might well have run away after getting so close to real battle, Anton couldn't be sure. He still thought of the Southerners as cowards that needed a mob to show any form of resistance. As these thoughts went through his mind, Anton remembered Haghuf's words, *never assume anything.*

Latham wandered away then and ate his food. Anton was very aware as he watched the large man's retreat that each of them was uncomfortable in the other's company. He ruminated to himself that they were like two cats who had fought. Once the hissing and spitting starts, there can never be real forgiveness. They were enemies, bound for the moment by a common cause. If by some miracle they should both survive this invasion, they would still be enemies. Anton remembered again Haghuf's words, *watch your back.* As if he could hear the thought, Latham turned just then and looked at Anton from under his heavy brows. Anton could see that Latham would be watching his own back. The question was, could they work together with the agitation of murderous intentions towards each other distracting them?

Anton had no time to think about it further. There was a sudden ruckus from the direction of the river as the man called Rolf rounded the building where Latham had appeared earlier, followed closely by two of the other Southern men who had formed Latham's sniper unit running at full speed. Anton didn't have time to struggle to remember their names as the pounding of hoof beats echoed from behind them on the river path. He began shouting orders to rouse the men. The battle was upon them.

Dani and Latham echoed the orders as they ran to awaken sleepers and assemble those at rest in the food tent. Anton drew his goblin sword and ran directly towards the river path, passing the snipers as they ran towards the protection of men rested and ready for battle. They were unarmed, having dropped their weapons to flee at full speed.

Anton was vaguely aware of men just behind him – men who ran with him to face the enemy. He was not alone, but it was the magic coming from the sword that gave him the confidence to strike hard as the riders appeared round the curve in the path. His small force was greatly outnumbered by the oncoming army as expected, yet the sword sang in his ears. Somehow, just on the edge of hearing, a song of battle emanated from the blade as Anton fell into a perfect rhythm of movements that took the sword into spirals of slashing that cut down the lead riders without missing a beat. It was as though he was caught up in a dance of warfare, possessed by the sword he carried so that he became a whirling shield of flying sword-edge, protecting the meagre force of men behind him.

Those riders who managed to gallop past to engage with the ordinary troops found themselves fighting men who were heartened by the performance of their leader as much as they were defending their homes and families.

They moved as a horde, knocking men from horses to face them on equal terms. The horses were mostly allowed to run on unhurt. It had been part of Anton's battle plan; unhorse them and commandeer the steeds for their own use. With the unexpected use of large wooden poles, it was working. The path between the river and the derelict buildings was too narrow for a large army to attack all at once. Count Michel's men had made the mistake of being predictable.

The horses could not ride more than three abreast on the narrow path. Anton slew enough men in the first few moments of battle to show the commander that his first attack was doomed. They had been too intent on riding down the snipers to consider that an effective resistance might lurk just around any bend in the river. A horn sounded in the distance. Those still on horseback turned and rode back the way they had come. Men who had been unhorsed tried to follow and might have been allowed to retreat honourably by Anton's tired defence force, but the goblin sword refused to stop.

Anton watched himself as if from a distance as he continued to swirl and lunge, cutting down every last opponent. His own men melted away back to the camp, fearing for their lives as their leader's frenzy took him further down the path, chasing down terrified soldiers.

At last the only remaining man cowered against a low brick wall, cringing in anticipation of pain at the final stroke. The sword stopped within a hair's breadth of his throat. Frozen in stillness for the first time since the skirmish had started, Anton recognised Count Michel. The little man was wearing no ornament of rank this time. He had cloaked himself within the troops, wily enough to avoid drawing attention to a leading officer.

Count Michel held no weapon. At some point during Anton's assault he had dropped it and tried to run. Anton grasped him by the shoulder and pulled him up, keeping the goblin sword ready in his hand in case of resistance. This time there was no ambiguity to his status as a prisoner.

As Anton recovered his conscious thought processes, he wondered to himself what role Haghuf had played in the carnage lying on the ground. More men had got past him than he had realised. They all lay dead, victims of a strategic miscalculation. Anton wondered how many men the ships had carried. They had been caught by surprise resistance twice now. If their commander was any good at all, there wouldn't be a third time.

Anton also wondered about the power of the sword in his hand. He had used it for sparring many times, even against Haghuf. It had never vibrated with such magic before. Anton had always felt that there was some form of dormant power untapped within the artefact. The manner of its acquisition suggested that it was something significant, yet the complete oneness he had felt with the blade as it guided his movements beyond his will or conscious thought concerned him.

Dani and Jerak approached him quickly in a half trot. Count Michel would get no opportunity to escape this time. Anton's biggest worry now was how long it would take the enemy to work out that there were many old streets near the river where they might attack the camp from several directions at once, now that they knew where to find their quarry. He pushed Count Michel into Dani's hands, then turned in a reflexive crouch at the sound of an arrow twang behind them.

All of the men, even Count Michel, reacted defensively to the sound. As Anton turned, he saw Rolf standing with a bow in his hand, apparently having just let loose the arrow. Anton wondered whose bow Rolf had stolen as his eyes followed the direction of Rolf's gaze just in time to see Haghuf fall. The goblin's legs failed him as he dropped the goblin sword in his hand, stained with the blood of men.

Anton sprinted towards his fallen friend, leaving Count Michel to the others. His thoughts jumbled together as he tried to hope that the arrow too close to the heart might have missed that vital organ and saw his chance to avenge his friend stolen as the arrows of the enemy began to fly through their camp, one of them striking Rolf straight through the eye. There would be no opportunity to regroup or to move the camp. The enemy was upon them again, and this time they came from too many directions to thwart them as they had done on the river path.

In the midst of the fracas, his friend was dying.

Chapter Fourteen

'The enemy moves, and so must we.'

Namah looked up at the sound of Alinea's voice, unsurprised that she had not heard the goblin girl enter the tent. She looked back to the mirror to assess the effect of the woad she had applied to her face. It had been Alinea's suggestion that the women dress in furs and paint their faces blue in the way of an ancient tribe of warriors who had once so adorned themselves to frighten enemies. The effect was truly disturbing.

'My stomach feels tight,' Namah responded in a girlish voice.

'That is fear,' Alinea explained. 'It is natural. You will forget about it when you remember your training and push yourself to move as you have learned to do.'

Namah accepted Alinea's assessment and forced herself to stand and pick up the spear that she had chosen as her favoured weapon. The tightness in her stomach felt a little less constricting with the movement and now she felt that she could manage it.

'Let's go then. Is Laura ready?'

Alinea smiled at her friend's sudden resolute bravery and she led Namah out of the tent by the hand. As they pushed through the flaps, Namah saw a familiar face.

'Alaric! What are you doing here?' Namah's mouth dropped as she watched the boy struggle with an armload of swords he was carrying. The monkey sat in its usual place on his shoulder, screaming objections to the unsteady wobble that had taken over his perch. Alaric grinned at the girls.

'Degrading, isn't it?' he lamented in his usual good humour. 'I'm not big enough yet to fight with the men, but I'm heir to this land. I couldn't allow myself to be packed away with the *children*! Especially with my own mother fighting among the Amazons.'

Namah struggled to think what an appropriate course of action would be to protect a prince in times of war.

'You can't go into battle can you? Even among the women you would be in too much danger, and you're only ten after all.'

'Some children grow up faster than others, don't they Alinea?'

Alaric shot a look at his half-sister. He knew something, that was clear, but Alinea showed no sign of acknowledging the provocation. Namah wondered what secret they shared. It was unlike Alinea to tell Alaric anything in confidence. Namah assumed it was something he had learned on his own. Alinea wasn't rising to the bait though. She artfully manoeuvred the conversation back to the task at hand.

'Namah, go straight to Laura and I will join you in a moment. Alaric, women are waiting for those swords and time is passing. We may be needed even now. I will get a report of events.' Alinea nodded goblin fashion and disappeared behind a tree. Alaric shrugged as best he could.

'Father tells me that taking orders from women isn't unusual, even for a ruler. I guess I'd best get used to it, you'll be giving me orders when you're my wife some day.' He grinned and winked at Namah, then walked on to deliver the weapons. The monkey had settled and casually observed the movement all round him as Alaric shifted the load and gained better control of his cargo.

Namah wondered what plan there was to protect the prince or if he would travel with the Amazons. She looked around at the scattered tents and the painted women milling about. She could see Laura just a few yards away, gathering her tribe of Amazons into an organised unit as she moved toward Namah's tent, the last one of the encampment. The furs and blue paint had transformed more than the appearance of these normally docile women. There was a new spirit apparent among them. They shouted and raised weapons, ready to take on any threat to their people. Namah wondered if the enthusiasm would last when they saw their neighbours dying.

At that moment Alinea came running back, shouting to Laura excitedly. Namah followed her so that they met Laura at the same time. Alinea was out of breath and looked more excitable than Namah had ever seen her. A compelling intensity exuded from her as she spoke quickly to Laura, drawing lines in the dirt on the ground as she issued commands.

'We must come in here and here, along the back streets away from the river. The invaders are circling around after their first charge was thwarted by Count Anton.'

Laura took in a quick breath at the mention of Anton. Alinea's penetrating look as her eyes shot up to meet Laura's brooked no interruption.

'Do not fear for him, he is protected by something... unexpected.' Namah caught the slight nod as Alinea seemed to look inward, deciding what information to reveal to the women.

'Whatever you do,' Alinea continued. 'You must not breach the men's camp. The Amazons are needed for peripheral flanking. We must strike and retreat quickly, then take cover.' Her eyes flicked up to Namah for a split second. 'Remember that movement draws the eye of a hunter. Take cover and be still when... you will know the time.'

Alinea stood up from her drawings and turned to lead the women towards the battle, then turned for one last warning.

'Stay away from the river as well. We are not needed there.'

Alinea's eyes met Namah's just for an instant as she turned again, falling into step with Laura so that both led the Amazon troops.

Namah fell into step just behind them, spear in hand. She suddenly envied the archers who could pick off the enemy from a distance. The thought of killing a man with her spear and of the danger of fighting a trained soldier who might as easily kill her made her stomach tighten up again. More than that, she wondered what information Alinea had held back. Something momentous had shaken the girl, Namah was sure of it. She had not seen her friend react so edgily since the time she had warned Namah not to move in the caverns, when doing so would have made her become a young dragon's prey.

ANTON LENT OVER HAGHUF'S pierced body in the makeshift infirmary that had been a food tent only moments before. The unconscious goblin still breathed, but the breaths were shallow and uneven. He was afraid even to break off the end of the arrow so that Haghuf could lay back comfortably, lest doing so would tear something delicate within the goblin's physiology.

The hoof beats became louder. He was needed outside to lead an army, yet he could not leave his friend's side as he lay dying. Anton thought of Leap. He knew the young goblin was a healer, but not whether his skills would be sufficient to stem the bleeding from this wound. Either way, Kraapneerg was too far away. Anton had pressed bandages around the protruding arrow vainly to try to stop the blood from flowing, but there was no one to help him or to advise him. The men outside were preparing to fight for their lives as a superior army drew closer. All seemed lost.

A movement in the corner of his eye caused Anton to turn. Someone stood in the opening of the marquee. Even with the light behind her turning her into a silhouette against the late morning light, Talla was easy to recognise with her white hair reflecting the sun as Anton had never seen it sparkle in the daylight.

'I can help him,' she said simply. Anton moved aside to allow her to come closer to her injured guardian. Anton was very aware that Talla loved Haghuf as much as he did himself. The memory came to him of another of those who looked like Talla, the river creatures called *Kol'ksu*. The female had covered a rather severe injury with her mouth and it had healed almost instantly. Anton wondered whether Talla had a similar ability.

'You must go, Anton,' Talla said coldly. 'Invoke the power of the sword.'

Her eyes looked up at him at the same moment that her deceptively strong hands broke the back end of the arrow so that it was even with Haghuf's back.

'How do I do that?' Anton's brow wrinkled in confusion. He had never been given instructions regarding the goblin sword at his side.

'Present it to Kahjak, tell him it is time to call on Kralic.' Talla spoke calmly, as if she were issuing a simple instruction. Anton felt the blood leave his face.

'Just present it to him, the words will come to you,' Talla encouraged. 'The sword is a promise, among other things. Distraction comes, all will be chaos. But *they* do not know friend from foe. If you do not seek help, he will die and so will you, and all your people. It is a time to act, not to think.'

Talla turned then and placed her mouth over the wound. Anton saw her lips stretch much as the fish-mouth of the female *Kol'ksu* had done, although not as far. There was no time to indulge in fascination for goblin culture or abilities. Talla's instruction had sounded urgent towards the end.

Thoughts raced through Anton's mind competing for attention. A ruler did not leave his people in the midst of battle. Talla's reference to '*they*' had sent a cold chill down his spine. It was not in his nature to act without thinking – if anything he was given to thinking out every detail.

Now Talla was telling him to ignore his nature and do the insane, to enter Lirrewot and seek Kahjak, the goblin who had thrown him down a pit to die the last time he had breached the entrance. It was strictly forbidden for humans to enter the training grotto of the goblin warriors, yet Talla had suggested that he would gain some protection by presenting the sword that had been given to him so long ago.

The thoughts collided in a mass of confusion until Anton stepped outside of the marquee and looked into the northern sky. Suddenly Talla's words made perfect sense. It was time to act, not to think. All was about to become chaos, and the lives of his people as well as the enemy depended on him moving quickly. Ignoring the terror in his heart, Anton sprinted towards the old underground train station entrance, stopping just in front of the opening to the ancient tiled corridor.

The entry to Lirrewot gaped before him. Over ten years slipped away as Anton remembered the night he had been chased into the first level by Southern men. Their blood-lust had overcome their recognition of authority as well as their natural sense of self-preservation. Any half-sensitive fool could feel the magical barrier that marked this place as completely forbidden to humans. It was the one thing that had kept Anton from exploring it himself before he had received the warnings from Haghuf.

Haghuf had always been adamant; *Don't go into Lirrewot. The goblins there will not tolerate humans, and there would be nothing I could do to protect you. Guest status does not extend to Lirrewot.* So Anton had heeded the warning, until certain death had chased him in. At least there had been an element of the unknown within the cavern.

The sound of his own screams echoed through his memory. He didn't remember hearing them at the time, only those of the two men who had been careless enough to chase him into the cavern and down the first steps into goblin hands. Anton's hiding place near the entrance had saved him from his pursuers, but not from the goblins inside, who had fashioned the hidden ledge. The goblins knew their own tricks.

Anton wondered if there was a sentry on that same ledge as he pulled the goblin sword from its scabbard and placed it across his palms in a gesture of supplication, then forced himself to plunge into the entrance without thinking of the danger. He knew from experience that the goblins guarded the opening closely and even those few steps would place sentries behind him, cutting off any chance of escape. He summoned his most confident tone as his voice boomed out to announce his intentions.

'I seek Kahjak. Let him come to speak with me.' Anton immediately wished that he had thought to empty his bladder first as he felt the presence of goblins closing the only path to freedom behind him.

THE RIDERS BORE DOWN on their quarry, confident in their superior numbers and the training that made them King's soldiers. Captain Kantor looked upon the derelict streets with distain and some concern for the safety of his horsemen as they galloped over the rough surfaces, hemming the quarry in.

To his mind, a society of farmers was meant to be enslaved to serve the needs of their military masters. In fact, victory should have been no more than a short invasion and the business of taking over control. It was the diplomats who complicated things. Count Michel had insisted on trying to take command with nothing more than bravado, while ships full of troops might have hit fast and hard and brought the local residents to heel before they could have attempted to organise.

In the end, Count Michel had been left no choice but to concede to measures of force. Kantor hoped that the little fool had got himself killed in the riverside attack. It could become inconvenient if his absence in the retreat meant that he had been taken prisoner. If the man hadn't been cousin to the King, Kantor would have simply employed a sniper to avoid diplomatic entanglements. As it was he would have to ascertain whether the Count lived or not and attempt a rescue if he was being held captive again. Kantor snorted at the thought of a member of the Royal Family walking into a tactic so obvious as drugging his drink.

Count Michel's delusions of invincibility had fallen away after finding the second diplomatic contingent in a drugged stupor. Kantor vowed to himself that he would make an example of this Count Anton and his household, hanging them all from the castle walls. That would surely subdue any rebellion from the local farmers and craftsmen. They would be of great service to the empire once they knew whom they rightfully served.

Kantor turned his horse to lead his unit down one of the streets that would lead to the encampment. He rode as fast as he dare on the terrain, brandishing his sword and signalling to the archers to prepare to release a volley. As he drew near to the encampment, he could see the fear on the faces of men who would soon fall to his sword as they raised their poor weapons to defend themselves. Kantor raised his arm. Another few hoof beats and they would be upon the camp. No amount of preparation would save them now. When the arm dropped, their pathetic resistance would be squashed.

Suddenly all was confusion. The horses reared without apparent cause, screaming in mindless panic. The voices of the horses were joined by the banshee screams of a tribe of warrior women attacking from all sides. The women wore primitive furs and had blue faces that put the fear of something worse than death into the hearts of men. They attacked ruthlessly, shooting arrows and hacking with swords and spears in apparent random attacks on any man who fell from his horse. Those still on horseback could not gain control of the simple beasts to allow them to deal with the wild women.

Kantor held onto the rearing back of his own steed, but he was baffled. These horses were trained for warfare, a horde of screaming women should have no effect on them. He turned just in time to see a gargoyle seemingly come to life from where it perched on the edge of a rooftop. It launched into the air with a single leap just in time to join in flight with a fearsome creature out of mythology... a dragon. Kantor blinked. He couldn't believe what he was seeing.

His men ran in panic as the claws of a much bigger dragon clutched a man from the back of a horse and flew away with him. Kantor looked up to see the sky filling with more huge dragons, soaring right over his troops. His horse reared again and shook him off before galloping wildly back the way they had come.

Two more men were taken from their terrified horses by huge claws. One of them met a grisly fate as the dragon ascended and met another dragon that tore half of the meat from the savage claws, swallowing the fresh prey before death could toughen the morsel. More riders were taken as they tried to control their mounts, too horrified to think clearly and see that men on the ground stood a better chance. Kantor tried to shout orders and warnings, but the sound was lost among dragon screeches and the terrified screaming of horses still trying to find direction through their own panic.

Men all around him were in chaos, alternately trying to run from the dragon attack or to fight the savage women. Kantor had never seen men fight as these women did, spearing men left and right as if their only purpose was to kill. No rules of war applied here. He felt his own panic rising as one after another of the dragons flew between the buildings, reaching for prey.

Those on horseback were the inevitable targets. The dragons were too big to fly low among the old buildings and were reaching with claws to grab whatever morsel came into their grasp most easily. Kantor looked around and realised that the women had suddenly disappeared. There was nothing but men running in all directions and a few dragons left in the sky. He sighted the gargoyle again, but it was riding on the back of the small dragon, apparently herding the larger ones away now that they had enjoyed their feast on his men. The encampment was also deserted. Kantor assumed that the men had taken cover from the aerial attack.

He looked for a place to take cover himself. There were many places between buildings that might conceal a man from the creatures in the air, but as he looked down the main road a new threat approached. He pinched himself to ascertain that he was not having a nightmare. Too many creatures out of legend had appeared for any of this to be real. It had happened so quickly that he hadn't been able to think.

His remaining men appeared to recover themselves enough to pick up their weapons again and brace themselves for the new assault as they watched it approach, coming closer with every heartbeat. Everything seemed to happen in slow motion as if the monsters before them had all the time in the world to finish off what the dragons had left behind.

Chapter Fifteen

I *must be mad*, Anton thought to himself. Every nerve in his body felt on edge. Only desperation could have brought him to enter this forbidden world again. The hair on his back prickled with his 'wolf' senses. His shape-shifting ability would be useless here, at least if he wanted to achieve his purpose. Even if he used it to run he would probably be surrounded and captured regardless of what form he chose. Goblins were no strangers to such physical changes.

Desperation had not saved him before. Identifying himself had made no difference then and asking for the goblin who had sent him to his death before might only lead to a repeat on that incident. Anton's only hope was that the sword he presented would have meaning to the goblins. It had seemed to have a great deal of significance to all who had seen it. He wished that he knew what the nature of that significance was.

Anton was gambling rather a lot on subtleties in a goblin society that he actually knew too little about. Everything he had learned about Haghuf's people might be different among *Those Who Protect*. He felt the eyes on him as he stepped gingerly along the unfamiliar paths. His 'wolf' sense of smell detected their presence, although none had made themselves visible. Anton knew that a single step back towards the entrance would show weakness and probably result in the sudden appearance of a substantial number of sentries.

'I seek Kahjak,' Anton said aloud. 'I must speak to him of a matter that concerns your people and mine. There must be co-operation for survival. I seek Kahjak.'

Anton repeated the words over and over again. He consciously controlled his breathing, willing himself to take slow, deep breaths as he had learned to do through his magician training. Fear must not be allowed to win in this gamble. His awareness grew sharper with every step, as well as his feeling of being watched. There was a dank taste to the air, growing stronger with every step. The sound of his own controlled breathing seemed to echo back at him from the walls. Occasionally he could hear other sounds, just on the edge of hearing. He couldn't make out what they were, yet he knew within himself that they were the natural sounds that occur within the caverns. The goblins would make no perceptible noise.

The light dimmed as he gingerly walked further into the cavern. Still no goblins showed themselves, but he had no doubt of their presence. He hoped that his voice didn't betray the shaking he felt from his hands on the sword. As a weapon, he knew it would not serve him well against a grotto full of hostile goblins. He gripped it only as a talisman, and because he didn't know what else to do with his quaking hands. Whatever façade he expected to present to the goblins, he had to admit to himself that he was completely terrified.

Anton stopped suddenly. He had passed the musty smell of the mouldy tiled walls near the entrance and come through more recently dug out rock to a place that he had seen once before. Despite his disorientation, it seemed that his feet had remembered the one familiar path in this labyrinth. He peered over the edge of the precipice, appreciating for the first time the complete blackness of the pit that he knew led through a very long fall that ended in a pool of deadly water. Memory surged. Lack of air. No light to see which way the bubbles of his exhaling breath floated. Something engulfing his face... acceptance of his own death.

Then the rough ground knocking breath into him before he slipped into unconsciousness. Haghuf's welcome presence when he awoke. Haghuf's fear of the sparkles in the water. *You asked me once what we do with our dead. Now you know.* Haghuf's words haunted Anton's memory now. This was a pit into which they threw their dead, and their captives. He had been unceremoniously pitched into it himself, but he had lived. He still didn't know why.

Anton felt his lower spine vibrate as two goblins appeared behind him and two others approached slowly from either side. A shadow near the rim of the pit was suddenly lit with the reflection of a large pair of yellow eyes. They rose slowly as the huge goblin emerged from the darkness. Anton thought to himself that it boded well that Kahjak approached him within sight this time, moving slowly and turning his head from side to side as if he regarded the intruding human with curiosity. Anton didn't bother to speak in the goblin tongue. He knew that Kahjak would understand the words that tumbled out as he spoke. He held the sword up, the blade still flat across the palms of his hands.

'I invoke the sanction of the *Foringen*, and seek brother to fight with brother against our common foe. Let our blood mingle without enmity, and our common cause transcend the wrongs of our ancestors. Let it be so.' Anton did not know where the formal words had come from, but he felt the sword vibrate in a similar manner to the way it had felt when it had led him into battle. Only this time, there would be no clash of steel. The sword could not be used as a weapon against goblin-kind.

For a moment, Kahjak did not respond. He stood directly in front of Anton, meeting his eyes and staring directly into them with an expression that kept no secret of Kahjak's distain for humans. It was a challenge. Anton looked up and met the troll-like goblin's eyes, but nodded in obeisance as he raised the proffered sword a little higher.

Several minutes seemed to pass slowly as Kahjak held Anton's eyes, then at last he spoke in the human dialect.

'You have more nerve than sense coming in here. There is nothing to stop me from throwing you in that pit again.'

Every fibre of nerve jumped as the booming voice of Kahjak assaulted him from the near silence. This, too, was a familiar scenario. *No humans in the caverns.* Anton only just managed not to jump into the pit himself from his own reflexes. He met Kahjak's eyes, trying his best to look relaxed.

'But you haven't yet, so you've obviously decided to listen to what I have to say.' Anton flashed his disarming grin at the massive goblin. He hoped it looked convincing. It was an old mind trick, to suggest to someone that they had followed a course of thought themselves. The process of deja-vu worked on the simplest minds most easily. Anton could only hope that it would work on a goblin.

For a moment he wasn't sure if it had. The goblin looked him in the eye angrily. It was not a good sign. Goblins only made that level of eye contact when engaging an enemy. He was standing right on the edge of the pit, but there was more than one way to confer death on a fragile human. Some of them had the potential to be extremely painful.

Slowly, the goblin's face pulled itself into a hideous and unreadable grimace. The long, sharp teeth gleamed dully in the dim light of the forbidden cavern.

'You dare to come to me, to breach the forbidden entrance in defiance of our law to ask me to fight for your pathetic humans?'

Anton stood his ground. This was no time to show weakness.

'Other humans come in greater numbers with weapons and training. It is time to call on Kralic.'

The mention of Kralic got a visible reaction. Kahjak's iron expression faltered as his eyes widened at the mention of the name.

'What do you know of Kralic?' Kahjak demanded.

'I know nothing,' Anton admitted quickly. 'But others of your kind have good reason to trust me and to see that the invading humans are more trouble than my people will ever be for your kind. We have common cause. The invaders must be stopped before they learn of your world.'

'You are a magician, why don't you fight these humans with your magic?'

Anton visibly relaxed at the question. He had Kahjak's attention now and a chance to debate his way through this.

'My people use magic to help things grow and to keep the rhythms of the Earth, as you do with *The Dance*. We can create illusion, but magic is about working in tune with nature. It is not like the stuff of stories where great and mighty wizards can shoot flashes of thunderbolt out of their fingers like the old gods. We are humans and can die like any other creature of the Earth.'

Kahjak regarded him, still turning his head slightly as if inspecting a curious insect.

'You admit that you are mortal, yet you come to my grotto, knowing that you will surely die for the trespass.'

Anton felt himself gaining the upper hand.

'The creatures of the forest live in harmony with us. Your own people who live in the water refuse to eat us.'

At this Kahjak blanched. The fact that the *Kol'ksu* had not eaten the arrogant human when he threw him down the pit to them had disturbed the warrior goblin greatly at the time. Anton continued quickly.

'The forgers of fire gave me this sword and even now the air is full of dragons helping to defend this land from hostile invaders.'

Kahjak's mouth actually dropped open at the news of the dragons. Anton felt a secret elation that the goblin hadn't already known about them and pressed the advantage, speaking vehemently.

'You who are so close to the Earth have good reason to distrust my species, but I come to you not to ask you to fight for me, but to join with us as brothers – as my brother – to defend our shared land from those who would ravage it for their own purposes.'

Kahjak snorted like a bull preparing to charge. He still stood very close to Anton, their noses nearly touching. Anton pulled his one Ace out of his sleeve.

'Haghuf has taken an arrow from these humans. Talla helps him now, but I do not know if he will live. The invading humans have attacked goblin kind.'

It was a lie. Anton knew very well that it was the Southern man, Rolf, who had deliberately shot Haghuf, but it was the one thing that would invoke the goblins' defensive laws. There was a risk that they would attack all humans rather than just the invaders, but it was a risk that Anton had to take.

The snorting increased as Kahjak flexed his muscles and started shifting his weight from one foot to another in a sort of dance that spoke of anger rising. Anton held the massive goblin's eyes as he steeled himself against whatever might happen when the eruption lashed out.

Suddenly Kahjak stopped. Without taking his eyes from Anton, he issued an order.

'Klurdan, send a runner to Kralic. Call the Dunai. It is time to kill humans.'

Anton still stood firmly, holding the eye contact, as he waited to find out if he would be the first kill of the day by *Those Who Protect*.

NAMAH LOST HER SENSE of self for a moment as the Amazons attacked in a horde. She did not look to see where her closest friend or her sister were or how they fared. Instead she gave herself over to her reflexes and operated as part of the larger unit, taking down men with her spear and working in co-operation with any woman near her.

The first time the spear penetrated flesh brought her back to herself for a moment, long enough to feel a little sick. However, there was no time to give in to the momentary weakness. Other men on horseback were trying to bear down on the women. Namah's training to pull and twist so that the spear came loose of the body, ready to be used again, saved her life as a horseman neared with his sword ready.

Namah turned at just the right moment with her freed spear so that he nearly rode right into it. He pulled up and the horse screamed in sudden fury. He might have recovered the assault, but then suddenly he was no longer on the horse. Namah blinked, unable to make sense of what she thought she had seen. It was as if a giant claw had suddenly grasped the man just as she was turning to defend from another rider behind her, but as she turned the other man was gone as well. His horse bolted in panic, running from the scene of battle.

In the meantime a third horseman had been unhorsed and his steed was also running away. Namah wasn't sure what had knocked him off. It was as if the horse itself had decided to dump its burden and be gone. She started to engage with the soldier, but an arrow appeared in his chest and he was down. Namah turned quickly to look for more of the enemy. She saw them looking to the air and her Amazon sisters running for cover as Alinea had instructed. A quick glance to the skies told her why.

The air was full of dragons, huge ones. Men were being plucked from horseback by giant claws. Namah understood now why Alinea had said to attack, retreat and take cover. She turned and ran for a building with a stairwell ramp that would give adequate cover from the aerial attack. When she reached it she found several women already cowering under the protective masonry as well as two of the enemy soldiers. Namah looked at them huddling among women she knew and almost took a step backwards.

'It's alright, they've surrendered.'

Namah turned towards the voice and found herself addressed by the Countess Ariane.

'I have their weapons,' the Countess assured Namah.

Namah turned and watched as several soldiers tried to attack the giant claws with their small swords, only to be carried away by the giant beasts. In the distance she saw Drazek riding on the back of Jezza, completely fearless as they flew through the melee in the sky. Together they appeared to dance on the edge of the flight of dragons as if Drazek were shepherding them or conducting a dance in the skies with the graceful and terrifying creatures.

Namah turned back to the Countess.

'Where is Alaric?'

The Countess had that look that mothers could get when their children were in the care of others, as if knowing they were safe were not enough.

'Alaric is protected, and probably having the time of his life.' There was a haunted sound in the Countess' voice as she spoke. 'It's the first time the goblins have allowed him to go underground.'

Namah understood. Alaric was much like his father. The world his father had embraced had been a fascination for the boy all of his life, but he had not been allowed to taste the world of the goblins. Namah knew too well how intoxicating the secret world within the caverns could be. She wanted more than anything to go back, to have another chance at the goblin culture she had so tentatively tasted. She also wanted to see Ja'imos again.

Suddenly everything was too quiet. The dragons were mysteriously gone from the sky and the remaining soldiers in the street were re-grouping. Namah glanced at the captives behind her. There was no dilemma in their eyes. They looked very happy to remain where they were and let the wars of men play out without their participation. However, the Amazons were taking up their weapons and making ready to join the battle again.

Namah noticed the soldiers in the street looking Westwards and came far enough out from her hiding place to see what they were looking at down the street. Her mouth dropped open at the unexpected new threat that bore down on the broken invading army. Namah saw what looked like a wall of massive goblins walking shoulder to shoulder, forming a procession of green flesh and coming closer with every step. They held swords in their hands and angry expressions, and right in the middle of them was Count Anton with his goblin sword in hand as if he led this army of trolls.

Namah went back under shelter to tell the Countess what she had seen, hoping that the Amazons would not be needed in this next stage of the battle.

Count Anton felt the energy building within himself as goblins marching on all sides of him drew their strength from the earth. It was much like *The Dance*, this slow march in a natural cadence emphasised on every other step with a release of a low guttural sound as the warrior goblins exhaled in unison.

Anton had read of ancient human armies using cadence to prepare themselves for battle. He understood now. When Roman soldiers had used their swords to drum on their shields, it was similar to the drumming preceding *The Dance*. Ancient Celts had used not only drums, but also their voices as the goblins did now. With a deep, resonant "Huhm" on those alternate steps, the goblins were invoking an ancient warrior magic.

The books had also pointed out that when warfare had become too technological to send men to war on foot, the warrior spirit within men had expressed itself through competition sports. Some of them had been intentionally bloody, like the gladiatorial amusements of those same Romans. Some had turned to bloodshed occasionally when the mob spirit would overtake groups of men in support of one team or another playing with a ball. Anton speculated that men were every bit as savage by nature as the goblins they feared and despised.

He could see it in men like Latham and even in himself when a weapon was in his hand. He felt it now, as the magic of the goblin sword sang along with his grunts in time with the goblins. Anton had felt the magic pulsing already when Kahjak sent the runner to Kralic. The runner couldn't have gone three steps before a drum echoed from the deeper cavern and a swarm of massive goblins had appeared from seemingly nowhere. Anton had been pushed along with the wave of warrior energy rising to express itself. He was very aware that marching in the centre of the front row of what had quickly become a horde of trolls would look to the other humans as if he were leading them.

Anton understood that the goblins did not operate on hierarchy, not even the warriors, and smiled to himself that the enemy could not know this as the wall of frightening creatures neared. It was only when Kahjak had sent the runner to seek Kralic that Anton had worked out that Kahjak was a *Wise One* among the goblins, like Haghuf, only in the area of warfare rather than a librarian and planner. The other goblins among *Those Who Protect* would follow his commands because he knew his business and it was in their interest to listen. There was no compulsion as there was in the armies of men. Goblins co-operated with each other for survival.

The cadence quickened as the goblin horde drew near to the gathering remains of the human army. There were still many men among the human invaders, although none sat a horse now. Anton felt the magic from the goblin sword travelling up his arm and connecting with the Earth below him. He felt that same invincibility that had allowed him to thwart the riverside attack. Before him he spotted a commander, a proud man with a strong jaw-line and stripes on his uniform. Knowing the ways of humans, Anton had no doubt that the bearing of the man was that of a military officer. The well-crafted sword in the foreigner's hand was too decorative to belong to a common soldier. Anton hoped that the goblins wouldn't get to him first.

Men appeared from the alleyways... men that Anton recognised. With the dragons gone from the skies, they had come out to finish off the scattered invading army. Anton thanked Dani in his heart. He knew that as second in command, Dani would have organised and heartened these men for the next stage of the battle. Anton also spared a thought for Haghuf, wondering how his friend fared while the battles of men were fought outside. He had some concern about the mixture of men and goblins. How would the goblins know which men were on which side? Or would it matter to *Those Who Protect*?

Suddenly Anton understood why Haghuf had so adamantly insisted that he could not have raised the warrior goblins despite his own position as a *Wise One*. The dance of the warrior was much different than that of the intellectual. The rhythm was different – more intense and angry than the dancing that took place after the storytelling. Anton felt the difference in the rhythm as his body prepared to swivel and lash limbs where required to achieve maximum effect with what strength he possessed.

The goblin sword swung and met with the foreign commander's sword in an arc that denoted the start of what was effectively a dance of battle. At the same time, Anton became aware that the magicians among the men on his side had moved close to his vicinity and were sharing in this dance as they engaged the invading soldiers in battle. The goblins fighting by their sides shared the rhythm of this dance in harmony. It was very probably the first time they had co-operated with humans in many centuries. Some of the opponents before them entered the battle rhythm as well, none more so than the commander.

Anton's eye caught a glimpse of an amulet at the commander's throat. It was identical to the one he wore himself as well as the one he had given to Haghuf so long ago. By this Anton knew that the commander was a magician, as were probably some of his elite guard. They could feel the rhythms of the Earth pulsate through the movements of battle just as Anton and the goblins did. Other men further from the crush of the fight fought with what skills they had learned, but the psychic connection that kept the goblins operating as a unit was perceptible only to the goblins themselves and to the magicians on both sides.

Captain Kantor had not expected this. What should have been an easy conquest had been hindered by unknown predatory creatures in the river, surprise attacks, nothing short of dragons attacking from the skies and now this alarming troll army. What else did the leader of the farmers and craftsmen have in store for them?

Kantor had noticed the magician's amulet at the first ring of their swords together. Even the sword of Count Anton looked like something that had manifested out of ancient legends. He would not allow his doubts to show in battle, but inside Kantor was feeling overwhelmed. Even the warrior women, though they had taken few of his men, had been disconcerting with their sudden furious attack and their unnatural blue faces. They had disappeared as if by magic as the dragons attacked. This, too, was disturbing. Kantor was becoming concerned that the magic of Count Anton might be far superior to his own.

Suddenly one of the big trolls stepped between him and Count Anton. Anton's sword was mid-swing and might have fallen hard on the troll, but it glanced sideways and did not connect. Kantor admired the skill that could control a weapon with such instant perception and redirection. He took the opportunity to fall back and put some distance between himself and Count Anton. At that moment in time, he preferred to fight the trolls.

Anton had been sure that he was about to finish the commander. He gave himself completely over to the magic that flowed through him, through the sword, through the Earth – and let the movement of the blade come down in what would be a bone-crunching blow that could fell the largest of the goblins that fought beside him. Then Kahjak himself had stepped in front of the blade when it was too late to divert the blow. For a split second Anton feared that he would kill the goblin and bring confusion to the battle that would surely end in *Those Who Protect* turning on all the humans with disastrous results.

The sword diverted its motion as if there were a force field around the goblin that it would not penetrate. It was as if Anton's own will was overridden by a conscious energy within the sword itself. Before he had much time to think about it he was engaged with more enemy swords from the throng, but the commander had disappeared behind an onslaught that Kahjak was pushing through the centre of what had been their reorganised force. Anton saw the strategy. The goblins were splitting the army and pushing half of it towards his own men while the other half were cut off from them.

Anton turned to see a muscular female goblin fighting near him, noting her presence to himself for later reference. The other goblins didn't appear to take any special notice of her. She fought among them as an equal. Out of curiosity, Anton made his way closer to her while clashing blades with any of the enemy that stood between them. Suddenly she whirled around and met Anton's eyes as the blade came crashing down towards him. At the same moment a sword slashed towards her from behind and Anton called out in the goblin tongue without thinking.

'dniheb uoy!'

The blow that had been intended for Anton sailed in a complete 180 degree arc that slashed the head from her would-be assassin's shoulders. Her eyes turned back to Anton momentarily as she nodded an acknowledgement, then carried on fighting the enemy humans. Anton made a mental note to himself to never sneak up on a goblin in battle, especially a female. They appeared to be more psychically sensitive than the males.

Kantor felt himself being herded along with his men, pinched between the trolls and the men that had come to fight for their homes. His own men were falling fast. Blood dripped from the swords of the massive green warriors that assaulted his forces, the blood of his own men. The men among the enemy fell easily, but he saw no green skins among the bodies that lay on the ground. The trolls were much bigger and stronger than his soldiers and at least as well trained. Their only hope lay in a complete retreat and in the soldiers on the other side of the street that the trolls had divided escaping to regroup with them later when they could plan according to their new knowledge of the opponents they faced.

Kantor reached for the horn at his side and blew the retreat signal, but just as he did so those damnable blue women attacked again, spearing his soldiers as they ran or engaging with some who stopped to fight, only to have his men dropped with arrows from yet another new threat that crawled across the rooftops of the buildings. He looked up to see another form of green creatures... ones who were strangely exotic in appearance. They were as tall as small men but of a slim, muscular build that was very different from the hefty trolls. They climbed across the thinnest ledges of the buildings, placing themselves on crumbling window ledges or decorative masonry as if they weighed nothing and had the balance of a spider crawling across a wall.

The green skin was tattooed with unreadable designs. The graceful pointed ears were pierced and adorned with rings of gold, sometimes with small stones that glittered in the grey cloudy light of this misty land. They had large, strangely beautiful yellow eyes with a look of intensity in them that turned Kantor's blood cold. Something about them brought more terror to his heart than the massive trolls as the unnaturally accurate arrows zinged from their bows, each one landing in a specific target's chest.

These were assassins, not mere snipers. Kantor began to accept that his mission and his army were doomed. He looked for a place to hide. The least he could do was to survive and report back to the king what had happened. He might even attempt a rescue of the king's worthless cousin if he lived to make the effort.

Anton heard the word whispered among the goblins closest to him... *Dunai!*

He worked out that the archers that had appeared on the rooftops and windows of the derelict buildings were of this tribe, but he had no reference to draw from to understand their significance. They reminded him of Ja'imos, with their tattoos and piercings as well as the slim, muscular build of their species and the accuracy of their archers. Some of the newcomers mixed in with the larger goblins, fighting near enough to Anton to get a close look at them. Some had fair hair, but not the white hair of the *Kol'ksu*... or of Talla. Anton had seen few of such goblins on the rare instances when he had been allowed to participate in *The Dance* and had wondered about them on the few occasions when he had noticed one mixed in with the more familiar goblins.

As the battle progressed, Anton followed the surge to the left, away from the men of his camp where more of the smaller goblins were appearing. He found himself fighting very close to one of the elf-like goblins that seemed familiar. The goblin turned as the thought occurred to Anton. He dipped his sword in a salute, smiling momentarily before resuming the dance of battle that was pushing back three of the enemy soldiers with the expert whirling of his deadly blade.

The look in the goblin's eyes in that brief glance triggered Anton's memory. It was from his first time at *The Dance*. He had been offered a small cup by this graceful, androgynous goblin. The cup had contained a strange liqueur that Anton had later learned the goblins called *Rabenis*. Its nature was one of the many puzzles he had yet to unravel about the goblin way of life. The goblins had no alcohol as far as Anton knew, but this one substance had some sort of hallucinogenic property that was conducive to *The Dance*. It tasted of apples and of cinnamon, and something else that he was never able to quite determine.

Anton had never been sure of the pretty goblin's gender and could not remember enough later to know if their encounter had been intimate enough to have found out. He had assumed in the battle that the newcomers were male, but he realised now that it had been an arrogant assumption. The female goblin he had encountered earlier should have been enough to teach him that females could fight alongside male goblins in the way that would be impossible among men.

As the battle progressed, Anton found himself back to back with the ethereal goblin, hoping they would get a chance to talk later.

Namah felt strangely compelled to join the fight with her fellow Amazons, but Countess Ariane had prevented her.

'No, Namah,' the Countess had said. 'We have prisoners to guard and we will be needed when it's all over, especially the magicians among us. You will get a chance to learn more about healing magic when the wounded are gathered.'

The Countess had gone on to plan a strategy as the wave of battle took on a definite pattern. Soon the action would pass their hiding place, then it would be safest to lead their prisoners down a nearby alley back to the camp by the river. The women would completely transform the food tent into an infirmary in preparation for casualties from both sides. Medical supplies had been stored in the tent in advance for this purpose.

Namah had taken the precaution of binding the wrists of the captives. Ariane had agreed that however compliant they appeared, the men were trained soldiers and could not be trusted to remain so in the ever-changing fortunes of war. The women waited patiently for their opportunity to escape their shelter.

Namah stood just at the entrance next to the street where battle raged, making herself unnoticeable to fighters from both sides as they passed while whistling out a pre-arranged signal to any of the Amazons that came close enough to hear. Those who heard it quickly fell back out of the fighting and looked for an opportunity to make their way to the riverside camp. There they could wash their faces and change back into ordinary clothing before the men returned. Hopefully some would have a chance to arrange food for the returning men while others prepared to nurse the wounded.

Namah looked at the man coming towards her without comprehension. She had learned the trick of being still and undetected from Alinea. It should have been nearly impossible to detect her unless a man had looked directly at her, specifically looking for a woman to be standing there. He wore a uniform with stripes on it that seemed to have some significance. Namah thought it odd that he should be running from a battle that he had been leading only moments before. He drew very close before Namah realised that it was not her he was running towards, but her hiding place. The man was looking for cover.

She melted back into the shadow of the stairwell and made her way back to the other women. Namah was about to report the immanent arrival of the enemy commander to Ariane when her attention was diverted to something happening by the back wall of their hiding place. The women looked as terrified as the captive men as chunks of concrete fell away to form a hole in the floor. Strange creatures began to emerge that were unlike anything Namah had seen before. The other women had seen even less of goblins than Namah had, but even during her brief exposure to *The Dance* she had seen nothing that remotely resembled what she was witnessing now. A part of her wondered if they were goblins at all... yet they must be.

The claws appeared first. They were as long as Namah's arm and thick – strong enough to tear rock and even concrete. As the first head emerged, the ground itself seemed to develop a subtle thrum. Namah could not be sure if it was an actual sound emanating from the newly formed tunnel or if she was hearing it on the subtle level where the rhythm of *The Dance* drummed its music.

Short dark hair covered the skull that emerged as if it were being birthed from its mother's womb, followed by a rodent-like face. Namah took a step backwards, unable to stop herself from responding to the goblin's ugliness. Powerful arms emerged as the goblin pulled itself through the barely adequate opening. Its body appeared to be complete muscle, covered by a tough skin and the short dark hair that continued from its head like the spiny coat of a hedgehog.

More of the strange goblins followed. The humans backed slowly away as one after another emerged, forming a close unit of stocky, spiky, hair-covered creatures. They were no taller than the women, but they made up for it in the bulk of rounded muscles. Namah counted five of the creatures as they emerged one after the other. Then to her surprise a small grime-covered boy emerged followed by one last goblin. The boy turned and brushed dirt from his face, flipping mud-covered hair away from his face. Alaric grinned up at Namah and at his mother, looking very pleased with himself.

Chapter Sixteen

'The dragons!' Haghuf thrashed his arms about, still only half conscious as the fever raged. 'I hear the dragons!'

Talla embraced him as a mother might embrace a sick child. She spoke to him gently as she tried to calm her own fears and sooth his.

'Yes, Haghuf, the dragons fly. Drazek is herding them. All will be well.'

Count Michel and his guard watched the exchange between the goblins with some trepidation. They could not understand the words as they were spoken in the goblin tongue, but Haghuf's goblin appearance was sufficiently disconcerting to them to make his palpable fear all the more frightening to the men. They, too, had heard the dragons, though they didn't know what creature emitted the sounds. They knew only that their natural instinct was to flee and hide.

'Drazek is a youngling,' Haghuf insisted. 'Herding a flight of dragons is not so easy as coercing a single young dragonet through the caverns!'

'Yet he holds his own.' Talla spoke soothingly, still ignoring her own terror. 'Remember, Haghuf, that it has been countless generations since one was born who could speak to the dragons.'

'To speak to them is one thing, to control them another.' Haghuf was coming back to himself now, but the fear of the dragons only grew with his returning consciousness.

'Shush, listen!' Talla perked up her pointed ears. 'The sounds are fading. Drazek is leading the dragons away.'

Haghuf began to calm a little.

'I feel the vibration of diggers,' he said more calmly, as he wiped the sweat from his brow with the back of his clawed hand.

Talla tried to feel through the ground. The vibrations were faint. She could not have identified them so easily as Haghuf did.

Haghuf's panic began to subside as confusion took over. *What are the diggers doing so close to all this?* he wondered silently. But his obsession with the dragons was not to be so easily distracted.

'You do not understand, Talla. The dragons have tasted freedom. They may never be content to remain in the caverns again.'

Talla's eyes widened a little as she took in the implications of what Haghuf said. The humans who observed them began to feel a deep-seated sensation of dread. If the goblins were afraid, how much more should they be terrified?

DIGGERS! Ariane recognised the strange goblins immediately, despite the fact that no human in history had ever seen one. She forgot her fear of the strange looking goblins as her mother's instinct took over. She moved to Alaric protectively.

What are you doing here? It's dangerous!

'Mother,' Alaric answered derisively as he gestured to his companions. 'Do I look as if I'm unprotected?'

At that moment one of the digger goblins laid a massive paw gently on Alaric's shoulder. Ariane was taken aback by the gentle gesture from the menacing looking claws. The slashing of such claws would be far more deadly than any sword.

'Anything can happen in a battle,' she said defensively. 'There are arrows flying everywhere out there.'

'That's why we came up under here,' he responded. 'These guys are incredible, they always know exactly where they are!'

Ariane remembered her manners and curtsied to the diggers. She had never mastered the art of the undulating bow that Anton had learned from the goblins. Namah had picked it up quickly as well, but Ariane felt too stiff when she tried to let her body flow into the motion. She found it difficult to think of these brutish looking creatures as goblins, despite the green skin and tiny pointed ears. They resembled giant moles more than anything else.

'Come, mother, the tunnel is wider inside. You'll be able to stand up.' Alaric smiled proudly, as if he had provided the escape route himself. Ariane looked confused as she answered her precocious son.

'You want us to travel underground?'

'As you said, mother, there are arrows flying everywhere out there.' The disarming grin, so like his father's, removed any doubt as to the wisdom of his plan. Ariane smiled in response.

'Lead on then, young Prince Alaric. I suppose you'll expect a fanfare and take credit for bringing in the first prisoners of war yourself.' Ariane winked as her son's grin widened.

One of the diggers returned to the passage first, then Alaric ushered first his mother, then the other women and the prisoners into the small opening. Each looked tentative as their turn to pass through the small opening occurred, but all complied and Alaric was just about to leap down into the newly dug cavern behind them, when there was a disturbance.

CAPTAIN KANTOR STILL had his sword in his hand as he ran for the promise of shelter. The space beneath the staircase of an old derelict building wound far enough around the steps that a man could hide there unobserved by the battle that raged outside. His one worry was that others might have thought the same and the refuge could already be occupied, but if it were so it was at least half possible that it would be by his own soldiers. He could simply take command of them and use them for protection while they all made their escape.

If he found enemies within, well, he still had his sword in his hand.

He plunged into the dark shelter with the attitude that he was ready for any eventuality... except for the one that he found. They were hideous creatures, more animal than humanoid. Four of them stood close together, apparently giving their attention to something behind Kantor's line of sight, but they turned towards him as he rushed into their sanctuary. A small boy with dirt on his face grinned up at him and was summarily pushed down into the pit by one of the creatures. Kantor was confused by the spectacle. The first thing that the soldier in him noticed was that they were unarmed. The monster had handled the child roughly, yet the boy had not appeared to be afraid of his captors.

Kantor quickly assessed his chances at taking on four unarmed but strong looking beasts. They were no taller than himself, but they looked muscular. It was then that he noticed the long, substantial claws. As one they took a step towards him. Kantor screamed in a high pitched voice that might have come from a little girl as he turned and ran.

The wedge that Kahjak had forged through the enemy had broken up into random skirmishes. Dead men covered the old street so that the remaining fighters were forced to move further down the rows of confining buildings continually to avoid tripping over the bodies. Men from both sides slipped away down side roads, melting away from the doomed battle.

Hulking goblins filled the streets, grunting and growling with glee as they searched out new opponents to hack to pieces. The lithe goblins that had appeared on the rooftops and window ledges had disappeared as silently as they had come. Arrows no longer filled the eerie surroundings, apart from the occasional random shaft from a human bow.

Kahjak raised an arm and the goblins of Lirrewot began to skulk away, disappointed that the pickings had been too easy. Many of them had seen the ancient goblin wars when a battle would last for days. Not enough men remained in this changed world to provide real sport.

Anton found himself standing alone as the retreating sounds of *Those Who Protect* faded into an unnatural silence. He wondered if there were some protocol to give thanks to his comrades in arms. No opportunity presented itself as they simply disappeared down side roads, moving more slowly than the men who had run from their swords.

Anton's eyes searched for hidden enemies as he trotted further down the street checking for stragglers. He was about to turn towards the riverside camp when a prickling on the back of his neck warned him. He spun round, sword arcing to meet the blade that might have slain him from behind had his instincts not alerted him. The blades clashed with an almost musical ringing sound. Anton found himself looking into the eyes of the commander of the invading army.

Kantor pressed his advantage of surprise, bearing down with all of his strength as he struck the other magician's sword. He had hoped the single stroke would have felled this strange man who fought his battles with monsters, but the quick reflex was not altogether unexpected. The Count wore the amulet after all.

Count Anton's sword sung with magic as the blades clashed and spun, drawing their wielders into a dance of battle once more. Kantor heard the song, just on the edge of perception, and matched the tune with his own humming. He was a magician too and considered that he might be able to steal this strange magic from his opponent. Capturing the sword would surely give him power over the monsters as well.

Anton heard Kantor's humming and felt the magic of the sword falter to some dark magic. Surely its power could not be so easily consumed? *If only I understood its power*, he thought as he, too, began to hum, remembering the strain of melody from the song of the *Kol'ksu*. The amulet on his chest burned as if the proximity to the matching one at the commander's throat was releasing a conflicting power. The song created by their humming as the magicians fought became discordant, one hearing the tune more precisely than the other. Anton wanted free of this battle to go study the books in his library again, to refresh his memory as to the nature of the amulets and his ancestral power.

The distraction of his own thoughts was causing him to lose the tune. The enemy sword bore down on the *Foringen* blade unceasingly. Anton was losing the advantage. The enemy sword flashed in an arc that came down impossibly fast, forcing Anton to use the flat of his own blade to stop the cutting edge from reaching his collar-bone. His eyes stared up at the amulet dangling from his opponent's throat, then raised to see the promise of victory in the seas of blue looking back at him from above the arrogant smile.

A sudden sword thrust through Kantor's abdomen from behind spilled blood all over Anton as the commander's expression changed through a variety of emotions that included pain and anguish, but most of all surprise. Kahjak pulled his goblin sword back roughly, slinging the limp body of the man onto the broken pavement to shudder into death as the goblin wiped his blade on the smart uniform.

Anton stood up quickly, sheathing his own sword. There were no words sufficient to thank the goblin for saving his life. A smile of elation broke out on his face. He was grateful to be alive, as well as very aware of the irony that it should be Kahjak that saved him.

Kahjak returned the smile. At least Anton assumed it was a smile. He always wondered when a goblin showed his teeth if it was entirely a friendly gesture. At last Anton found his words.

'It is an honour to fight beside you and your people, Kahjak. I hope this will forge new understandings between us.'

Kahjak lost his smile quickly and looked at Anton suspiciously.

'You are still human. Nothing changes.'

The sudden change in Kahjak's demeanour perplexed Anton. His brow furrowed as he took the amulet from his dead enemy's neck and attempted to keep Kahjak in conversation.

'Why did you choose to help?'

Kahjak smiled a little again as he gave a brutally straightforward reply.

'Curiosity, and the chance to blood some of my younger warriors on their first humans. I wanted to see what the *Foringen* sword would do in the hands of a human. You should learn to use it, *human*, you let him steal the power. In truth, I protected the sword from falling into the hands of an unworthy human. The *Foringen* chose you.'

Anton considered a moment, turning the captured amulet over in his hands.

'Perhaps your people could teach me its magic, Kahjak?'

The goblin's head flew up with anger in his eyes. He stepped closely to Anton and met his eyes with the disconcerting stare that goblins use when confronting an enemy.

'Do not visit Lirrewot. Haven't you worked it out? Lirrewot is a training grotto for *Those Who Protect*. Most live deep within the Earth, like those you saw today. Goblins never stop growing, especially the ears. Big ones are very old. They were killing your ancestors before humans were writing down the histories.'

Kahjak looked as if he might spit at Anton's feet, but he just turned and began to walk away. Anton felt just bold enough to call out one more question.

'How did they know which men were on which side?'

Kahjak stopped and half-turned in a way that reminded Anton of Haghuf.

'They smell different. Aggressors smell of arrogance. Defenders just smell of fear. Including you.'

With that the hefty goblin turned and walked away with long strides, quickly turning down a side street. Anton was sure Kahjak had chosen the route that would take him out of the presence of a stinking human as quickly as possible.

Chapter Seventeen

I f there was anything that Latham had learned young, it was how to watch his own back. It had been no accident that he had volunteered for the position that was intended to cut and run when they went out on the first raid. When the major battle began to get too close for comfort in the street, he slipped away quietly and stayed out of the way while other men died to protect their homes.

As soon as things calmed down, he wandered back to the camp, appearing to have just returned from a hard day of battle. In fact, he had watched much of it from a balcony in one of the old buildings, although he had gone back inside the protective walls when the dragons had appeared.

First demons and now dragons from Hell, he thought to himself. *This is getting out of hand.*

He wanted to slip into the food marquee to refresh himself, but the danger of getting recruited to help with the makeshift hospital tasks was a deterrent. *Besides*, he thought, *that damnable goblin is in there.*

Latham scowled to himself. Rolf had missed the heart and then had been killed before he could get a second shot in. They had been over and over the plan to rid themselves of the goblin, but the invaders had struck too quickly. Losing one goblin in a sea of warfare should have been simple. Unfortunately losing a man was just as easy.

His remaining men, Matthew and Zak, returned one at a time. Latham had instructed his hand-picked cohorts to stay out of harm's way if possible. They still had important work to do. Now that they were all safely back at camp, they shared proximity casually as if they were being companionable after a shared battle. Each of them feigned weariness in their own way, but all of them had taken cover somewhere while the battle had been raging.

Any thoughts that Latham had of Count Anton falling to an unfortunate accident had been abandoned when the unpredictable ruler had appeared with the massive trolls flanking him. Getting anywhere near him would have been almost impossible and very dangerous. He also had trained fighters guarding his back. Latham didn't need reminding that the fighter goblins knew their business. He remembered all too clearly the last time they had come above ground.

With the skies completely overcast, there was no chance of the bright sunlight that had turned the tide of battle against the goblins all those years ago. Latham didn't fancy joining them on the battlefield again, even if they were supposed to be on the same side this time.

Latham pretended to clean his sword as he spied the harlot, Namah, sitting and drawing outside the marquee. Where she had found parchment and quill he did not know, but it was her serenity that annoyed him. Her father and her promised husband were both dead. Latham had seen Gareth fall to the enemy's sword. Namah appeared completely oblivious of her loss, although in fairness he had protected her from the knowledge of her father's death himself.

Still, her brazen appearance among the people enraged him. She offered no explanation as to where she had been or why she had run away from her wedding. She had been mourned as if dead. The girl clearly had no soul.

Latham gestured with a slight flick of the chin and the shifting of his eyes as the girl Alinea emerged from the marquee. She stopped to speak with Namah, handing her an apple. Latham remembered his hunger, but it would have to wait a little longer.

Matthew and Zak followed their leader's gaze and understood. That was the girl... the half-goblin. They stood as one, still pretending to have their attention elsewhere. After a few whispered words between them, Zak wandered off in one direction while Matthew disappeared behind some buildings the opposite way. Latham tried to act natural as he observed which direction the goblin girl chose. He prayed to himself that she would not simply disappear back into the marquee.

Namah watched as the lines her hands drew slowly became a likeness of the one person she had in mind most, Ja'imos. She had looked for him among the smaller goblins who had scaled the buildings so easily. They reminded her of him and she had speculated that he might be of their tribe. However, if he had participated in the battle she had not seen him. It had been some time since she had enjoyed so much as a glimpse of him. He had not appeared at the full moon bonfires since that first night. Namah thought of their last encounter in the caverns and sighed.

Alinea suddenly appeared at her side. The girl had a way of stealth that not only made her footsteps unheard, but also defied detection with psychic sensitivity. Namah had learned to simply accept her friend's unexpected appearances.

'You draw well,' Alinea declared as she handed Namah a perfect golden apple. 'Eat this, it will make you feel strong.'

Namah smiled up at Alinea's compliment as she accepted the apple and bit into it, chewing her first mouthful before she responded.

'I must thank you for the parchment. We have little that we can draw on remaining in our world.

Alinea returned the smile.

'Yet Count Anton has many books in his library. Perhaps your people should recover the skill of making paper.'

'Yes, you're right,' Namah agreed. 'When I was a small child, my father found rolls of old paper in a factory and I was allowed to draw on that, but it has long since run out.'

'Ja'imos would probably be pleased to see how well you depict him.' Alinea moved to a position behind Namah's shoulder so that she could see the drawing upright.

'Will you take it to him for me?' Namah implored. 'Only... I don't think I would be allowed to seek him out myself.'

Alinea nodded goblin fashion to acknowledge the truth of Namah's words.

'To seek him you would have to penetrate the world of *Those Who Protect* and even Kralic's forces. No human would be allowed so far.'

'Who is Kralic?' Namah asked quickly.

Alinea hesitated. To speak openly of such things to a human, even a friend, would be to break the only law that bound the goblins. Yet some response was required. Eventually she decided on a compromise.

'You witnessed goblins of great skill today. We have no leaders, but some have the skill of training. You must ask me no more.'

So I was right, Namah thought. *He is like those goblins on the rooftops.*

Suddenly Alinea's eyes were alert. She did not jerk her head up or respond in any visible way, but Namah could see that she had sensed something.

'We are being observed,' Alinea said simply. 'I feel malice among your people. I cannot be sure if it is towards you or to myself, but there are strong emotions.'

Alinea slowly straightened up and looked around casually as if she were unaware of her observers.

'I will walk a little and see if they follow me, but I will be close in case you require assistance.'

Namah nodded slightly. She tried to send her awareness out to determine the origin of this impression of malice, but to no avail. Her eye fell on Latham standing alone. She speculated that it might well be him. There were few of the Southern people among those who returned to the riverside camp, but Latham moved his family to their side of the river after the incident with the goblins ten years hence and was known for his ill temper and judgmental attitude. Namah was very aware that her presence might well be the cause of unfriendly vibrations emanating from him.

Alinea had deliberately walked slowly in plain sight as she disappeared down an alley. Namah felt a growing sense of foreboding as Latham pretended to casually wander, following her friend's path. She watched him out of the corner of her eye as she pretended to attend to her drawing and finished eating her apple.

DANI APPROACHED ANTON as the Count sat by Haghuf's side with Talla, willing his friend to awaken.

'Sir, all that you ordered has been accomplished.'

Anton nodded to acknowledge Dani's report.

'I am sorry to have asked more of the men after they've been wearied with battle, but moving with haste was necessary.'

Dani returned the nod.

'They understand, Sir, and many are glad of their new... acquisitions.'

Anton exchanged a smirk with Dani. Ordering the confiscation of all weapons and the potato liquor from the Southern homes was something of a gamble, but he was not going to leave those people armed and feeling over-confident after their success of the day. They owed their victory to the goblins, but the ignorant fools were just arrogant enough to forget that quickly.

It had been essential that the task was accomplished before the Southerners returned to their homes. Dani had had to move quickly as many of the Southern men were crossing the river even now and a message had been sent to retrieve their women and children. What remained of the enemy troops had disappeared onto the ships that were sailing away into the evening light. Tales would be told that Anton hoped would dissuade any future attempts to invade his small kingdom.

A kingdom ruled by a Count, Anton thought to himself. He frowned, as dark thoughts played on his mind.

Talla's presence was both comforting and disconcerting to him. Whatever healing skills she had, Haghuf still lived because of them. Still, she was the woman who he would have made his Countess if their cultural differences had not been so irreconcilable. As much as he loved Ariane in his way, Talla was forever engraved on his heart.

The silence between them was deafening. Dani withdrew discreetly, his eyes moving one to the other as he turned. Anton was aware of far too many people around him when he wished he could be alone with his thoughts. Not least of all was the prisoner, Count Michel, sitting with his guards in the corner. Anton wondered if the little man knew that his ships had sailed without him. He knew that he would have to make a decision about what to do with the diplomat soon. Anton understood now that he had been right about Michel's position and the military command, but the foreign commander was dead now. Anton wondered who gave orders on their ships for the return journey.

'Your thoughts race from one thing to another, even now.' Talla's voice spoke quietly with a calm assurance that Anton remembered fondly.

Anton smiled, flashing the familiar grin that had so often charmed the ladies.

'You know my responsibilities, Talla. I have much to think about. Not least of all Haghuf's words before he fell back to sleep. Do you think that dragons will be a new problem for my people?'

'You mean as they have been for ours for so long?' A touch of the old defiance touched her tone.

'That's another thing, Talla, I have met *your* people.'

The implication hung in the air between them. The emphasis on the word 'your' made it clear that he spoke not of the ordinary goblins, but of those who resembled Talla so much, the *Kol'ksu*.

Talla's eyes looked up at Anton with an unreadable expression. For a moment he thought he saw the predator in them, as he had seen in the eyes of the female *Kol'ksu* who had warned him of his own vulnerability.

'Some things we do not speak of,' Talla said coldly.

Anton found himself hypnotised by the deep, white-irised eyes. He was vaguely aware that Ariane tended the wounded nearby and was trying her best not to watch her husband sitting with his previous lover, but at that moment all he knew was Talla and the siren song that he remembered so well, just on the edge of hearing. He almost thought that he could hear it, even now. Then he decided consciously to break the spell.

'I've missed you, Talla. Although with all I've learned of late, I suppose I should be grateful that you didn't devour me when first we met.' The old attitude of amusement took over his features and sparkled in his eyes. Talla lowered hers as she suppressed a smile.

'I never draw blood on a first date,' she said flippantly.

The familiar grin spread openly across Anton's face for a moment, then settled into a more serious expression.

'I wonder if you can tell me one thing though, Talla. Kahjak said that *Those Who Protect* could tell which humans were the foreign ones by their smell.'

Talla acknowledged the question with a slight incline of her head and looked as though she would speak, but it was the gravely voice of Haghuf that responded.

'They stink differently.'

Haghuf's eyes opened then and looked at Anton with the old expression that Anton knew from their past discussions of goblin habits and abilities. The goblin pushed himself up a little to rest on his elbows, then continued.

'What you eat affects your scent directly. The invaders haven't cultivated food as you have, they eat too much vermin.'

Anton was too grateful to see his friend fully conscious to take up the old game. Instead he gave a sigh of relief.

'Welcome back, Haghuf, you've missed all the fun.'

Haghuf struggled into a sitting position as he responded.

'Not all of it. Are the dragons gone? I do not hear them.'

Talla stroked his hand reassuringly.

'They are safely back in the caverns, Haghuf, all of them.'

Haghuf eyed her suspiciously.

'For how long?' he asked rhetorically.

Anton could see that Haghuf was disturbingly worried about the dragons and wondered if he, too, should be concerned.

'You spoke of *Those Who Protect*,' Haghuf continued. 'How did you get them to come?'

Anton smirked as he realised that he had the advantage of his old friend this time.

'I went to Lirrewot and asked Kahjak,' he replied casually as if it were the most ordinary thing in the world to do. 'He saved my life in the end. Ran the foreign commander through as he was just about to overcome me.'

If dark green skin could turn white, Haghuf's face tried its best. His shock at this news was far too apparent to even be a good joke for Anton, but Haghuf's next question surprised him even more.

'How did this man get the upper hand if you fought with the sword of the *Foringen*?'

At that Anton frowned, then he fished the commander's amulet out of a pocket and showed it to Haghuf.

'He wore this, and he knew the rhythm of *The Dance*.'

Haghuf's eyes shot up at Anton's. His clawed hand reached for the matching amulet at his own throat.

'How well do you know the history and magic behind this trinket you gave me?' Haghuf's eyes were deadly serious as he awaited Anton's response.

'I read the full histories when I was young, but it has been many years. I think it is time I read them again.' Anton put the amulet back in his pocket and looked back at Haghuf. 'Perhaps you would join me and we can study them together and look for anything I might have missed.'

Haghuf nodded.

'I know the way to your library.'

Anton thought he saw a twinkle of amusement in Haghuf's eye before the goblin continued more seriously.

'It is also time you learned more about the sword you carry. It had been prophesised that war would come. It falls to me to teach you this. I have been remiss.'

'We have many powerful weapons now, Haghuf, invaders will not be so quick to return.'

Haghuf took in Anton's meaning and looked at him sadly.

'Do not rely on goblins to come to your aid, Anton, or dragons. Both are unpredictable and must not be counted among your weapons of war. You can sharpen a sword to a finite point, but then you run out of blade.'

The old goblin proverb was not lost on Anton. He nodded goblin style to show that he understood.

At that moment there was a scuffle in the corner. Count Michel had apparently tried to bolt, but had been quickly subdued by his guards.

'I must attend to this,' Anton explained as he left his friend's side to investigate.

'Coward!' The Count Michel shouted at Anton as he approached. 'You have broken the rules of war. I claim your castle by right of compensation!'

Anton looked at Michel quizzically before responding.

'You are in no position to make demands, Michel.'

The little man shook off his subduers and stood proudly to face Anton.

'That is *Count* Michel, just as you are *Count* Anton. You have no king, so by right of succession you must yield to mine.' Michel took another step closer to Anton, glowering at him as he made further demands.

'You started the war with your attack on my ships. Therefore your lands and properties are forfeit. It is the rules of war.'

Anton flashed his disarming grin, enjoying his captive's discomfiture as the bravado failed to impress.

'Rules are for games. You invaded my territory with full intent to take it from me and my people. My men fought for their homes and families and many have died. I don't even know how many as yet.'

Anton frowned as the weight of his own words brought the unknown devastation to the forefront of his thoughts.

'You put a lot of stock in a title, but such things are artificial. My son is a prince and will be king after me. This land does not lack a ruler.'

Count Michel reacted to Anton's reason with outrage.

'We of the continent are civilised men! We do not train monsters to do our fighting for us, where is your honour? War *must* have rules!'

Anton whirled and looked at Haghuf as the word 'monsters' was practically spat from Michel's mouth. His eyes flashed with anger at the insult to his friends. He whirled back quickly with his sword in his hand.

'You are in no position to make the rules!' Anton declared. His arm seemed to move of its own volition as it plunged the goblin-forged blade through the body of Count Michel. The foreigner's eyes opened wide in surprise, then faded quickly in inescapable death. Anton felt as if he were watching someone else perform the bloody deed. It was an execution by any definition, yet Anton could not feel sympathy for the silenced prisoner.

'Bury him with the commoners,' Anton ordered the shocked guards. It was his last insult to the irritating little man.

It's only a pity that he didn't stay alive in agony a little so that he could hear it, Anton thought as he strode away from the bleeding corpse.

He had intended to go back to Haghuf, but the goblin was no longer on the cot where he had left him. Anton turned and strode towards the marquee door to look outside for his friend. He was thinking that perhaps Talla had taken him out for some fresh air and a walk, then he remembered that open spaces were not a comfort to a creature that spent its life in enclosed places. Anton hoped that he was not too late to see Haghuf again before he disappeared into one of the secret cavern entrances.

ALINEA WALKED SLOWLY, allowing her pursuer to follow easily. He struggled just a little to quiet his resounding footsteps, but Latham was not built for stealth. Alinea was grateful for the confirmation that it was herself who was of interest to whatever malice lurked within this man and not Namah, but it could mean only one thing. Someone knew that she was goblin-kind.

The human women had washed the woad from their faces and changed into their usual clothing. Alinea still wore her primitive goblin furs, although she had washed with the others. There was some possibility that her follower could be intending rape on what he thought was a helpless girl, but the sheer force of the anger he projected suggested murderous intent.

Alinea tried to think what indiscretion might have given her away as she examined the walls of the buildings that lined the alley. Climbing was certainly an option, but it was also a dead giveaway. If there were any doubts, her ability to scale walls in ways that human girls could not would dispel them. For the moment, she relied on her ability to walk extremely fast to keep herself consistently ahead of the hostile man.

What she needed was a place to disappear, unobserved. There was little to work with in the alley. The buildings had windows, but only above the first level so that climbing would still be necessary. The occasional stairwell led down to a lower level that might offer some opportunity, or one of the old discarded rubbish bins could offer a means of climbing that would give the appearance of something possible for a young human to do.

Alinea had to think quickly as she observed every option while walking increasingly quickly past them. She was observant enough to have noted that Latham had accomplices and meeting one of them at the end of the alley was almost certain. She wondered for a moment where Alaric and the diggers had gone, but she felt no vibrations in the ground to suggest they were nearby. A quick underground escape would have been welcome at that juncture.

Suddenly she noted dislodged bricks in the wall of a building just as she was passing one of the old industrial-sized bins. It was enough for goblin eyes to see a weak wall and a possible escape route. Alinea ducked faster than a human eye could follow behind the old wheelie bin and climbed into the opening, hoping that it would go all the way through the wall. Enough bricks had been broken to make tearing out the last of the material of the interior wall reasonably easy. She worked at the bricks and plaster quickly now that she was out of the line of her followers' sight, but there would not be much time before they were upon her. She heard two sets of feet running in the alley now. Whoever had been at the other end of the alley had noted her disappearance and come to join Latham.

Latham was well-known among the goblins, not least of all to Alinea as Talla had warned her about the brutal man long ago. Alinea had noted his presence, lurking in the camp. She did not have to turn and look to surmise that it was he who had followed her. His hatred for the goblins had caused trouble in the past. It was that hatred that Alinea felt from him now. Nothing but bloodlust could feel so strong. It was this that made him dangerous.

Alinea broke through to the inside of the building, keeping the opening in the wall just big enough for her small figure to slip through. The men would be slowed by having to break a larger hole to crawl through without tools. With the freedom to run unobserved, she flew from one room to another, looking for stairs. She would be able to leap up them too fast for her human pursuers to follow and could travel across the rooftops if necessary, but she did not know the layout of the inside of the building. She quickly became confused. Her sense of direction was intact but she didn't know where one wall would open to another and could not decipher the logic of the seemingly random doors that might lead to a small enclosed room as easily as to a main corridor. Precious time was lost as she opened one door after another until she finally found one that led to a fairly open space that she could cross quickly.

This only led to more small enclosed rooms. Worse, these had no windows. Alinea began to feel trapped within the labyrinth.

At last she opened a door to a long corridor that had windows all along one side. Stairs were visible at the end, just through another door that had glass next to it so that she could see them through the barrier. She ran, moving swiftly with her bare feet. They flapped on the tiled floor like proper goblin feet, one of the few features that marked her as what she was. Among humans, they would only be perceived as fairly large feet as long as no one examined the toes closely.

Alinea slammed herself into the door, expecting it to open. It didn't. Some form of locking mechanism kept it solidly in place. The glass on either side was too narrow to slip through, even for her small frame. She looked at the larger windows along the wall of the corridor, speculating on how much force it would take to break one and the certainty that the shatter of breaking glass would give away her position.

Then she spied a locking mechanism on the window itself. She climbed up the window frame using the suckers on the bottom of her feet. There was no point in pretending to be human now. She quickly worked out the mechanism and the window swung open, allowing her to drop to the foliage below. The fresh air smelt good. She was in a courtyard area and still confined by walls, but the long grass and weeds gave her a form of cover that was more familiar to her and offered better possibilities for concealment.

Still, she would be visible from above. She could not just sit here and wait for them to give up the chase, but climbing the walls would make her too visible from all directions. Alinea didn't like the idea of re-entering the building. It was too confusing inside and she felt much more comfortable standing on actual earth, yet it was the logical course of action. Small windows at ground level on the opposite side of the courtyard led to lower rooms in the building. Alinea decided to crawl though one of them and see if she could either find a good hiding place or find her way to a window leading to the street where she could escape. A goblin could sit for long periods of time when it was necessary.

Her instinct told her to hide. As she crawled through one of the windows, she saw a large desk with a comfortable looking space beneath it as well as a partially open cabinet that she could fit inside. The men could not possibly search every space in the large building, yet if they happened to enter that particular room she would be trapped in either of the spaces. Her precognitive sense screamed at her to hide, but her logic could not accept being cornered.

She made her way quietly to the door and opened it soundlessly just a little to peer outside. There was no scent or sound of the humans. She opened the door a little further and sniffed carefully. Still no sign of them. Alinea made her way through another labyrinth of rooms that was designed very similarly to those she had passed through before. Following the memory of that pattern, she found herself looking at the street at last through another wall of large windows.

Again, her instinct pressed her towards concealment. There were many ways through the openings from one room to another, but Alinea didn't know them well enough, even with her exceptional memory for pathways, to feel comfortable. She wanted the freedom of the outside world, away from the confining walls. She had never felt so claustrophobic in the caverns, but she knew her way through those and even the secrets of their design that would allow her to find passages in grottos where she had never travelled. The ways of ancient humans were a mystery to her.

The stench of humans came to her nostrils. At least one of them was nearby. Alinea could not determine whether they had simply passed this way or were still lurking, but the possibility that they might catch her unaware within the confusing walls pushed her decision to get out. She regarded the window as opposed to a door that appeared to lead out to the street. A human would certainly choose the door and that could be her one defence if she were to be observed. Her feet made no sound as she crept across the room and opened it gradually as she had done with the other door, sniffing and sending her awareness out before her.

There was no sign of movement outside. Still, the human scent was uncomfortably close. The entrance to Lirrewot was not far, she would be safe there. If she were to run at full speed, no human could catch her. She would just have to avoid trees or other hiding places where someone might conceal themselves. The street before her offered far too many such places, but running down the middle to avoid every doorway and obstacle would make her extremely visible. She spied an alleyway across the road, just a few sprints away. The chances that someone would be hiding in that particular place were slim, but not impossible. If she were to dart left to make use of the cover of the wall and then leap across the road into the alley, she would all but disappear in a flash. She decided to risk it.

One bounce off the wall would give her the momentum she needed. She opened the door the rest of the way, cringing at the subtle sounds despite knowing that human ears could not hear the soft grinding of grit in hinges. She gave herself two strides across the room to build speed and one across the threshold from which she bounced back to push with both feet against the wall of the door she had just shot through... and right into the swinging club of a man who had stepped from just around the corner of the building. Her last thought was that she should have listened to her instinct.

'Is she dead?' Matthew asked as Zak picked up his crumpled prize.

Zak listened to the soft whisper of her breath.

'She's breathing. Hell of a bash in the head though, I never saw anything move so fast.'

'Good job swinging round the wall like that, I'd call it a lucky hit.' Matthew glinted at his companion, sharing in the pride of the hunter. 'At least Latham was right, she had to come out sometime.'

Zak frowned as he gazed at the limp girl in his arms.

'She really does look human. I hope he knows what he's doing.'

Just then Latham appeared from around the same corner that Zak had rounded to block Alinea's leap to freedom.

'The demons are deceptive, don't let her appearance fool you.' He looked down at the angelic face of a young girl. She resembled Count Anton far too much to elicit sympathy from Latham.

'Let's get her across the river before someone sees her. Matthew, can we wrap her in your coat?'

Matthew nodded in compliance and removed his coat, wrapping it around the body of the goblin girl.

'She ain't dressed decent anyway, I reckon we better get your missus to look after her.'

Latham nodded and took Alinea from Zak as all three men turned towards the river, slinking away in the growing darkness of night.

Chapter Eighteen

Esther had never been entirely happy when Latham had insisted that they move to the Southern side of the river. It wasn't so much that she was required to dress more modestly than she had done before, but there was so much expectation of conformity in small ways that made it difficult to quite grow accustomed to all of it.

She had attended worship services in their old life, but there were subtle differences here. It was as if instead of worshipping their God with love in their hearts, they were constantly given sermons that felt angry and demanding, her new acquaintances closing their hearts to her old neighbours across the river for their tolerance of those who were different and especially towards the magicians, even their ruler Count Anton himself.

She had been expected to cook for functions decreed by a group that surrounded their minister and to participate in events for which she had no interest, showing a face of kindness to what felt like a hierarchy of women comprised of the other Southern wives, some of whom she did not like at all. They were haughty and self-important within their little community, at least until their husbands came home when they turned into snivelling chattels to their men. Not least of all among the local customs that Esther despised was the assumption that she would comply with her husband's wishes, no matter what.

This time Latham had gone too far. Esther wasn't sure if she was more outraged that he had kidnapped a young girl, or at the thought that he had saddled her with the responsibility of what he explained was the goblin abomination that they had all thought killed so many years ago. If the girl was indeed part goblin, Esther was frightened for herself and their children, should the whelp's goblin kin come to rescue her. If Latham was mistaken and the girl was no more than just a human child, then Esther herself was now an accomplice to a heinous crime.

The goblin girl looked innocent enough in her unconscious state. She was even rather pretty. It was not difficult to imagine that she really was the daughter of the handsome Count Anton, but that gave Esther even more concern. Count Anton might come to get her himself if he got wind of where she had been taken.

Alinea stirred. Latham had said not to speak with her, but as the girl looked up with those large, multi-coloured eyes, Esther could not help thinking that there could be no harm in responding to a few simple questions. No doubt the captured girl would ask where she was and what had happened to her.

Esther was surprised when instead of waking slowly, the first glance up was followed by the girl springing into a fighting position and looking around quickly at her surroundings. Now it was easier to imagine her as a goblin as she crouched, looking as though she might leap and attack at any second. Her eyes flashed with anger and defensiveness. Her hands were held as if they had claws at the ends of the delicate fingers, instead of the ordinary human fingernails that Esther could see. Most frightening was the low snarl that came from her slightly open mouth. Esther feared that she could take a nasty bite from this wild girl.

'Please,' Esther pleaded, hoping the girl would understand her language. 'Don't hurt the children.'

Alinea whipped her head round, noting the hallway behind her that appeared to lead to other rooms. The door to freedom lay just behind the woman who was apparently placed to guard her. She could see the outside world beckoning through curtain-framed windows.

'Go to your children, woman. I will not stop you.' Alinea's tone was authorative. Both women knew the goblin girl had the superior strength of will, although Esther was unaware of the physical strength that came with Alinea's goblin heritage.

Esther's instinct was to run to her children as commanded, but she could see the girl eyeing the door. There was no doubt that if Esther stepped out of the way, the wild girl would escape quickly.

'I was charged to keep you here. If I move, you'll escape.'

Alinea could see the woman trembling as she tried to persuade herself to maintain her guard despite her fear. Alinea admired her courage. Many human women would have crumpled and run away before now, but escape was imperative. There was no time to sympathise with the frightened human.

'Nothing you can do will prevent that. I will not be your prisoner.'

Esther hesitated. Alinea's confidence began to seem incongruous from a girl who appeared to be no more than twelve or thirteen. *Perhaps I can reason with her*, she thought to herself. Esther had a certain strength of her own that allowed her to survive her marriage to a man such as Latham. She wondered if a half-human child could have a soul. Perhaps the girl could even be redeemed. Esther held her position in front of the door as she tried to speak soothingly.

'There is no need for all this upset. Won't you sit down and speak with me a while? I have heard that your... your people... are friendly to us and even helped us win the war with the invaders.'

Alinea was not fooled by the delaying tactic. She looked at the colour of the night through the window, assessing how long she had been unconscious. She did not know where the men had gone or what their customary habits might be, but there was no doubt that they would return all too soon.

She flopped down on the floor, sitting cross-legged. She could play this game... for a little while.

'So be it,' Alinea declared. 'Let us speak to each other. What would you have us speaking about? Be careful, woman, I am told I am a bad influence.'

Alinea's open stare as she spoke was disconcerting. Esther struggled to think of some way to keep her distracted long enough for Latham and the other men to return.

'Perhaps we can speak about you,' Esther hazarded. 'You look very human to me, though they tell me you are only half. Surely you must have a soul, a need to find spiritual peace in your life?'

Alinea looked at the woman curiously, cocking her head as the question hung in the air.

'You surprise me, woman. What is your name?'

'I am Esther,' came the reply. 'Wife of Latham.'

'I thought as much. I am Alinea of Krapneerg. You are correct of course, I am half human, though that is not unusual among my people, and I lead a deeply spiritual life as we all do who live close to the Earth. Have you ever danced?'

Esther was openly shocked by the direct question, as well as the implication that cross breeding was not unique to this girl.

'Certainly not! Dancing is forbidden, it stirs carnal desires... '

'You see such desires as unsuitable? The pattern of life; birth, breeding, death... is part of nature. You breed.' Alinea nodded towards the corridor leading to the children's bedrooms. 'Why not enjoy dancing as well?'

Esther hesitated a moment. She wished the minister was here to help answer such questions.

'Humans breed within the sanctity of marriage. Desire is for animals.'

Alinea snorted.

'Breeding and giving birth are no more tidy for having enclosed them within social customs. Do you not allow yourself the joy of feeling life as it begins?'

'I find joy in obedience to God,' Esther returned quickly. 'And in caring for my children. The pleasures you hint at are sinful. We are meant to resist the temptation to descend into animal lust and other such gratification, including dancing. In doing so, we can be sure of our reward in Heaven.'

Again, Alinea cocked her head as she looked for some form of logic in the woman's self-denial.

'And in your Heaven, you will be allowed the pleasures you have deemed as sinful in life? Or will you find pleasure in continued denial?'

Again, Esther struggled to find an answer for the wild girl's questions, but Alinea continued expressing her radical ideas.

'Sanctity is found in expression of the natural rhythms of life, of the Earth. We dance to celebrate what we are... creatures of nature. Human and goblin are essentially no different in this. Humans can dance, humans can know pleasure, yet many deny themselves for an abstract idea of a personified deity from ancient mythologies that were distorted by men to gain control of their tribes long ago. There is no spiritual benefit in self-denial, apart from the occasional fast or temporary abstention that is practised by the magicians of both our peoples.'

This was too much. Esther drew back, her face contorting into a mask of self-righteous fear and anger.

'You are possessed by demons!' she screeched abrasively.

'My good woman,' Alinea answered calmly as she stood up. 'I *am* the demon!'

Alinea walked languidly towards Esther, holding steady eye contact in a hypnotic manner that weakened the woman until she collapsed to her knees, whimpering. Alinea continued walking towards her, maintaining awareness of the proximity of the door just behind the woman in her peripheral vision. Any second she could sprint and run...

The door flew open and three men stepped inside as Esther screamed.

'Nooooo!'

Alinea felt the woman's arms wrap around her leg when she would have leapt past her captors. She nearly turned to bite, then thought to save that weapon for the men who had more strength. Latham strode in quickly, followed closely by Matthew and Zak. Alinea thrashed but even her strength was not enough to fight off four pairs of hands as her arms and legs were restrained by all of them at once. They lifted her off the floor and held her as she struggled in frustration, grunting as she pulled first one limb and then another to no avail.

Zak had the other leg besides the one Esther still held securely. The goblin furs left most of their length exposed.

'Latham, this girl is marriageable age and I have no wife. You don't suppose...'

'Don't be stupid,' Latham growled to Zak. 'She is half goblin! She would eat you before she would lie with you. We must kill her, now!'

Matthew looked at the struggling girl from his position holding an arm while Latham secured the other. Her childish appearance softened his heart so that he tried speaking to Latham reasonably.

'What do the details of her bloodlines matter? Can you look on her and not see that she is inescapably human? Our own laws forbid murder.'

Latham's exasperated response brooked no argument.

'She is a wild animal and an abomination. She should have died with her mother years ago. We cannot be weak over appearances, she is demon spawn.'

Esther looked at the girl sadly. As she opened her mouth to speak, Latham rolled his eyes expecting the weakness of a woman to defend the repugnant half-breed, but the soft words of his wife surprised him.

'She spoke blasphemy. My husband is right. There is no redemption for such a creature.'

The men looked at her, then at each other. Slowly, each of them nodded in agreement. The demon must be destroyed.

NAMAH WAS STILL SITTING outside the marquee as Count Anton emerged, scanning the immediate area for any sign of Haghuf or Talla. The light had long since failed so that she had put her drawing materials away and sat in the moonlight thinking wistfully of Ja'imos.

'Did you see Haghuf come this way?' Anton asked Namah. 'Or a female goblin with white hair?'

Namah stood to speak with Count Anton.

'Goblins have a way of getting about unnoticed in the dark and I've been attending to my drawing, but there is something else of importance that you should know about. I am concerned for Alinea.'

Anton turned and gave the girl his full attention.

'What of... Alinea?' He stopped to correct himself as he had been about to refer to her as *my daughter*. The unspoken words echoed in his mind.

'She was followed, over there, just as the sun was going down.' Namah pointed to the derelict buildings and the alley where Alinea had led her pursuers. 'She felt anger and hostility near us and I thought it might be directed at me because there are a few Southern men here, but they followed her. It was Latham and his men.'

Anton felt the adrenaline course through his system at the mention of Latham's name. He looked in the direction that Namah had indicated as every muscle in his body twitched, waiting for instructions from his brain to run or shift. Wolf could track her, yet Anton needed to retain his sense of logic. Time could be lost following an old trail and if she hadn't given them the slip in ways that even his wolf senses couldn't follow, there was only one place that Latham could take her.

'Namah, find Dani,' Count Anton commanded. 'Tell him what you've told me and tell him that I'm going across the river. If you see any goblins, *any* of them, tell them too.'

With that, Anton rested his hand on the goblin sword at his side as he bent down to give Namah a kiss on the cheek, then he sprang towards the river. Namah touched her cheek where the Count had kissed her, lost in a childhood dream for a moment. Then she turned to look for Dani. Before she had taken a second step she ran into Alaric emerging from the darkness.

'Alaric! Where are your friends, the diggers? We need help.'

Alaric's eyes darted in all directions as he turned a moment to look behind himself as if to find the diggers still following him, then he turned back to answer Namah.

'They left me here a while ago and filled the tunnel we came through. I've had time to wash, as you can see.'

Alaric half bowed, presenting his properly clean appearance to his friend with a proud grin.

'So what is this help we require?'

'We need to know if Alinea got away. Latham was following her. Count Anton is crossing the river to look for her. I have to tell Dani.' Namah turned one way and the other as she tried to decide which direction to go first. Alaric put his hands on her shoulders.

'First calm yourself, Namah Remember what you've learned.'

Namah nodded affirmation then closed her eyes, taking a deep breath. She pulled her shoulders down to stretch her neck muscles as she exhaled slowly, willing her body into a controlled, relaxed state that would allow her to think clearly.

'I've called Drazek and Alinea before, just with the power of thought and sending out awareness. I must keep my promise to Count Anton and then we can seek our friends among the goblins.' Namah spoke with confidence now that she had decided what to do.

'Come on then, Dani is just on the other side of the marquee,' Alaric said enthusiastically as he grabbed Namah's hand and pulled her after him. They ran around the makeshift hospital and spotted Dani speaking to a small group of men. Namah recognised two of them as Southerners.

Alaric noted Namah's unconscious hesitation as her steps refused to walk right into the group.

'Do you want me to deliver the message?'

Namah looked into the kind eyes, so much like his father's. For a moment she wondered if his teasing about marriage could ever become real intent.

'Yes,' she answered. She described exactly what had happened and what Count Anton had said, then retreated to a shadowy place beneath a tree as the children often did at the bonfires. As she sat on the moist grass she sent her awareness into the ground, seeking contact with Drazek. She felt nothing in response.

Alaric returned with a serious expression on his face that Namah had never seen on him before. He looked all too much like his father when the Count was puzzling out a problem.

'Alaric, we need to dance!' Namah exclaimed before the boy could speak. 'Not here so close to people, but there are other green places along the river. Come!'

Namah sprang up and pulled Alaric along by both hands.

'Did you tell Dani everything?' she asked, then she noticed his expression. 'What's wrong?'

Alaric looked at her sadly.

'I've learned something, that's all. But it will have to wait, you're right. We must dance to call the goblins and haste may be essential to rescue Alinea. We can speak of other things when she is found. Let's go.'

The children held hands as they ran together down the path by the river. The night stillness was broken only by the gentle lapping of small waves on the river shore and the soft chirping of crickets that took no notice of the light steps of children as they ran in their soft leather boots. They did not have to run far before they found a patch of greenery far enough from the camp to escape observation in the partial moonlight as they reached into the Earth with their minds, finding the rhythm that would take them naturally into *The Dance*.

'ESTHER, GO DOWN TO the basement and get a machete,' Latham ordered.

His wife looked up at him with fear in her eyes as she continued to hold the goblin girl's struggling leg.

'They're gone, Latham, all the weapons and the liquor too. I figure those invaders had a good raid while we were away from our homes.'

Latham swore, then looked at Matthew.

'Your arm is strongest and we've got the weapons we took with us. If we hold her down on the wood block outside you could cut off her head.'

Alinea went limp. Struggling wasn't working so a little subterfuge was in order. Meanwhile, Matthew's face had lost all it's blood at the suggestion of what Latham wanted him to do. Latham was correct that Matthew was the strongest of them, yet Latham was the instigator. Alinea looked from one to the other, assessing which would be better to incapacitate first. She would only get one shot at it.

'Latham, I don't know that I can do this,' Matthew whined.

Alinea noted the weakness. Latham it was then. Take out the leader and the followers would crumple. Zak and Esther she could fight on even terms easily enough.

Latham glared derisively at Matthew as he struggled to open the door with one hand while holding onto Alinea's arm with the other. She shut her eyes quickly just as he looked down at her, hoping that he would believe she had fainted.

She heard the door slam open and felt herself carried several steps as Latham derided Matthew.

'That kind of cowardly talk could get us killed. We're in it now, the goblins would come after us all if she got away and told them. She ain't human! Don't fall for that goblin glamour trick.'

Suddenly Latham swore again as Alinea heard the voice of Count Anton.

'Latham!'

The sound of swords being drawn followed and Alinea made a fast decision. She jerked loose from Latham's hold as he was distracted by drawing his sword and pulled Matthew's arm to her mouth, biting deeply into his flesh. At the same time she kicked wildly against her other captors.

Latham's sword rang against the steel of Anton's goblin sword. Alinea dismissed Latham as out of the picture for the moment and concentrated on her struggle with Zak and Esther, but Esther lost her hold as she saw the bite on Matthew's arm and the way he staggered back, falling into some form of paralysis.

Alinea silently thanked her mother's people for the venom that had been passed down to her, a trait of the *Kol'ksu* that was used both as a weapon and in their mating rituals. Esther backed away in her fear of the alien creature which left only Zak. He drew his sword, but looked unsure of himself against the angry glare of a girl who could flatten his strongest cohort with her bite. Alinea knew that she could only paralyse one man before the venom was spent and would need time to collect in her glands again, but the man didn't know this.

Still, the tiny fangs that transferred the venom might have a little toxin left, and pulling her lips back as far as she could to hiss at the shaken man played on his fear as he saw their points halfway back in her otherwise human-looking set of teeth.

His eyes widened, but it was not Alinea's teeth that drew his gaze and caused the look of terror to take over his face. Esther also looked suddenly petrified and both pairs of eyes rose and looked above Alinea's head. Cautiously, Alinea turned, still positioned to spring. It was then that she noticed that the clanging of swords had stopped. She understood why as the scene behind her came into view. Latham and Anton were standing, mouths open, staring at the same creature that had captivated the others' attention. Standing just in front of the men and towering over them was a dragon.

Chapter Nineteen

'Why have we come here?' Talla asked Haghuf as she looked around herself. Rows of wood bookcases lined the walls of Count Anton's library. Talla had seen the room only once before, when the housekeeper had attempted to lock her in after guards had captured her on the castle grounds when the first conflict had occurred long ago. They had thought Talla was human as she had kept her green skin covered with a borrowed cloak. The wall outside the window had proven easy to scale for goblin feet and hands... up or down.

'There is something I must know.' Haghuf kept his face very close to the book spines as he read across the titles along the bookcase shelves. The walls held bookcase after bookcase, yet Haghuf read quickly as he searched for something that might lead him to the information he sought.

'Tell me what you seek and I will help,' Talla offered.

Haghuf stopped, thinking a moment, then turned to Talla.

'I had forgotten that you can read as well as I, but it is your aetherial senses that could be of most use for this. I seek a book of magic.' Haghuf touched the amulet that he wore, identical to the amulet worn by Count Anton. 'One that will tell the history of this trinket.'

'As you taught me the skill yourself,' Talla began as she reached out to touch the amulet, 'I know that you appreciate that the ability to read provides meat for the Storytelling. Why else would so many of our people learn?'

Talla touched the purplish stone embedded in the silver necklace lightly and closed her eyes, then opened them again as she turned to see a wooden box sitting in the corner of the room. She began to walk towards it, but felt some sort of resistance and stopped. Haghuf stepped up beside her.

'I feel it too,' he said in his matter of fact tone. 'It is like the resistance in the last turn to Le'ina's pool, a protection spell of some kind.'

Haghuf began to step deliberately forward, pushing his way through the resistance. Talla reached forward, shaping her hands like claws.

'If it is like the magic of my mother's people, I should be able to bypass it.' Talla reached with her mind, seeking a path between the tendrils of magic she could feel. She stepped forward, passing Haghuf.

'Just don't disable it,' Haghuf cautioned. 'We must leave this place untouched.'

Talla nodded slightly to acknowledge the warning, but kept stepping forward until she reached the box. To her surprise, she found it unlocked. Apparently the Count relied on the protection spell to guard whatever secrets lay within. She opened the lid easily and scrutinised what she found inside. Old, hand-bound books dominated the right hand side of the contents while the left side was stacked with odd items that reeked of magic. There was a metal chalice, a dagger with symbols carved upon it, a folded cloth with other symbols embroidered on it that Talla recognised as symbolic of the moon and stars, metal candle holders and a supply of fresh candles, and various other items buried under those she saw near the top of the pile. It was the books that interested her.

Many were leather bound, with no title showing anywhere on the cover. Talla flipped through the pages of the first few books, then stopped when she saw a drawing of the amulet on a page.

'This may be the one.' She turned towards Haghuf, noting that he hadn't come much closer. She stepped towards him and handed him the book, then went back to look through others as Haghuf settled down on the rug to read. It was a thick book and looked as if it would take some time to read all of it. Talla amused herself looking through the secret magic of humans for a while, but soon became weary of the subject and longed to be back in the caverns.

She moved towards the window, looking out at the quiet night beyond. The moon was bright and illuminated the land within view as well as the endless sky. Talla saw a shape that she recognised moving silently in the stillness. She knew then that something more was afoot among humans from the events of the day.

'I can come back if you need my help to replace the book, but I think Anton will return soon.'

She turned to see Haghuf nod acknowledgment, then slipped over the window ledge to climb down the familiar side of the tower. Talla decided that it was best not to tell Haghuf what she had seen or where she was going. She had learned early in life that that the *Kol'ksu*, like the dragons, must never be mentioned aloud to the land-dwelling goblins except in extreme circumstances. Haghuf's casual mention of Le'ina's cavern had been out of character for the old goblin. Talla made no mention of her mother's people in the river as she went to them now. They were the only other thing in this world besides the dragons that Haghuf had good reason to fear.

ANTON HAD ONLY JUST begun entering into the dance of swordplay with murder in his heart. The goblin sword led him smoothly through the hypnotic spirals of movement that he had learned to associate with the talisman. The sword swirled in an arc that met Latham's blade and swung back easily to block a kick, slicing a line of blood into the side of Latham's calf. Anton had been intent on the fury within his soul as he had seen his daughter's danger, then on another down swing a feeling of foreboding led him to turn to see the dragon.

His emotions swirled into a maelstrom of confusion; he had felt anger when he first saw the Southerners dragging Alinea away with ill intent, fear that he would be too late, as he had been the last time he had seen her thrown to what was meant to be her death when she had been only an infant, but not least of all, the questioning... what could Alinea do to defend herself?

Anton had never been told how the baby Alinea had survived being thrown into the river with the creatures that had eaten grown men. Talla had shown him that his daughter lived, but she had never explained how. Haghuf was always reticent about giving out information about the goblins. Now, when the one clear thing in his mind was that Latham was the enemy and must be destroyed, Anton found himself looking into the eyes of a dragon.

The dragons had helped in the battle with foreign invaders, yet this seemed to be a matter of feeding on those who had been most in reach of their fearsome claws. Anton felt no particular loyalty from the dragon. He hadn't even had that of the goblins who had fought beside him.

Both men stood frozen, but Anton's thoughts were racing. Was it a stray? Did the goblins have some way of controlling the dragons? Did his sword have any special power for this? Would the dragon simply choose a victim at random, or eat them all?

An eternity seemed to pass as the two men waited for something to happen as if they had no will of their own. The other humans had disappeared, either into the house or far beyond it, apart from

Matthew who was coming out of the temporary paralysis and struggled to crawl back to the relative safety of Latham's home. The dragon sat still, regarding them all and softly snorting. Anton's blade was held up, partly because that was where it had happened to be when he had seen the dragon and he hadn't moved, but also because some instinct drove him to hold it up as a talismanic shield.

At last the dragon nudged its nose forward to sniff the goblin sword. The crystalline glare of its eye was unreadable as Anton looked up into its soft glow. He hadn't realised how hypnotised he had been by that glow until his daughter's voice broke the spell.

'Jezza! Get the ball.'

A ball made of skins rolled past Anton's foot to the dragon's claw just a step in front of him. The massive head came down, nudging the ball with its snout. Every instinct Anton had told him to run and to shout at Alinea that she should disappear down a goblin passage, but she ran straight towards the dragon as she intercepted the ball that it nudged back towards her.

'Whatever you do, don't run,' she ordered her father.

Latham, however, had not heard the instruction. With the spell broken by the dragon playing with the ball, he lunged forwards and shoved his sword into the ground just in front of Anton and pushed the Count forwards so that he tripped, falling in front of the massive jaws. Jezza's mouth opened in a snarl, but his eye was trained on Latham. Latham screamed and ran.

Jezza reacted instantly. He sprang into the air and lifted Latham with claws embedded deeply into the human prey's shoulders. Latham screamed louder from pain and fear as rivulets of blood dribbled down his legs, flowing from the deep gouges in his torso where dragon claws had been embedded into his flesh. Jezza flew low, just above the tree tops and circled round towards the river with his prey. Anton tried to run to follow.

'No, Anton,' Alinea insisted. The panic in her voice was sufficient to stop him in his tracks. 'We must leave here, now!'

Anton heard a low shuffling in the brush. The gait suggested creatures like the diggers, whom he had seen only once before. Alinea picked up the ball and grabbed Anton's hand, pulling him away from the house and further to the south, away from the river. He followed without question.

The stillness of the night was broken by the screams of a man as the dragon that carried him dipped near to the surface of the river. Those who lived north of the river heard little and chose to ignore what might have been the inhuman cry of a bird... or something else. They had returned to their homes now and wished to rest and enjoy the company of their families, now restored to them.

There was no one to witness the silhouettes of the creatures in the river as their shapes broke above the surface to feed on the morsel the dragon offered to them. Like the land goblins, the *Kol'ksu* did not mark time, but there were few among them old enough to remember the last time a dragon had brought them meat in such a way. They ripped off his clothing with sharp claws, feasting on the flesh they could reach until he was naked and sufficiently bloodied, his legs gone from the thighs downward. Then the dragon swallowed what was left of him. Latham had long since stopped screaming.

ANTON FOLLOWED ALINEA into the opening for Oolretaw Grotto. It was a grotto that he had never visited, as were all those south of the river with only one exception, an unmarked cavern that might have been used only for *Those Who Protect* to gather when the goblins had fought humans on the Southern lands a decade before. There was no formality at the entrance as he would have expected from Haghuf and no way to predict what sort of reception he would receive from any goblins they might encounter, but Anton trusted Alinea implicitly and followed as quickly as he was physically able.

They saw no one as they descended the stairs of the old underground train station, yet Anton felt eyes on them. He had replaced the goblin sword into its sheath before they had entered the station, but any eyes that followed their progress would see the handle showing distinctively outside of the protective cover as well as Alinea leading him through the goblin territory. Human as she might look, the goblins always knew their own.

As soon as they were past the human-built structures and into goblin-dug caverns, Alinea stopped to allow Anton a chance to get his breath. He gasped heavily for a few minutes before he felt able to speak.

'You called the dragon by name...'

Quickly Alinea moved forward and pressed her fingertips to Anton's lips.

'We do not mention the dragons, ever,' Alinea whispered. The urgency in her words imparted to Anton that this was no small matter. He nodded to show that he understood.

'Where did you get the ball?' he whispered back.

'Drazek was in the trees, you won't have seen him. He brought it with him.' Alinea turned to lead Anton further.

He still had many questions, but there would be no answers within the caverns. Anton had had many lessons over the years about goblin secrecy. To be allowed into the caverns at all was pushing things enough. Discussing their mysteries openly would be too much to ask of the watching eyes. Anton considered that next full moon bonfire night on the surface he would ask them separately – Haghuf and Alinea. Perhaps he could piece together some information between the answers he received from each.

For the moment he kept his eyes and other senses active, taking in the sights and sounds of a goblin grotto that he had never before traversed. He listened closely for any hint of drumming. It had been some time since he had last enjoyed *The Dance*. However, he heard nothing other than the sound of his own booted footfalls. Even Alinea's steps made no sound as she passed through her own world. Anton was suddenly struck by the realisation that he was in fact in his daughter's company in her own world for the first time. There was much of her life as she had grown up that he would never know.

The caverns grew dark. As much as caverns were always dark, a complete blackness engulfed them as they travelled further downwards. Anton could see nothing and had to rely on his fingers brushing along the wall to his right to follow the path. His wolf senses felt the open space of the cavern before him, yet he could not be sure if any side passages might have gone by on the other side as they travelled forwards. His fingers reached no openings. The scent ahead was dank and musty as the echo of his own boot steps became the only clear indication that the passage continued forwards.

Anton began to wonder if Alinea was still with him, when suddenly her soft fingers entwined with his and she led him away from the comfort of the solid wall, presumably into one of the side passages on the left that he could not see. Slowly, light began to penetrate the darkness. It was no more than a soft glow at first, then shapes began to become apparent in the darkness and soon Anton was able to see the walls. A staircase leading off to the side told him that they had reached another old underground train station. He felt no eyes following him now. They had come to a station that appeared to be completely derelict.

The rails had long since been scavenged as they had been throughout the underground network, but the walls of the station itself were completely in ruins. Anton and Alinea emerged from a tunnel into what had once been a platform for passengers waiting for the train in the human civilisation of Anton's ancestors. It was still dark as no lights illuminated the platform as they would have done in that other age. Still, Anton's eyes had adjusted through the complete darkness so that the minimal light that glowed from the world above supplied enough visibility to take in the ancient artefacts.

The platform was lined with benches and posters on the wall, now torn and yellowed with age. One of them showed a map of the network of underground trains that had once provided transport in what was then a large city. Anton noted the goblin grottos he knew, automatically reading the names of the places backwards as the goblins would do. It had become habit to reverse the words as their world had become so familiar to him.

A sign on the wall proclaimed the station they stood in now. This one he read forwards as there was no grotto here. *Westminster*. It was a name that hailed from an age gone past when the city had been called *London*. That city was long decayed, and only the civilisation that Anton's people had built near the castle and the settlement just across the river remained to bear witness that men had ever lived here, along with these artefacts of a dead city.

Anton felt weary. He knew now that the dark caverns had taken them beneath the river and back to the Northern shore. There would be a long walk still to come when they reached the surface. Anton hoped that it would not be obstructed by dragons.

DANI STOOD AMONG THE magicians in Count Anton's receiving room, watching the door. He exchanged a look with Laura, who also looked too frequently for any sign of their leader's return. The Countess Ariane helped Jerak to serve refreshment to their guests. She glanced at the doors frequently, anxious for her husband's return, like the others.

A momentary ripple of excitement surged through the gathered assembly as the big double doors started to move, but it was only

Namah who entered. Alaric bounded up to her quickly, speaking in a whisper.

'Have you heard or seen anything? Have you spoken to Drazek?' Namah shook her head.

'He assured us he could find Alinea after he came to us in response to our dance, but I do not know what he planned.' She took Alaric's hands and pulled him to a corner away from the adults to speak to him seriously.

'Alaric, twice I've seen him in control of dragons and I'm sure I saw the shape of one flying across the river tonight.'

Alaric thought for a moment, looking very much like his father when the Count was puzzling out a situation. After a moment he appeared to come to a conclusion.

'If Drazek has some control of the dragons, he is better armed than any opponent he or my father might be facing. Also the goblins will surely be on our side in this. Alinea is one of theirs. We must wait, and try not to worry.'

Namah was not sure if the reassurance was more for her benefit or for his own. The marks of worry were on the boy prince's face. For a moment, it was easy to forget how young he was and see the ruler that he was destined to become. A few lines of the song that Namah had heard round the bonfire came back to her then, from *The Saga of Alaric*.

> *...Alaric took his place with his people*
> *Their spirit only leadership could bring*
> *Neither gold nor riches made a tribe thrive*
> *Alaric wore the mantle as their king...*

Namah thought about that first full moon bonfire, the night she had first seen Ja'imos. She gazed towards the window now, wondering where he was and whether he had taken any part in the war with the invaders.

'Look,' Alaric said suddenly. The old playful note was back in his voice. 'I see Damon over there.'

Namah looked across the room where Alaric indicated. Their young friend was standing with his magician parents, laughing at some joke amongst the conversation. They started to move towards him when the big double doors moved to open again. Count Anton stepped inside. The tiredness showed behind the familiar grin as he greeted his people. The Countess Ariane ignored the dirt on his clothing as she threw her arms around him to welcome him home. A loud cheer grew among the other magicians in the room, expressing pure joy at their leader's return.

Dani strode towards him but was passed by Alaric as he threw himself into his father's arms, just as Anton disengaged from his embrace with Ariane. Anton swung the boy round once, noting that he was becoming too heavy to be picked up so easily. He put his son down and embraced his second in command briefly before speaking.

'Dani, we must speak of important matters.' Count Anton turned to Ariane.

'You and I must also speak privately, as soon as our guests have departed.'

Ariane curtsied to her husband, recognising that he wished to speak with Dani immediately. She returned to attending to their friends, but Alaric stayed by his father's side.

'Father, if you are to discuss matters of state I should stay with you, to learn.'

Anton crouched to speak to his son at eye level.

'Alaric, no ruler is ever entirely prepared when his time comes. You must learn to rule from your head and your heart in balance, and to take good advice from trusted advisers like Dani here. I see one of your own trusted friends is here behind you.'

Alaric turned to see Namah approaching tentatively.

'Namah,' Anton addressed the approaching girl. 'Alinea waits outside. It was your warning that led to her rescue, although I wonder still if she truly needed rescue at all.'

Anton beamed an amused smile at Namah, but his thoughts were of Matthew, whom he had seen suffering the familiar paralysis of a goblin bite. It reminded him of Alinea's conception, as well as the seemingly never-ending surprise defences of the goblins. His own daughter had skills far beyond anything he had anticipated. He found it easy to believe that she might well have fought her way past four humans, including Latham, without his interference.

'Come, Alaric,' Namah entreated. 'Let's go to Alinea.'

'A moment, Alaric.' Count Anton stopped his son with a gentle hand on his shoulder. 'There is one thing I do wish to discuss with you immediately.'

'You go ahead,' Alaric instructed Namah. 'I will bring Damon and any of the others I can find in a few moments.'

Namah nodded goblin style without realising she did so, then scurried quickly out through the big doors to seek her friend outside. It would be a great relief to her to see her well and whole with her own eyes.

'Alaric,' Anton said seriously to his son. 'There is something I have not had a chance to say to Namah. I charge you now to deliver a sad message to her.'

Alaric nodded curtly and awaited his father's instruction, though he guessed the message as he had learned about Rab's death from Dani just before the search for Alinea. Suddenly he looked much older, a young prince who would take important matters seriously. Anton regarded his son with both affection and scrutiny. He was pleased with Alaric's attentiveness when called upon to attend to a serious matter.

'Namah's father was killed in the first raid. He sacrificed himself to help the others in the party to get away.' Anton watched his son's face as the boy assimilated the information. 'I charge you to tell her what has happened, in as gentle a manner as you are able.'

Alaric's eyes penetrated his father's composure so that for a moment, Anton felt as if his son were the stronger ruler and himself only a subject awaiting a pronouncement.

'I will do as you ask, father, as soon as I can arrange a moment alone with her.' Alaric's composure impressed his father. It was easy for Anton to imagine a time when Alaric would be grown and in charge of the kingdom... a kingdom ruled by a king... the time of King Alaric.

Father and son exchanged a formal bow that was no more than a slight bend from the waist. Both were aware of the effect that such a gesture had on those among their people who watched. Then Alaric gave his father a subtle wink and bounded off to find Damon and his other friends.

Anton turned his attention to Dani.

'What's happened to those Southern girls? I don't see any of them here.'

Dani's expression flirted with a sardonic smirk as he replied to the question.

'Most of them returned to their parents. Despite your efforts, they will likely be re-married quickly.'

'They've lost many men, as have we,' Anton speculated.

'Then perhaps they will be married to younger men this time,' Dani returned.

'Let's hope, Dani. Let's hope. If they change the habit of many generations, it will save us changing it for them.' Anton sighed before continuing.

'You said most, what about the others?'

Dani smiled genuinely this time.

'A few of them got to know families in exile and have been adopted as you had hoped. Several sons returned home today to find themselves with new sisters... or potential future wives.'

Anton nodded.

'So we are rid of them one way or another?'

Dani grinned at the relief on Anton's face.

'I do believe you are growing weary of solving problems, Anton. You grow soft in your old age.' Dani winked quickly, smirking at his own joke.

Anton returned a smile, one that was heavy with weariness.

'More than you know, Dani,' he replied after a moment. 'Come, there is a serious matter that we must discuss. It cannot wait.'

The Countess Ariane looked across the room to see her husband leaving with his trusted adviser. She felt her heart sinking as the doors closed behind them. Laura watched them leave also, then looked at Ariane.

A heaviness seemed to fall upon the room. She crossed the floor to go to Ariane. The guests were beginning to leave, a few at a time. Laura helped Ariane to see them out, occasionally resting a supporting hand on Ariane's arm. Nothing was spoken between them, yet both took comfort from the nearness of the other as they shared an inexplicable sense of loss.

Chapter Twenty

Anton hesitated in front of the library door, sensing the familiar presence of Haghuf within. He had become particularly attuned to the presence of his old friend over the years and was beginning to understand a little about the instincts of the goblins.

He opened the door as silently as he could. Anton knew a thing or two about stealth himself. Haghuf sat quietly in the middle of the rug, intent on reading a book. As Anton crept up behind him, he noted that the goblin was reading one of the old Alchemy tomes from the fourteenth century, before the Turning.

Haghuf did not show any surprise as Anton's voice broke the still, evening silence.

'I've often wondered if your people learned writing from these old books of magic, Haghuf.'

Haghuf didn't flinch, or even look up as he replied.

'It goes back farther than that, but you are astute, Anton. The writing in books of magic formed the most recent basis of my people's language and records.'

Damn his enormous goblin ears, Anton thought to himself. *He probably heard me coming from two floors down.*

'The Alchemists wrote their words backwards like that to protect their secrets.'

'Hmph,' Haghuf responded. 'Some secret. It is not so difficult to read a word forwards as easily as backwards, or even scrambled. Your Alchemists depended a lot on the ignorance of their own kind.'

Anton speculated on the literacy of men in an age gone by as he walked around in front of Haghuf.

'Can many goblins read, Haghuf?'

Haghuf looked up with his old suspicious expression at the direct question. Then his eyes went back to the page as he replied.

'About half. Intelligence is a survival tool and the intelligent become curious. Those who wish to read, learn. Others, like Kahjak, see no need when what he chooses to do is better taught by doing.'

There had been a time when Anton would have been surprised at the direct answer, but things had become more open between him and his old friend over time. Still, Anton could not resist pressing for more information whenever he felt the advantage... except this time. He had something else to say to his most trusted friend.

'I'm leaving, Haghuf.'

At this Haghuf looked up at last, but there was still no surprise on his face.

'I know.'

'How could you know that? I've told no one my decision!' Anton was flustered by the goblin's uncanny knack for knowing things that he couldn't and even questioned in his mind whether Haghuf was being entirely honest with him.

'Goblins listen, goblins pay attention.' Haghuf explained. 'You call yourself a Count, and so someone who calls himself a King gives the other humans the power to invade your land. This is why goblins don't use titles. Your son, because you call him Prince, will become King when you are gone. Tell me, Anton, will you someday return and settle down to a trade, as your father did before you?'

Anton flashed his familiar grin.

'You read my mind too well, Haghuf.'

But Haghuf's expression remained serious as he stood and looked Anton in the eye.

'I don't think you will. You like freedom too much, like goblins. I hear you fought back to back with Kralic.'

The sudden change of subject discombobulated Anton more than the first statement. His face contorted as he tried to picture fighting near any goblin that might have been the great warrior, Kralic. He had only fought back to back with one of the trained warriors – the little goblin that he had met before in the caverns, at *The Dance*.

Slowly understanding stole over Anton's face.

'*That* was Kralic?'

A wicked smile slowly spread across Haghuf's face.

'You did not know.' It was a statement rather than a question.

'I never even knew the gender of the little blonde goblin, never mind his name.'

Haghuf looked as if he would laugh at Anton's discomfiture.

'Kralic is *gorna*, like many of the Dunai. I do not know a human word for it... they can change gender. They do not reproduce as do some animals with this ability, but it can make some of the males... more comfortable.'

'You are full of surprises today, Haghuf.'

Haghuf looked at Anton seriously then.

'I have one more.'

Anton watched attentively as Haghuf flipped to a page in the book he had been reading. Haghuf stopped on a page with a drawing of the design of the amulets they both wore. He looked up to watch Anton's reaction.

'There are more of them. They were worn by leaders among your people who travelled in different directions after the Turning, to seek others of your kind who might have survived.'

Anton took in the information, half remembering a time when he had read this same book as a young man. He remembered his horror when he had discovered that the amulets were originally worn by a group of young people who had only played at rank and titles, one of whom was his ancestor Count Victor. Anton mentally noted that the amulet he had retrieved during the battle had been worn by a ranking warrior among the people who had come over the sea from what had once been Europe, not by their king.

'Does it say how many there were?' Anton asked, straining to remember if he had read that information before.

Haghuf shook his head.

'It says only that a sacred number of them was created and that magic was infused into them by a magician among them. There are many sacred numbers. Why did you have two of them?'

'The story that was passed down to me was that Count Victor and his brother both wore them. The one you wear was his brother's.'

Haghuf nodded to acknowledge the information. The gift had always held significance for the bond between them, but the implication of brothers touched Haghuf more than he would show. No one could replace his lost twin, least of all a human, but the bond between Haghuf and Anton had long been closer than anything he had ever shared with one of his own kind since the loss of his twin, save Talla, and perhaps Leap.

'It's my turn to ask a question, Haghuf.'

Haghuf looked at Anton suspiciously. Brother or not, he would always be human... one that asked too many questions about goblins.

'I need to know, Haghuf, are my people in any danger from the dragons?'

Haghuf appeared to flinch, something that Anton had never seen him do before. Then the old goblin shook his head.

'The diggers have to open the caverns wider for them to get out. They are back in their own natural world now, even Jezza.'

'Alinea called a dragon by that name, what is different about him?' Anton had pounced quickly on the slip of information. Haghuf hesitated a moment, struggling between a long habit of silence and the fact that this human had already witnessed the dragons in full flight.

'Only that he is a young one and was kept as a pet by one of our kind. He has grown too big now to run free in the caverns. Drazek has led him to join his own kind again.'

'Why does Drazek have some special power over the dragons?' Anton pressed.

This time, Haghuf turned his back to Anton, refusing to speak for a moment. When he turned back, he spoke with a resolve that suggested that he had prepared exactly how much information to impart before beginning to speak.

'Long ago, you and I discussed theoretical possibilities that may lie behind the legends of both your people and mine.'

Haghuf walked up to Anton, meeting him face to face very close up.

'You are a shapeshifter. Your ability to change between man and wolf is not spoken of openly, but we may speak between us.'

Anton nodded. Some of the magicians knew of his ability, yet Anton had never been told how Haghuf first learned of it or how many of the goblins shared the secret.

'The legend among my people says that those who could change form were affected during a Turning,' Haghuf continued. 'Some bore young ones after radiation from the Earth's changes prevented them from changing back to goblin form, but their young were born with traits of both. Goblins who were part shark became the *Kol'ksu*. Goblins who were part dragon became the first *Foringen*.'

Haghuf made a dismissive gesture and walked a few steps away as he finished his story.

'They are tales for younglings. Still, it is known that among my people... my mother's people... that one who is born with the wings of a dragon has mind-to-mind communication with the dragons. Such a one is Drazek.'

Anton nodded, taking in all that he heard.

'Can Drazek control the dragons then?'

Haghuf shook his head quickly.

'Not control, communicate. I do not know what incentive he used to get them to return to their caves after the battle, but it is only his art of persuasion that has prevented a new threat from taking over your world.'

Anton took a moment to assimilate this, then tried one more question.

'What do the dragons...'

'Do not ask me more about the dragons,' Haghuf barked. 'They are of no danger to you, I can say no more.'

Haghuf appeared to stare off into empty space, as if he were looking within himself.

'Some secrets are buried very deeply indeed.'

Anton watched his friend a moment, letting Haghuf's last words echo in memory before changing the subject.

'Is there anything more of use about the amulets in that book?' He gestured to the tome Haghuf had left lying on the rug. 'I learned much of magic as a child, but there seems to be some shroud of mystery over their power. It is said that the stones were made when the universe first came into being as the result of a giant explosion.'

'Bah!' Haghuf replied quickly in his usual gruff tone. 'The universe was always here, it will always be here. Only the details change. Planets and stars are born and they die like all life, but the universe continues through all time. Time itself is only an illusion – a concept that humans brought to us. We speak of it for convenience, yet it means nothing to the eternal struggle.'

Anton was about to ask what struggle he was referring to when Haghuf changed the subject again.

'Do you remember, Anton, long ago, there was a prophecy. You read it on parchment in my library.'

Anton nodded. He knew the prophecy well and had often ruminated on the meanings within the words.

'I have often wondered,' Haghuf speculated. 'Which of us was meant when it said *One who walks between the worlds*.'

'Perhaps,' Anton conjectured. 'It did not refer to either of us at all. We both walk between the worlds of human and goblin, but there is a greater difference in the shifts of a shapeshifter. Beast and man are alien to each other... of different minds.'

'But it is Drazek who can touch the minds of beasts.' Haghuf finished Anton's speculation. Suddenly Haghuf had another thought.

'Why did you call your son 'Prince' Alaric?'

Anton smirked and shrugged as he replied.

'It sounded better.'

Haghuf chuckled.

'And so the futures of men are written on a whim.'

'You are not so without hierarchy, Haghuf. What of *Those Who Protect*?' Anton accused.

Again, Haghuf walked up and looked Anton in the eye, with their noses nearly touching, before he answered.

'There is a vague form of hierarchy, but not a formal one. The goblins know who has most experience, and whom to follow. Kahjak and Kralic are often consulted in matters of war because they have experience. It is not unlike my own position as a recognised *Wise One*. In nature, it is instinct to follow the *one who knows*.'

Anton thought about this for a few moments as Haghuf slowly backed away, leaving him to work this new idea into his thoughts.

Anton recognised that the opportunity for obtaining information was fading and pressed just one more question.

'Who... how is it decided that it is time for *The Dance?* You have allowed me into the Storytelling more than once, Haghuf, but I have never known what signal decides at the end when it is time to pick up a drum and begin the transition.'

Haghuf nodded to himself human fashion as he formulated a reply in his mind.

'*The Dance* is at the heart of what we are. Some of your religious leaders objected to it because they felt that it stirred sexual responses, but it is so much more than that. Yes, it is so much more than that.'

He paced a few steps away from Anton and turned back to speak to him face to face before he continued.

'*The Dance* decides itself. There is no conscious signal. There is no number of stories to tell before it is time. We just *know*, and then the drummers begin.'

Anton nodded as he unconsciously stroked his chin in thought. A moment passed before his friend's voice penetrated his ruminations again.

'Do you go tonight?'

'The wolf travels at night.' Anton had not realised his intention until he heard the words from his own mouth. 'I must say goodbye to my family. Dani has instructions to act as Regent in case of my disappearance.'

Haghuf bowed to his friend, goblin style.

'I am sure we will meet in the wild places.'

Anton returned the deep, undulating goblin bow.

'If you can, tell your people in the wild Northern places not to eat me.' Anton winked as he finished speaking, but a small part of him wondered if he meant it entirely as a joke. He saw the goblin smile a little before he turned and sat down to read again. It would not occur to Haghuf to politely ask permission to peruse the books of Anton's private library.

Anton turned and walked out, descending the stairs to the room he shared with the Countess Ariane. She, too, would play a part in teaching his son to rule a kingdom. He felt strangely disassociated with her, as if he could not remember loving her. They both knew that he had never stopped loving Talla, but still they had been close once. Now it was as if he had mentally separated her from his life to come, even before he had told her his plans.

Ariane looked up at him as he stepped inside the door. She had been sitting on the bed, waiting for him. Despite his remembered love for her and his own inherent courage, he could not meet her eyes directly. Her penetrating gaze saw through all of his being in a way that was still un-nerving. He could not meet that gaze with his own eyes, but lowered them slightly. She would see all, it was unavoidable.

'Ariane, I've come to a decision. I can't revoke it.'

Ariane looked at him shrewdly, seeing through the nervous exterior into his heart... a heart that she knew all too well. There could be no secrets between them. She already knew what he intended to say next.

'You're leaving,' she said flatly.

Anton nodded, almost imperceptibly. *Does everyone close to me know my thoughts before I know them myself?* He thought silently.

'And I must stay here with our son,' Ariane finished.

Quickly, Anton rushed to embrace her. Ariane stood to meet him, feeling the loss that she knew they must both bear for the good of the people.

'It wont be forever,' Anton continued. 'My own parents came back quietly after a time of exile. We must see each other, the goblins have ways.'

'When my son is established as King, you will have more freedom,' Ariane stated encouragingly. She noted her own words, *my son*. She had already let Anton go in her heart and was prepared herself to raise Alaric alone.

'Yes!' Anton latched onto the advantages without noticing Ariane's reference to her son. 'And the time away will do me good. I can practise my art more, and be a man without a kingdom to serve for a time. I will miss you, but there is no other way. Our son must be king, and he cannot do it while I live within the city. At least it's better than the only alternative.'

Ariane looked down then, but only for a moment. She pulled away from him slightly.

'You will send word of your well-being?' Her tone suggested caring, yet she felt coldness in her heart.

'Yes, of course. It does *not* have to be forever.' Anton repeated.

When Ariane turned and looked at him again, the distance was already there. They were linked no more.

'You must do what you have to,' she said finally.

Anton backed away then, leaving her.

'Goodbye, Ariane. For a little while.'

He passed through the door, looking back only once. Ariane did understand. It was clear in her expression, if not in the link which seemed to have suddenly turned into a void.

Ariane looked at the coldness of the closed door, her expression unchanged. A single tear that had waited for his departure flowed unheeded as she whispered to the empty space softly with a note of finality that spoke of the foreknowledge that she would never see him again.

'Goodbye, Anton.'

She sat on her bed for a time, her mind too busy thinking out issues of state that would now fall to her to share with Dani and to teach her son, as he grew to rule the kingdom.

After a while the door opened gently and Alaric entered, silent in his bare feet and nightshirt. He went straight to the window. Ariane followed him, wrapping her arms around her son's shoulders. Their eyes followed the shape of a black wolf as it crossed the courtyard in the faint light of a partial moon.

'Will father ever return?' Alaric asked his mother. His eyes continued to penetrate the darkness, watching the spot where his father had disappeared.

'Change is the only constant in life, my son,' Ariane answered him philosophically. 'You will likely see your father again, but nothing will ever return to how it was. The world moves forward, we must move with it. Never turn to look back. There is nothing behind you but memories. Resurrecting them is like resurrecting the dead. Even the memories themselves change with time.'

Ariane gently pulled her son from the window and turned him so that she could look him in the eye as she sat on the bed.

'There is a new time before us. The time of King Alaric.'

Alaric stood proudly for a moment in the realisation that he now held that title, then he hugged his mother like the child that he was.

Ariane held her son close as she turned her mind to planning the ceremony to come that would proclaim Alaric as ruler of their people.

'WHY DO THE GOBLINS wish to avoid another Turning so much?' Namah asked her friend. 'I should think they would be pleased to see the humans cleansed away more thoroughly.'

Namah had never learned to refer to Alinea as one of the goblins, despite Alinea's own assertions that she was very much one of them. Her human appearance set Alinea apart in Namah's perception.

'A Turning does not only affect the surface,' Alinea explained. 'What do you suppose happens to the deep places when ocean beds rise and mountains crumble into the sea?'

Namah thought of this for a moment, imagining the tumultuous land changes that would happen underground as much as on the surface.

'I see what you mean. So that is why Kahjak chose to help?'

Alinea nodded affirmation.

'He is more intelligent than he will ever allow a human to see. It is an old goblin survival trick, to allow your enemy to underestimate you.'

Namah saw the wisdom in Alinea's words. She was a little surprised that her friend had spoken of it so casually when the one purely goblin trait that she usually exhibited was the habitual secrecy that they kept for their own protection. Namah supposed it was a result of the long conversation they had been enjoying as the night had worn away. They had shared thoughts and speculations about the future as the moon had moved from one part of the sky to another and Namah at least had begun to feel the weariness of the day.

She turned to Alinea, about to mention her appreciation of her trust when she noted a faraway look in the goblin girl's eyes. She stopped with her mouth open in preparation to speak, very aware that her friend had been transported into some form of psychic vision.

Namah had seen some among the magicians go into trance and prophesy, but it had been nothing like this. Points of light sparkled in Alinea's eyes, much like the stars in the sky. Her pupils had dilated into oval slits, almost like something reptilian. Her voice, when she spoke, took on an ethereal quality that was beyond the usual soft otherworldly tones that Namah had heard from her friend before.

'The wind changes. I can see new land from the distance. Still hidden between dense mists, yet so promising...' Alinea stopped a moment, her lips poised as if to continue speaking.

'But can you see the future for yourself?' asked Namah. Alinea smiled wistfully, her hand dropped unconsciously to her abdomen.

'Yes...' she said, as her eyes looked into worlds unknown.

'What is it Alinea?' Namah queried anxiously.

'I will bear a child of *The Dance*,' she answered, still smiling. 'And he will live.'

Namah reached out, touching her friend's arm lightly to share her vision. She saw Alinea, a few years older, sitting and singing to an infant. The baby looked human, like his mother. She held the naked child closely, rocking gently. Namah could just see the small protrusions on his back. The child her friend bore, was going to grow up sporting a pair of wings.

The Goblin Series Complete!

Look for the short story collection

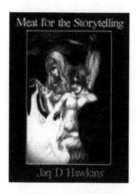

A COLLECTION OF SHORT stories set in the goblin world. Stories that fill in the history of how Count Anton's ancestors became the ruling family and of the different goblin species, how their lives differ from others of their kind and how they learned to survive.

The Author

J aq D Hawkins is the author of several Fantasy novels, which include *Dance of the Goblins*, *To Dance With Dragons* and *Power of the Dance* as well as *The Wake of the Dragon*, first of the *Airship Mechanoids Steampunk* series and *The Chase for Choronzon*, an adventurous farce through time and space.

For updates of upcoming projects and samples from various projects, follow the *Goblins & Steampunk* blog at:

https://goblinsandsteampunk.wordpress.com/

Amazon page:

http://www.amazon.com/Jaq-D.-Hawkins/e/ B0034P4BFI/

Facebook: https://www.facebook.com/GoblinSeries

Twitter: https://twitter.com/JaqDHawkins

Also by Jaq D Hawkins

The Wake of the Dragon :
A Steampunk Adventure

An exhilarating airship pirate adventure!

No sane airshipman will fly near a storm, but the cover of storm edge offers effective concealment for airship pirates who can strike quickly from above before anyone knows a ship is near. With the protection of Aide, the goddess of air travel, one airship defies the elements to seek fortune for the rag tag aerialists who make up the pirate crew.

The elements are the least of their problems when they find themselves saddled with an airsick clerk, a crewmember suspected of working for the East India Company and a love sick farm girl whose headstrong misconceptions compel her to seek adventure where no decent woman would wander unescorted.

Battling businessmen, mechanoids and villagers armed with torches and pitchforks, Captain Bonny must decide who to trust, and whether the only rational course of action is one of apparent madness.

The Chase For Choronzon

TWO REINCARNATED MAGICIANS go on a zany chase through time and space and between the worlds to put the universe back in order, if they live to accomplish their task!

The demon Choronzon was supposed to keep the gate between the worlds, but he has abandoned his post and it's up to two reincarnated magicians, Karl Spare and Alei-Cat, to capture him and return him to his post.

A romp through time and space takes these two unlikely heroes through some harrowing portals and surreal adventures where they meet a variety of bizarre personages along the way, but there can be only one finale to the chase for Choronzon!

Milton Keynes UK
Ingram Content Group UK Ltd.
UKHW010808080923
428296UK00004B/302